HOT ROCKS

Nora Roberts

HOT ICE	HOMEPORT
SACRED SINS	THE REEF
BRAZEN VIRTUE	RIVER'S END
SWEET REVENGE	CAROLINA MOON
PUBLIC SECRETS	THE VILLA
GENUINE LIES	MIDNIGHT BAYOU
CARNAL INNOCENCE	THREE FATES
DIVINE EVIL	BIRTHRIGHT
HONEST ILLUSIONS	NORTHERN LIGHTS
PRIVATE SCANDALS	BLUE SMOKE
HIDDEN RICHES	ANGELS FALL
TRUE BETRAYALS	HIGH NOON
MONTANA SKY	TRIBUTE
SANCTUARY	BLACK HILLS

Series

Born In Trilogy
BORN IN FIRE
BORN IN ICE
BORN IN SHAME

Key Trilogy
KEY OF LIGHT
KEY OF KNOWLEDGE
KEY OF VALOR

Dream Trilogy
DARING TO DREAM
HOLDING THE DREAM
FINDING THE DREAM

In the Garden Trilogy
BLUE DAHLIA
BLACK ROSE
RED LILY

Chesapeake Bay Saga
SEA SWEPT
RISING TIDES
INNER HARBOR
CHESAPEAKE BLUE

Circle Trilogy
MORRIGAN'S CROSS
DANCE OF THE GODS
VALLEY OF SILENCE

Gallaghers of Ardmore Trilogy
JEWELS OF THE SUN
TEARS OF THE MOON
HEART OF THE SEA

Sign of Seven Trilogy
BLOOD BROTHERS
THE HOLLOW
THE PAGAN STONE

Three Sisters Island Trilogy
DANCE UPON THE AIR
HEAVEN AND EARTH
FACE THE FIRE

Bride Quartet
VISION IN WHITE
BED OF ROSES

Nora Roberts & J. D. Robb

REMEMBER WHEN

J. D. Robb

NAKED IN DEATH
GLORY IN DEATH
IMMORTAL IN DEATH
RAPTURE IN DEATH
CEREMONY IN DEATH
VENGEANCE IN DEATH
HOLIDAY IN DEATH
CONSPIRACY IN DEATH
LOYALTY IN DEATH
WITNESS IN DEATH
JUDGMENT IN DEATH
BETRAYAL IN DEATH
SEDUCTION IN DEATH
REUNION IN DEATH
PURITY IN DEATH
PORTRAIT IN DEATH
IMITATION IN DEATH
DIVIDED IN DEATH
VISIONS IN DEATH
SURVIVOR IN DEATH
ORIGIN IN DEATH
MEMORY IN DEATH
BORN IN DEATH
INNOCENT IN DEATH
CREATION IN DEATH
STRANGERS IN DEATH
SALVATION IN DEATH
PROMISES IN DEATH
KINDRED IN DEATH

Anthologies

FROM THE HEART
A LITTLE MAGIC
A LITTLE FATE

MOON SHADOWS
(with Jill Gregory, Ruth Ryan Langan, and Marianne Willman)

The Once Upon Series
(with Jill Gregory, Ruth Ryan Langan, and Marianne Willman)

ONCE UPON A CASTLE   **ONCE UPON A ROSE**
ONCE UPON A STAR   **ONCE UPON A KISS**
ONCE UPON A DREAM   **ONCE UPON A MIDNIGHT**

* * *

SILENT NIGHT
(with Susan Plunkett, Dee Holmes, and Claire Cross)

OUT OF THIS WORLD
(with Laurell K. Hamilton, Susan Krinard, and Maggie Shayne)

BUMP IN THE NIGHT
(with Mary Blayney, Ruth Ryan Langan, and Mary Kay McComas)

DEAD OF NIGHT
(with Mary Blayney, Ruth Ryan Langan, and Mary Kay McComas)

THREE IN DEATH

SUITE 606
(with Mary Blayney, Ruth Ryan Langan, and Mary Kay McComas)

THE LOST
(with Patricia Gaffney, Mary Blayney, and Ruth Ryan Langan)

Also available . . .

THE OFFICIAL NORA ROBERTS COMPANION
(edited by Denise Little and Laura Hayden)

Turn to the back of this book for an excerpt from

BIG JACK

by #1 *New York Times* bestselling author J. D. Robb

HOT ROCKS

Previously published in *Remember When*

NORA ROBERTS

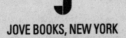

JOVE BOOKS, NEW YORK

THE BERKLEY PUBLISHING GROUP
Published by the Penguin Group
Penguin Group (USA) Inc.
375 Hudson Street, New York, New York 10014, USA
Penguin Group (Canada), 90 Eglinton Avenue East, Suite 700, Toronto, Ontario M4P 2Y3, Canada
(a division of Pearson Penguin Canada Inc.)
Penguin Books Ltd., 80 Strand, London WC2R 0RL, England
Penguin Group Ireland, 25 St. Stephen's Green, Dublin 2, Ireland (a division of Penguin Books Ltd.)
Penguin Group (Australia), 250 Camberwell Road, Camberwell, Victoria 3124, Australia
(a division of Pearson Australia Group Pty. Ltd.)
Penguin Books India Pvt. Ltd., 11 Community Centre, Panchsheel Park, New Delhi—110 017, India
Penguin Group (NZ), 67 Apollo Drive, Rosedale, North Shore 0632, New Zealand
(a division of Pearson New Zealand Ltd.)
Penguin Books (South Africa) (Pty.) Ltd., 24 Sturdee Avenue, Rosebank, Johannesburg 2196,
South Africa

Penguin Books Ltd., Registered Offices: 80 Strand, London WC2R 0RL, England

Previously published in *Remember When* by Nora Roberts and J. D. Robb.

HOT ROCKS

A Jove Book / published by arrangement with the author

PRINTING HISTORY
Jove mass-market edition / February 2010

Copyright © 2003 by Nora Roberts.
Excerpt from *Big Jack* by J. D. Robb copyright © by Nora Roberts.
Cover design by Richard Hasselberger.
Text design by Kristin del Rosario.

ISBN: 978-0-515-14799-5

JOVE®
Jove Books are published by The Berkley Publishing Group,
a division of Penguin Group (USA) Inc.,
375 Hudson Street, New York, New York 10014.
JOVE® is a registered trademark of Penguin Group (USA) Inc.
The "J" design is a trademark of Penguin Group (USA) Inc.

PRINTED IN THE UNITED STATES OF AMERICA

10 9 8 7 6 5 4 3 2 1

To Mary Kay McComas,
who sort of plays a musical instrument,
but who is the best of pals

Covetous of others' possessions,
he was prodigal of his own.

SALLUST

Who in the world am I?
Ah, that's the great puzzle!

LEWIS CARROLL

CHAPTER

1

A heroic belch of thunder followed the strange little man into the shop. He glanced around apologetically, as if the rude noise were his responsibility rather than nature's, and fumbled a package under his arm so he could close a black-and-white-striped umbrella.

Both umbrella and man dripped, somewhat mournfully, onto the neat square of mat just inside the door while the cold spring rain battered the streets and sidewalks on the other side. He stood where he was, as if not entirely sure of his welcome.

Laine turned her head and sent him a smile that held only warmth and easy invitation. It was a look her friends would have called her polite shopkeeper's smile.

Well, damnit, she *was* a polite shopkeeper—and at the moment that label was being sorely tested.

If she'd known the rain would bring customers into the store instead of keeping them away, she wouldn't have given Jenny the day off. Not that she minded business. A woman didn't open a store if she didn't want customers, whatever the weather. And a woman didn't open one in Small Town, U.S.A., unless she understood she'd spend as much time chatting, listening and refereeing debates as she would ringing up sales.

And that was fine, Laine thought, that was good. But if Jenny had been at work instead of spending the day painting her toenails and watching soaps, Jenny would've been the one stuck with the Twins.

Darla Price Davis and Carla Price Gohen had their hair tinted the same ashy shade of blond. They wore identical slick blue raincoats and carried matching hobo bags. They finished each other's sentences and communicated in a kind of code that included a lot of twitching eyebrows, pursed lips, lifted shoulders and head bobs.

What might've been cute in eight-year-olds was just plain weird in forty-eight-year-old women.

Still, Laine reminded herself, they never came into Remember When without dropping a bundle. It might take them hours to drop it, but eventually the sales would ring. There was little that lifted Laine's heart as high as the ring of the cash register.

Today they were on the hunt for an engagement present for their niece, and the driving rain and booming thunder hadn't stopped them. Nor had it deterred the drenched young couple who—they'd said—had detoured into Angel's Gap on a whim on their way to D.C.

Or the wet little man with the striped umbrella who looked, to Laine's eye, a bit frantic and lost.

So she added a little more warmth to her smile. "I'll be

with you in just a few minutes," she called out, and turned her attention back to the Twins.

"Why don't you look around a little more," Laine suggested. "Think it over. As soon as I—"

Darla's hand clamped on her wrist, and Laine knew she wasn't going to escape.

"We need to decide. Carrie's just about your age, sweetie. What would *you* want for your engagement gift?"

Laine didn't need to transcribe the code to understand it was a not-so-subtle dig. She was, after all, twenty-eight, and not married. Not engaged. Not, at the moment, even dating particularly. This, according to the Price twins, was a crime against nature.

"You know," Carla piped up, "Carrie met her Paul at Kawanian's spaghetti supper last fall. You really should socialize more, Laine."

"I really should," she agreed with a winning smile. *If I want to hook up with a balding, divorced CPA with a sinus condition.* "I know Carrie's going to love whatever you choose. But maybe an engagement gift from her aunts should be something more personal than the candlesticks. They're lovely, but the dresser set's so feminine." She picked up the silver-backed brush from the set they were considering. "I imagine another bride used this on her wedding night."

"More personal," Darla began. "More—"

"Girlie. Yes! We could get the candlesticks for—"

"A wedding gift. But maybe we should look at the jewelry before we buy the dresser set. Something with pearls? Something—"

"Old she could wear on her wedding day. Put the candlesticks *and* the dresser set aside, honey. We'll take a look at the jewelry before we decide anything."

The conversation bounced like a tennis ball served and volleyed out of two identical coral-slicked mouths. Laine congratulated herself on her skill and focus as she was able to keep up with who said what.

"Good idea." Laine lifted the gorgeous old Dresden candlesticks. No one could say the Twins didn't have taste, or were shy of heating up their plastic.

She started to carry them to the counter when the little man crossed her path.

She was eye to eye with him, and his were a pale, washed-out blue reddened by lack of sleep or alcohol or allergies. Laine decided on lost sleep as they were also dogged by heavy bags of fatigue. His hair was a grizzled mop gone mad with the rain. He wore a pricey Burberry topcoat and carried a three-dollar umbrella. She assumed he'd shaved hurriedly that morning as he'd missed a patch of stubbly gray along his jaw.

"Laine."

He said her name with a kind of urgency and intimacy that had her smile turning to polite confusion.

"Yes? I'm sorry, do I know you?"

"You don't remember me." His body seemed to droop. "It's been a long time, but I thought . . ."

"Miss!" the woman on her way to D.C. called out. "Do you ship?"

"Yes, we do." She could hear the Twins going through one of their shorthand debates over earrings and brooches, and sensed an impulse buy from the D.C. couple. And the little man stared at her with a hopeful intimacy that had her skin chilling.

"I'm sorry, I'm a little swamped this morning." She sidestepped to the counter to set down the candlesticks. Intimacy, she reminded herself, was part of the rhythm of small towns. The man had probably been in before, and she just couldn't place him. "Is there something specific I can help you with, or would you like to browse awhile?"

"I need your help. There isn't much time." He drew out a card, pressed it into her hand. "Call me at that number, as soon as you can."

"Mr. . . ." She glanced down at the card, read his name. "Peterson, I don't understand. Are you looking to sell something?"

"No. No." His laugh bounced toward hysterical and had Laine grateful for the customers crowded into the store. "Not anymore. I'll explain everything, but not now." He looked around the shop. "Not here. I shouldn't have come here. Call the number."

He clamped a hand over hers in a way that had Laine fighting an instinct to jerk free. "Promise."

He smelled of rain and soap and . . . Brut, she realized. And the aftershave had some flicker of memory trying to light in her brain. Then his fingers tightened on hers. "Promise," he repeated in a harsh whisper, and she saw only an odd man in a wet coat.

"Of course."

She watched him go to the door, open the cheap umbrella. And let out a sigh of relief when he scurried out into the rain. *Weird* was her only thought, but she studied the card for a moment.

His name was printed, Jasper R. Peterson, but the phone number was handwritten beneath and underscored twice, she noted.

Pushing the card into her pocket, she started over to give the traveling couple a friendly nudge, when the sound of screeching brakes on wet pavement and shocked screams had her spinning around. There was a hideous noise, a hollow thud she'd never forget. Just as she'd never forget the sight of the strange little man in his fashionable coat slamming against her display window.

She bolted out the door, into the streaming rain. Footsteps pounded on the pavement, and somewhere close was the crunching sound of metal striking metal, glass shattering.

"Mr. Peterson." Laine gripped his hand, bowed her body over his in a pathetic attempt to shield his bloodied face from the rain. "Don't move. Call an ambulance!" she shouted and yanked off her jacket to cover him as best she could.

"Saw him. Saw him. Shouldn't have come. Laine."

"Help's coming."

"Left it for you. He wanted me to get it to you."

"It's all right." She scooped her dripping hair out of her eyes and took the umbrella someone offered. She angled it over him, leaned down closer as he tugged weakly on her hand.

"Be careful. I'm sorry. Be careful."

"I will. Of course I will. Just try to be quiet now, try to hold on, Mr. Peterson. Help's coming."

"You don't remember." Blood trickled out of his mouth as he smiled. "Little Lainie." He took a shuddering breath, coughed up blood. She heard the sirens as he began to sing in a thin, gasping voice.

"Pack up all my care and woe," he crooned, then wheezed. "Bye, bye, blackbird."

She stared at his battered face as her already chilled skin began to prickle. Memories, so long locked away, opened. "Uncle Willy? Oh my God."

"Used to like that one. Screwed up," he said breathlessly. "Sorry. Thought it'd be safe. Shouldn't've come."

"I don't understand." Tears burned her throat, streamed down her cheeks. He was dying. He was dying because she hadn't known him, and she'd sent him out into the rain. "I'm sorry. I'm so sorry."

"He knows where you are now." His eyes rolled back. "Hide the pooch."

"What?" She leaned closer yet until her lips almost brushed his. "What?" But the hand she had clutched in hers went limp.

Paramedics brushed her aside. She heard their short, pithy dialogue—medical codes she'd grown accustomed to hearing on television, could almost recite herself. But this was real. The blood washing away in the rain was real.

She heard a woman sobbing and saying over and over in a strident voice, "He ran right in front of me. I couldn't stop in time. He just ran in front of the car. Is he all right? Is he all right? Is he all right?"

No, Laine wanted to say. He's not.

"Come inside, honey." Darla put an arm around Laine's shoulders, drew her back. "You're soaked. You can't do anything more out here."

"I should do something." She stared down at the broken umbrella, its cheerful stripes marked with grime now, and drops of blood.

She should have settled him down in front of the fire. Given him a hot drink and let him warm and dry himself in front of the little hearth. Then he'd be alive. Telling her stories and silly jokes.

But she hadn't recognized him, and so he was dying.

She couldn't go in, out of the rain, and leave him alone with strangers. But there was nothing to be done but watch, helplessly, while the paramedics fought and failed to save the man who'd once laughed at her knock-knock jokes and sung silly songs. He died in front of the shop she'd worked so hard to build, and laid at her door all the memories she thought she'd escaped.

She was a businesswoman, a solid member of the community, and a fraud. In the back room of her store, she poured two cups of coffee and knew she was about to lie to a man she considered a friend. And deny all knowledge of one she'd loved.

She did her best to steady herself, ran her hands through the damp mass of bright red hair normally worn in a shoulder-sweeping bob. She was pale, and the rain had washed away the makeup, always carefully applied, so freckles stood out on her narrow nose and across her cheekbones. Her eyes, a bright Viking blue, were glassy with shock and grief. Her mouth, just a hair too wide for her angular face, wanted to tremble.

In the little giltwood mirror on the wall of her office, she studied her reflection. And saw herself for what she was. Well, she would do what she needed to do to survive. Willy would certainly understand that. Do what came first, she told herself, then think about the rest.

She sucked in a breath, let out a shudder, then lifted the coffee. Her hands were nearly steady as she went into the main shop and prepared to give false testimony to Angel's Gap's chief of police.

"Sorry it took so long," she apologized as she carried the mugs to where Vince Burger stood by the little clinker fireplace.

He was built like a bear with a great shock of white-blond hair that stood nearly straight up, as if surprised to find itself on top of the wide, comfortable face. His eyes, a faded blue and fanned with squint lines, were full of compassion.

He was Jenny's husband, and had become a kind of brother to Laine. But for now she reminded herself he was a cop, and everything she'd worked for was on the line.

"Why don't you sit down, Laine? You've had a bad shock."

"I feel sort of numb." That was true enough, she didn't have to lie about everything. But she walked over to sip her coffee and stare out at the rain so she wouldn't have to meet those sympathetic eyes. "I appreciate your coming in to take my statement yourself, Vince. I know you're busy."

"Figured you'd be more comfortable."

Better to lie to a friend than a stranger, she thought bitterly. "I don't know what I can tell you. I didn't see the actual accident. I heard . . . I heard brakes, screams, an awful thud, then I saw . . ." She didn't shut her eyes. If she shut them, she'd see it again. "I saw him hit the window, like he'd been thrown against it. I ran out, stayed with him until the paramedics came. They were quick. It seemed like hours, but it was only minutes."

"He was in here before the accident."

Now she did close her eyes, and prepared to do what she had to do to protect herself. "Yes. I had several customers this morning, which proves I should never give Jenny a day off. The Twins were in, and a couple driving through on their way to D.C. I was busy when he came in. He browsed around for a while."

"The woman from out of town said she thought you knew each other."

"Really?" Turning now, Laine painted a puzzled expression on her face, as a clever artist might on a portrait. She crossed back, sat on one of the two elbow chairs she'd arranged in front of the fire. "I don't know why."

"An impression," Vince said with a shrug. Always mindful of his size, he sat, slow and careful, in the matching chair. "Said he took your hand."

"Well, we *shook* hands, and he gave me his card." Laine pulled it out of her pocket, forced herself to keep her attention on Vince's face. The fire was crackling with warmth, and though she felt its heat on her skin, she was cold. Very cold. "He said he'd like to speak with me when I wasn't so busy. That he might have something to sell. People often do," she added, offering Vince the card. "Which is how I stay in business."

"Right." He tucked the card into his breast pocket. "Anything strike you about him?"

"Just that he had a beautiful topcoat, and a silly umbrella— and that he didn't seem like the sort to wander around small towns. Had city on him."

"So did you a few years ago. In fact . . ." He narrowed his gaze, reached out and rubbed a thumb over her cheek. "Still got some stuck to you."

She laughed, because it's what he wanted. "I wish I could be more help, Vince. It's such an awful thing to happen."

"I can tell you, we got four different witness statements. All of them have the guy running straight out into the street, dead in front of that car. Like he was spooked or something. He seem spooked to you, Laine?"

"I wasn't paying enough attention. The fact is, Vince, I basically brushed him off when I realized he wasn't here to shop. I had customers." She shook her head when her voice broke. "It seems so callous now."

The hand Vince laid over hers in comfort made her feel foul. "You didn't know what was coming. You were the first to get to him."

"He was right outside." She had to take a deep gulp of coffee to wash the grief out of her throat. "Almost on the doorstep."

"He spoke to you."

"Yes." She reached for her coffee again. "Nothing that made much sense. He said he was sorry, a couple of times. I don't think he knew who I was or what happened. I think he was delirious. The paramedics came and . . . and he died. What will you do now? I mean, he's not from around here. The phone number's New York. I wonder, I guess I wonder if he was just driving through, where he was going, where he was from."

"We'll be looking into all that so we can notify his next of kin." Rising, Vince laid a hand on her shoulder. "I'm not going to tell you to put it out of your mind, Laine. You won't be able to, not for a while. I'm going to tell you that you did all you could. Can't do more than all you could."

"Thanks. I'm going to close up for the day. I want to go home."

"Good idea. Want a ride?"

"No. Thanks." It was guilt as much as affection that had her rising on her toes to press a kiss to his cheek. "Tell Jenny I'll see her tomorrow."

His name, at least the name she'd known, was Willy Young. Probably William, Laine thought as she drove up the pitted gravel lane. He hadn't been her real uncle—as far as she knew—but an honorary one. One who'd always had red licorice in his pocket for a little girl.

She hadn't seen him in nearly twenty years, and his hair had been brown then, his face a bit rounder. There'd always been a spring in his step.

Small wonder she hadn't recognized him in the bowed and nervy little man who'd come into her shop.

How had he found her? *Why* had he?

Since he'd been, to her knowledge, her father's closest friend, she assumed he was—as was her father—a thief, a scam artist, a small-time grifter. Not the sort of connections a respectable businesswoman wanted to acknowledge.

And why the hell should that make her feel small and guilty?

She slapped on the brakes and sat, brooding through the steady whoosh of her wipers at the pretty house on the pretty rise.

She loved this place. Hers. Home. The two-story frame house was, strictly speaking, too large for a woman on her own. But she loved being able to ramble around in it. She'd loved every minute she'd spent meticulously decorating each room to suit herself. And only herself.

Knowing, as she did, she'd never, ever have to pack up all her belongings at a moment's notice to the tune of "Bye Bye Blackbird" and run.

She loved being able to putter around the yard, planting gardens, pruning bushes, mowing the grass, yanking the weeds. Ordinary things. Simple, *normal* things for a woman who'd spent the first half of her life doing little that was normal.

She was entitled to this, wasn't she? To being Laine Tavish and all that meant? The business, the town, the house, the friends, the *life*. She was entitled to the woman she'd made herself into.

It wouldn't have helped Willy for her to have told Vince the truth. Nothing would have changed for him, and everything might have changed for her. Vince would find out, soon enough, that the man in the county morgue wasn't Jasper R. Peterson but William Young, and however many aka's that went with it.

There'd be a criminal record. She knew Willy had done at least one stint alongside her father. "Brothers in arms," her father had called them, and she could still hear his big, booming laugh.

Because it infuriated her, she slammed out of the car. She made the house in a dash, fumbled out her keys.

She calmed, almost immediately, when the door was closed at her back and the house surrounded her. Just the quiet of it, the scents of lemon oil rubbed into wood by her own hand, the subtle sweetness of spring flowers brought in from her own yard stroked her frayed nerves.

She set her keys in the raku dish on the entry table, pulled her cell phone out of her purse and plugged it into the recharger. Slipped out of her shoes, out of her jacket, which she draped over the newel post, and set her purse on the bottom step.

Following routine, she walked back to the kitchen. Normally, she'd have put on the kettle for tea and looked through the mail she'd picked up from the box at the foot of the lane while the water heated.

But today, she poured a big glass of wine.

And drank it standing at the sink, looking through the window at her backyard.

She'd had a yard—a couple of times—as a kid. She remembered one in . . . Nebraska? Iowa? What did it matter, she thought and took a healthy gulp of wine. She'd liked the yard because it had a big old tree right in the middle, and he'd hung an old tire from it on a big thick rope.

He'd pushed her so high she'd thought she was flying.

She wasn't sure how long they'd stayed and didn't remember the house at all. Most of her childhood was a blur of places and faces, of car rides, a flurry of packing up. And him, her father, with his big laugh and wide hands, with his irresistible grin and careless promises.

She'd spent the first decade of her life desperately in love with the man, and the rest of it doing everything she could to forget he existed.

If he was in trouble, again, it was none of her concern.

She wasn't Jack O'Hara's little Lainie anymore. She was Laine Tavish, solid citizen.

She eyed the bottle of wine and with a shrug poured a second glass. A grown woman could get toasted in her own kitchen, by God, especially when she'd watched a ghost from the past die at her feet.

Carrying the glass, she walked to the mudroom door, to answer the hopeful whimpering on the other side.

He came in like a cannon shot—a hairy, floppy-eared cannon shot. His paws planted themselves at her belly, and the long snout bumped her face before the tongue slurped out to cover her cheeks with wet and desperate affection.

"Okay, okay! Happy to see you, too." No matter how low her mood, a welcome home by Henry, the amazing hound, never failed to lift it.

She'd sprung him from the joint, or so she liked to think. When she'd gone to the pound two years before, it had been with a puppy in mind. She'd always wanted a cute, gamboling little bundle she'd train from the ground up.

But then she'd seen him—big, ungainly, stunningly

homely with his mud-colored fur. A cross, she'd thought, between a bear and an anteater. And she'd been lost the minute he'd looked through the cage doors and into her eyes.

Everybody deserves a chance, she'd thought, and so she sprang Henry from the joint. He'd never given her a reason to regret it. His love was absolute, so much so that he continued to look adoringly at her even when she filled his bowl with kibble.

"Chow time, pal."

At the signal, Henry dipped his head into his bowl and got serious.

She should eat, too. Something to sop up some of the wine, but she didn't feel like it. Enough wine swimming around in her bloodstream and she wouldn't be able to think, to wonder, to worry.

She left the inner door open, but stepped into the mudroom to check the outside locks. A man could shimmy through the dog door, if he was determined to get in, but Henry would set up the alarm.

He howled every time a car came up the lane, and though he would punish the intruder with slobber and delight—after he finished trembling in terror—she was never surprised by a visitor. And never, in her four years in Angel's Gap, had she had any trouble at home, or at the shop.

Until today, she reminded herself.

She decided to lock the mudroom door after all, and let Henry out the front for his evening run.

She thought about calling her mother, but what was the point? Her mother had a good, solid life now, with a good, solid man. She'd earned it. What point was there in breaking into that nice life and saying, "Hey, I ran into Uncle Willy today, and so did a Jeep Cherokee."

She took her wine with her upstairs. She'd fix herself a little dinner, take a hot bath, have an early night.

She'd close the book on what had happened that day.

Left it for you, he'd said, she remembered. Probably delirious. But if he'd left her anything, she didn't want it.

She already had everything she wanted.

Max Gannon slipped the attendant a twenty for a look at the body. In Max's experience a picture of Andrew Jackson cut through red tape quicker than explanations and paperwork and more levels of bureaucracy.

He'd gotten the bad news on Willy from the motel clerk at the Red Roof Inn where he'd tracked the slippery little bastard. The cops had already been there, but Max had invested the first twenty of the day for the room number and key.

The cops hadn't taken his clothes yet, nor from the looks of it done much of a search. Why would they on a traffic accident? But once they ID'd Willy, they'd be back and look a lot closer.

Willy hadn't unpacked, Max noted as he took stock of the room. Socks and underwear and two dress shirts were still neatly folded in the single Louis Vuitton bag. Willy had been a tidy one, and he'd loved his name brands.

He'd hung a suit in the closet. Banker gray, single-breasted, Hugo Boss. A pair of black Ferragamo loafers, complete with shoe trees, sat neatly on the floor.

Max went through the pockets, felt carefully along the lining. He took the wooden trees out of the shoes, poked his long fingers into the toes.

In the adjoining bath, he searched Willy's Dior toiletry

kit. He lifted the tank lid on the toilet, crouched down to search behind it, under the sink.

He went through the drawers, through the suitcase and its contents, flipped over the mattress on the standard double.

It took him less than an hour to search the room and verify Willy had left nothing important behind. When he left, the space looked as tidy and untouched as it had when he'd entered.

He considered giving the clerk another twenty not to mention the visit to the cops, then decided it might put ideas in his head.

He climbed into his Porsche, switched on Springsteen and headed to the county morgue to verify that his strongest lead was on ice.

"Stupid. Goddamn, Willy, I figured you for smarter than this."

Max blew out a breath as he looked at Willy's ruined face. *Why the hell did you run?* And what's in some podunk town in Maryland that was so important?

What, Max thought, or who?

Since Willy was no longer in the position to tell him, Max walked back out to drive into Angel's Gap to pick up a multimillion-dollar trail.

If you wanted to pluck grapes from the small-town vine, you went to a place where locals gathered. During the day, that meant coffee and food, at night, alcohol.

Once he'd decided he'd be staying in Angel's Gap for at least a day or two, Max checked into what was billed as The Historic Wayfarer's Inn and showered off the first twelve hours of the day. It was late enough to pick door number two.

He ate a very decent room-service burger at his laptop, surfing the home page provided by the Angel's Gap chamber of commerce. The Nightlife section gave him several choices of bars, clubs and cafes. He wanted a neighborhood pub, the kind of place where the towners knocked back a beer at the end of the day and talked about each other.

He culled out three that might fit the bill, plugged in the addresses for directions, then finished off his burger while studying the printout map of Angel's Gap.

Nice enough place, he mused, tucked in the mountains the way it was. Killer views, plenty of recreational choices for the sports enthusiast or camping freak. Slow enough pace for those who wanted to shake the urban off their docksiders, but with classy little pockets of culture—and a reasonable drive from several major metro areas should one be inclined to spend the weekend in the Maryland mountains.

The chamber of commerce boasted of the opportunities for hunting, fishing, hiking and other manner of outdoor recreation—none of which appealed to the urbanite in Max.

If he wanted to see bear and deer in their natural habitat, he'd turn on The Discovery Channel.

Still, the place had charm with its steep streets and old buildings solid in their dark red brick. There was a nice, wide stretch of the Potomac River bisecting the town, and the interest of the arching bridges that spanned it. Lots of church steeples, some with copper touches gone soft green with age and weather. And as he sat, he heard the long, echoing whistle of a train signaling its passing.

He had no doubt it was an eyeful in fall when the trees

erupted with color, and pretty as a postcard when the snow socked in. But that didn't explain why an old hand like Willy Young had gotten himself mowed down by an SUV on Market Street.

To find that piece of the puzzle, Max shut down his computer, grabbed his beloved bomber jacket and headed out to go barhopping.

CHAPTER

2

He bypassed the first choice without bothering to stop.
The forest of Hogs and Harleys out front tagged it as a biker bar, and not the sort of place where the customers talked town business over their brew.

The second took him less than two minutes to identify as a college den with strange alternative music piped in, and a couple of earnest types playing chess in a corner while most of the others performed standard mating rituals.

But he hit it on the third.

Artie's was the sort of place a guy might take his wife to, but not his side piece. It was where you went to socialize, to bump into friends or grab a quick one on the way home.

Max would've made book that 90 percent of the customer base knew each other by name, and a good chunk of them would be related.

He sidled up to the bar, ordered Beck's on tap and scoped out his surroundings. ESPN on the bar tube, sound muted, snack mix in plastic courtesy baskets. One very large black guy working the stick, and two waitresses handling the booths and four-tops.

The first waitress reminded him of his high-school librarian, which made him think she'd seen it all and wasn't too pleased with the view. She was short, heavy at the hip and on the high side of forty. There was a look in her eye that warned him she wouldn't tolerate lip.

The second was early twenties and the flirty type. She showed off a nicely packed body with a snug black sweater and painted-on jeans. She spent as much time tossing her curly blond hair as she did scooping up empties.

From the way she lingered at her stations, shooting the breeze, Max bet she was a fount of information, and the sort that liked to share.

He bided his time, then sent her a winning smile when she stopped by the bar to call in an order. "Busy tonight."

She shot a winning smile right back at him. "Oh, not too bad." She shifted her weight, swiveled her torso toward him in a body-language invitation to talk. "Where you from?"

"I move around a lot. Business."

"You got southern boy in your voice."

"Caught me. Savannah, but I haven't been home in a while." He held out a hand. "Max."

"Hi, Max. Angie. What kind of business brings you to the Gap?"

"Insurance."

Her uncle sold insurance and he sure as hell didn't decorate a bar stool like this one. Six-two, most of it leg, and a well-toned one-ninety, if she was any judge. And Angie considered herself a damn good judge of her eye candy.

There was a lot of streaky brown hair the humidity had teased into waves around a sharp, narrow face. The eyes were tawny brown and friendly, but there was an edge to them. Then there was that hint of dreamy drawl, and the slightly crooked eyetooth that kept his smile from being perfect.

She liked a man with an edge, and a few imperfections.

"Insurance? Could've fooled me."

"It's just gambling, isn't it?" He popped a pretzel into his mouth, flashed the grin again. "Most people, they like to gamble. Just like they like to believe they're going to live forever." He took a sip of his beer, noted she glanced at his left hand. Checking for a wedding ring, he assumed. "They don't. I heard some poor bastard got creamed right on Main Street this morning."

"Market," she corrected, and he made himself look puzzled. "Happened this morning on Market Street. Ran right out in front of poor Missy Leager's Cherokee. She's a mess about it, too."

"That's rough. Doesn't sound like it was her fault."

"It wasn't. Lots of people saw it happen, and there wasn't a thing she could've done. He just ran right out in front of her."

"That's hard. I guess she knew him, too. Small town like this."

"No, nobody did. He wasn't from here. I heard he was in Remember When—I work there part-time—right before. We sell antiques and collectibles and stuff. I guess maybe he was browsing on through. Awful. Just awful."

"It sure is. You were there when it happened?"

"Uh-uh. I wasn't working this morning." She paused, as if conducting a quick debate on whether she was glad or sorry to have missed it. "Don't know why anybody'd run out in the street that way. It was raining pretty bad. I guess he didn't see the car."

"Bad luck."

"I'll say."

"Angie, you waiting for those drinks to serve themselves?"

It was from the librarian and had Angie rolling her eyes. "I'm getting 'em." She winked at Max, then hefted her tray. "See you around?"

"You bet."

By the time Max walked back into his hotel room, he had a good handle on Willy's movements. He'd checked into his motel at around ten the night before, paid cash for a three-night stay. He wouldn't be getting a refund. He'd had a solo breakfast at the coffee shop the next morning, then drove in his rental car to Market Street and parked two blocks north of Remember When.

Since, at this point, Max couldn't put him in any of the other shops or businesses in that section, the most logical reason for parking that distance from his assumed destination, in the rain, was caution. Or paranoia.

Since he was dead, caution was the safer bet.

So just what had Willy wanted with an antique shop in Angel's Gap that had him making tracks from New York— and doing everything he could to cover those tracks?

A drop point? A contact?

Once again, Max booted up his computer and brought up the town's home page. In a couple of clicks, he linked to Remember When. Antiques, estate jewelry, collectibles. Bought and sold.

He scribbled the shop name on a pad and added *Fence?* circling the question twice.

He read the operating hours, phone and fax numbers,

e-mail address, and the fact that they claimed to ship worldwide.

Then he read the proprietor's name.

Laine Tavish.

It wasn't one on his list, but he checked anyway. No Laine, he verified, no Tavish. But there was Elaine O'Hara. Big Jack's only daughter.

Lips pursed, Max leaned back in the desk chair. She'd be . . . twenty-eight, twenty-nine now. Wouldn't it be interesting if Big Jack O'Hara's little girl had followed in her daddy's larcenous footsteps, had changed her name and snuggled herself away in a pretty mountain town?

It was, Max thought, a puzzle piece begging to fit.

Four years of living in Angel's Gap meant Laine knew just what to expect when she opened Remember When in the morning.

Jenny would arrive, just a hair late, with fresh doughnuts. At six months pregnant, Jenny rarely went twenty minutes without a craving for something that screamed sugar and fat. As a result, Laine was viewing her own bathroom scale with one eye closed.

Jenny would complement the doughnuts with a thermos of the herbal tea she'd become addicted to since conception and demand to know all the details of yesterday's event. Being married to the chief of police wouldn't stop her from wanting Laine's version to add to already accumulated data.

At ten sharp, the curious would start to wander in. Some, Laine thought as she filled the cash register with change, would pretend to be browsing, and others wouldn't bother to disguise the hunt for gossip.

She'd have to go through it all again. Have to lie again, or at least evade with the pretense that she'd never before seen the man who called himself Jasper Peterson.

It had been a long time since she'd had to put on a mask just to get through the day. And it depressed her how easy a fit it was.

She was ready when Jenny rushed in five minutes late.

Jenny had the face of a mischievous angel. It was round and soft, pink and white, and had clever hazel eyes that tilted up just a tad at the outside corners. Her hair was a curling black mass, often, as it was today, bundled any which way on top of her head. She wore an enormous red sweater that stretched over her pregnant belly, baggy jeans and ancient Doc Martens.

She was everything Laine wasn't—disordered, impulsive, undisciplined, an emotional whirlwind. And exactly the sort of friend Laine had pined for throughout childhood.

Laine considered it one of those golden gifts of fate that Jenny was in her life.

"I'm *starving*. Are you starving?" Jenny dumped the bakery box on the counter, ripped open the lid. "I could hardly stand the *smell* of these things on the two-minute walk from Krosen's. I think I started to whimper." She stuffed the best part of a jelly-filled into her mouth and talked around it. "I worried about you. I know you said you were okay when I called last night, just a little headache, don't want to talk about it, blah, blah, blah, but Mommy worried, sweetie."

"I'm okay. It was awful, but I'm okay."

Jenny held out the box. "Eat sugar."

"God. Do you know how long I'll have to work out to chip this off my ass?"

Jenny only smiled when Laine caved and took a

cream-filled. "You've got such a pretty ass, too." She rubbed her belly in slow circles as she watched Laine nibble. "You don't look like you got much sleep."

"No. Couldn't settle." Despite every effort not to, she looked through the display window. "I must've been the last person he spoke to, and I brushed him off because I was busy."

"Can you imagine how Missy's feeling this morning? And it's no more her fault than yours." She went to the back room, moving in the waddle/march she'd developed in the sixth month of her pregnancy and came back with two mugs. "You'll have some tea to go with your sugar hit. You're going to need both to fortify you for the onslaught when we open. Everybody's going to want to come by."

"I know."

"Vince is going to keep it quiet until he's got more figured out, but it's going to get out, and I figure you've got a right to know."

Here it comes, Laine thought. "Know what?"

"The guy's name? It wasn't the name on the card he gave you."

"I'm sorry?"

"It wasn't the name he had on his driver's license or credit cards either," Jenny continued excitedly. "It was an alias. His name was William Young. Get *this*. He was an ex-convict."

She hated hearing the man she remembered so fondly called an ex-con, as if it was the sum of him. And hated herself for doing nothing to defend him. "You're kidding? That little man?"

"Larceny, fraud, possession of stolen goods, and that's just convictions. From what I wormed out of Vince, he was suspected of a lot more. Like a career criminal, Laine. And he was in here, probably casing the joint."

"You're watching too many old movies, Jenny."

"Come *on*! What if you'd been alone in here? What if he had a gun?"

Laine dusted sugar off her fingers. "Did he have a gun?"

"Well, no, but he could have. He could've robbed you."

"A career criminal comes all the way to Angel's Gap to rob my store? Man, that website really works."

Jenny struggled to look annoyed, then barked out a laugh. "Okay, so he probably wasn't planning on knocking over the joint."

"I'm going to take exception if you keep calling my shop a joint."

"But he had to be up to something. He gave you his card, right?"

"Yes, but—"

"So *maybe* he was hoping to sell you stolen merchandise. Who'd look in a place like this for hot goods? Like I told Vince, he probably did a job recently, and maybe his usual fence dried up or something, so he had to find a way to turn the goods, and fast."

"And of all the antique stores in all the world, he walks into mine?" She laughed it off, but there was a twist in her gut as she wondered if that was indeed the reason Willy had come to her door.

"Well, he had to walk into one, why *not* yours?"

"Ah . . . because this isn't a TV movie of the week?"

"You have to admit it's strange."

"Yes, it's strange, and it's sad. And it's also ten o'clock, Jen. Let's open and see what the day brings."

It brought, as expected, the gossip hounds and gawkers,

but Jenny was able to exchange theories with a few customers while she rang up genuine sales. It was cowardly, but Laine decided to take the yellow feather and escape into the back with the excuse of paperwork while Jenny handled the shop.

She'd stolen barely twenty minutes of solitude when Jenny poked her head in. "Honey, you've *got* to see this."

"Unless it's a dog that can juggle while riding a unicycle, I need to update this spreadsheet."

"It's better." Jenny jerked her head toward the shop, stepping back with the door open.

Since her curiosity was piqued, Laine slipped out after her. She saw him, holding a green Depression glass water glass up to the light. It seemed entirely too delicate, too feminine, for a man wearing a battered bomber jacket and worn hiking boots. But he didn't fumble it as he set it down and picked up its mate for a similar study.

"Mmmm." Jenny made the same sound she made when contemplating jelly doughnuts. "That's the kind of long drink of water a woman wants to down in one big slurp."

"Pregnant married women shouldn't slurp at strange men."

"Doesn't mean we can't appreciate the scenery."

"Mixing metaphors." She elbowed her friend. "And staring. Wipe the drool off your chin and go make a sale."

"You take him. I gotta pee. Pregnant woman, you know."

Before Laine could object, Jenny nipped into the back. More amused than irritated, Laine started across the room. "Hi."

She had her friendly merchant smile in place when he turned, and his eyes locked on hers.

She felt the punch dead center of the belly, with the

aftershocks of it radiating down to her kneecaps. She could almost feel cohesive thought drain out of her brain, replaced by something along the lines of: Oh. Well. Wow.

"Hi back." He kept the glass in his hand and just looked at her.

He had tiger eyes, she thought dimly. Big, dangerous cat eyes. And the half smile on his face as he stared at her had what could only be lust pooling at the back of her throat. "Um . . ." Fascinated by her own reaction, she let out a half laugh, shook her head. "Sorry, mind was wandering. Do you collect?"

"Not so far. My mama does."

"Oh." He had a mama. Wasn't that sweet? "Does she stick to any particular pattern?"

He grinned now, and Laine cheerfully allowed the top of her head to blow off. "She doesn't—in any area whatsoever. She likes . . . the variety of the unexpected. Me too." He set the glass down. "Like this place."

"Excuse me?"

"A little treasure box tucked away in the mountains."

"Thank you."

And so was she, unexpected, he thought. Bright—the hair, the eyes, the smile. Pretty as a strawberry parfait and a hell of a lot sexier. Not in the full-out, warmly bawdy way the brunette had struck him, but in a secret, I'll-surprise-you way that made him want to know more.

"Georgia?" she asked, and his left eyebrow lifted a fraction.

"Tagged."

"I'm good with accents. Does your mother have a birthday coming up?"

"She stopped having them about ten years ago. We just call it Marlene's Day."

"Smart woman. Those tumblers are the Tea Room pattern, and in fairly short supply. You don't often see a set of six like this, and in perfect condition. I can give you a nice price on the complete set."

He picked one up again but continued to look at her. "I get to haggle?"

"It's required." She stepped closer to lift another glass and show him the price on the bottom. "As you can see, they're fifty each, but if you want the set, I'll give them to you for two seventy-five."

"I hope you don't take this the wrong way, but you smell really good." It was some smoky fragrance you didn't notice until it had you by the throat. "Really good. Two and a quarter."

She never flirted, *never* flirted with customers, but found herself turning toward him, standing just a little closer than was strictly business and smiling into those dangerous eyes. "Thanks, I'm glad you like it. Two-sixty, and that's a steal."

"Throw in the shipping to Savannah and have dinner with me and we've got a deal."

It had been too long, entirely too long, since she'd felt that little thrill swim through the blood. "Shipping—and a drink, with the option for dinner at a later time and place. It's a good offer."

"Yeah, it is. Seven o'clock? They've got a nice bar at the Wayfarer."

"Yes, they do. Seven's fine. How would you like to pay for this?"

He took out a credit card, handed it to her.

"Max Gannon," she read. "Just Max? Not Maxwell, Maximillian, Maxfield." She caught the slight wince and laughed. "Maxfield, as in Parrish."

"Just Max," he said, very firmly.

"All right then, Just Max, but I have a couple of very good framed Parrish posters in the next room."

"I'll keep that in mind."

She walked away and behind the counter, then laid a shipping form on it. "Why don't you write down the shipping information. We'll have this out this afternoon."

"Efficient, too." He leaned against the counter as he filled in the form. "You've got my name. Do I get yours?"

"It's Tavish. Laine Tavish."

He kept his smile easy as he looked up. "Just Laine? Not Elaine?"

She didn't flick an eyelash. "Just Laine." She rang up the sale and handed him a pretty gold-foiled gift card. "We'll include this, and gift wrap, if you'd like to write a message to your mother."

She glanced over as the bells rang, and the Twins came in.

"Laine." Carla made a beeline for the counter. "How are you holding up?"

"I'm fine. Just fine. I'll be right with you."

"We were worried, weren't we, Darla?"

"We certainly were."

"No need." With something like panic, she willed Jenny to come back in. The interlude with Max had driven the grief and the worry over Willy out of her mind. Now, it was flooding back. "I'll get those things I have on hold for you as soon as I'm finished here."

"Don't you rush." Carla was already angling her head so she could read the destination on the shipping form. "Our Laine prides herself on good customer service," she told Max.

"And certainly delivers. Ladies, you are a two-scoop treat for the eyes."

They blushed, in unison.

"Your card, Mr. Gannon, and your receipt."

"Thank you, Ms. Tavish."

"I hope your mother enjoys her gift."

"I'm sure she will." His eyes laughed into hers before he turned to the Twins. "Ladies."

The three women watched him walk out. There was a prolonged beat of silence, then Carla let out a long, long breath and said simply, "My, oh my."

Max's smile faded the minute he was out on the street. He had nothing to feel guilty about, he told himself. Having a drink with an attractive woman at the end of the day was a normal, pleasant activity, and his inalienable right as a healthy, single man.

Besides, he didn't believe in feeling guilty. Lying, prevaricating, pretense and guile were all part of the job. And the fact was he hadn't lied to her—yet.

He walked half a block down where he could stand and look back at the spot where Willy had died.

He'd only lie to her if she turned out to be part of this. And if she was, she was going to get a lot worse than a few smooth lies.

What worried him was the not knowing, the not intuiting. He had a sense about these things, which was why he was good at his work. But Laine Tavish had blindsided him, and the only thing he'd felt was that slow, sugary slide of attraction.

But big blue eyes and sexy smile aside, the odds were she was in it up to her pretty neck. He always went with the odds. Willy had paid her a visit and ended up splattered on the street outside her shop. Once he knew why, he was one step closer to the glittery end of the trail.

If he had to use her to get there, those were the breaks.

He went back to his hotel room and took the receipt from his pocket, carefully dusted it for prints. He had good ones of her thumb and forefinger. He took digital pictures and sent them to a friend who'd run them without asking irritating questions.

Then he sat down, flexed his fingers and went to work on the information highway.

He plowed through a pot of coffee, a chicken sandwich and really good apple pie while he worked. He had Laine's home address and, between the phone and the computer, the information that she'd bought her home and established her business on Market four years before. Previously, she'd listed a Philadelphia address. A bit more research located it as an apartment building.

With methods not strictly ethical, he spent more time peeling away the layers of Laine Tavish and began to get a picture. She'd graduated from Penn State, with her parents listed as Marilyn and Robert Tavish.

Funny, wasn't it? Max thought, tapping his fingers on the desk. Jack O'Hara's wife was, or had been, Marilyn. And wasn't that just a little too coincidental?

"Up to your pretty neck," he murmured and decided it was time for more serious hacking.

There were ways and there were ways to eke out tidbits of information that led to more tidbits. Her business license had been, according to law, clearly displayed in her shop. And that license number gave him a springboard.

Some creative finessing netted him the application for the license, and her social security number.

He stuck with it, using the numbers, intuition and his own insatiable curiosity to track down the deed to her house through the county courthouse, and now he had the name of her lender should he want to break several laws and hack his way to her loan application.

It would be fun because God knew he *loved* technology, but it would serve more purpose to find out where she'd come from rather than where she was now.

He went back to the parents, began a search that required a second pot of coffee from room service. When he finally pinpointed Robert and Marilyn Tavish in Taos, New Mexico, he shook his head.

Laine didn't strike him as a flower of the West. No, she was East, he thought, and largely urban. But Bob and Marilyn, as he was thinking of them, had a link to something called Roundup, which turned out to be a western barbecue joint, and they had a web page. Everyone did, Max thought.

There was even a picture of the happy restaurateurs beside an enormous cartoon cowboy with lariat. He enlarged and printed out the picture before flipping through the site. The attached menu didn't sound half bad, and you could order Rob's Kick-Ass Barbecue Sauce through the site.

Rob, Max noted. Not Bob.

They looked happy, he thought as he studied the photo. Ordinary, working class, pleased as punch to own their own business. Marilyn Tavish didn't look like the former wife—and suspected accomplice—of a career thief and con artist who'd not only gotten delusions of grandeur, but had somehow pulled it off.

She looked more like the type who'd fix you a sandwich before she went out to hang up the wash.

He noted Roundup had been in business eight years, which meant they'd started the place while Laine had been in college. Playing a hunch, he logged onto the local Taos paper, dipped into the archives and looked for a story on the Tavishes.

He found six, which surprised him, and went back to the first, in which the paper had covered the restaurant opening. He read it all, paying close attention to personal details. Such as the Tavishes had been married for six years at that point, and had met, according to the report, in Chicago, where Marilyn had been a waitress and Rob worked for a Chrysler dealership. There was a brief mention of a daughter who was a business major in college back East.

Rob had always wanted to own his own place, blah blah, and finally took up his wife's dare to do something with his culinary talents besides feed their friends and neighbors at picnics.

Other stories followed Rob's interest in local politics and Marilyn's association with a Taos arts council. There was another feature when Roundup celebrated its fifth anniversary with an open-air party, including pony rides for kids.

That story carried a picture of the beaming couple, flanking a laughing Laine.

Jesus, she was a knockout. Her head was thrown back with the laugh, her arms slung affectionately around her mother and stepfather's shoulders. She was wearing some western-cut shirt with little bits of fringe on the pockets, which—for reasons he couldn't fathom—made him crazy.

He could see a resemblance to her mother now that they were side by side. Around the eyes, the mouth.

But she'd gotten that hair, that bright red hair, from Big Jack. He was sure of it now.

The timing worked, too well. Marilyn O'Hara had filed for divorce while Jack was serving a short stretch, courtesy of the state of Indiana. She'd taken the kid and moved to Jacksonville, Florida. Authorities had kept their eye on her for a few months, but she'd been clean and had worked as a waitress.

She'd bumped around a bit. Texas, Philadelphia, Kansas. Then she'd dropped out of sight, off the radar, a little less than two years before she and Rob tied the knot.

Maybe she'd wanted to start fresh for herself, for the kid. Or maybe it was just a long con. Max was making it his mission to find out.

CHAPTER

3

"What am I doing? This isn't something I do."

Jenny peered over Laine's shoulder at their dual reflections in the bathroom mirror. "You're going to have a drink with a great-looking man. Why that isn't something you do is best discussed with a therapist."

"I don't even know who he is." Laine set down the lipstick she held before applying it. "I hit on him, Jen. For God's sake, I hit on him in my own shop."

"A woman can't hit on a sexy guy in her own shop, where can she? Use the lipstick." She glanced down to where Henry was thumping his tail. "See, Henry agrees with me."

"I should just call the inn, leave a message for him, tell him something came up."

"Laine, you're breaking my heart." She picked up the lipstick. "Paint," she ordered.

"I can't believe I let you talk me into closing a half hour early. I can't believe how easy it was for you to talk me into it. Coming home to change—it looks obvious, doesn't it?"

"What's wrong with obvious?"

"I don't know." Laine used the lipstick, studied the tube. "I'm not thinking straight. It was that moment, that *ka-boom* moment. I just wanted to yank off his shirt and bite his neck."

"Well, go to it, honey."

With a laugh, Laine turned around. "I'm not follow-ing through. A drink, okay. It'd be rude not to show up, wouldn't it? Yes, it would be rude. But that's it. After that, common sense will once more rule the day, and I'll come home and close the door on this very strange interlude."

She held her arms out. "How do I look? Okay?"

"Better."

"Better than okay is good. I should go."

"Go ahead. I'll put Henry out in the mudroom. You don't want to smell like dog. I'll lock up for you."

"Thanks. Appreciate it. And the moral support. I feel like an idiot."

"If you decide to . . . extend the evening, just give me a call. I can come back and get Henry. We'll have a sleepover."

"Thanks again, but I'm *not* going to extend the evening. One drink. I figure an hour tops." She gave Jenny a light kiss on the cheek, then, risking eau de Henry, bent down to kiss the dog's snout. "See you tomorrow," she called as she dashed for the stairs.

It had been silly to drive all the way home just to drive back to town, but she was glad she'd been silly. Though even Jenny hadn't been able to talk her into slipping into a little black dress—talk about obvious—she felt more polished out of her work clothes. The soft sweater in forest green was a good color, and just casual enough not to send the wrong signal.

She had no idea what sort of signal she wanted to send. Yet.

There was a little bubble of panic when she walked into the hotel. They hadn't actually confirmed they were meeting for drinks. It had all been so off the cuff, and so out of character for her. What if he didn't show or, worse, happened into the bar while she was waiting and looked surprised—chagrined—annoyed?

And if she was this nervous about something as simple as a drink in a classy, public bar, she'd definitely let her dating tools rust.

She stepped in through etched-glass doors and smiled at the woman working behind the black oak bar.

"Hi, Jackie."

"Hey, Laine. What can I get you?"

"Nothing yet." She scanned the dimly lit room, the plush red sofas and chairs. A few businessmen, two couples, a trio of women starting a girls' night out with a fancy drink. But no Max Gannon.

She chose a table where she wouldn't actually face the door but could observe it. She started to pick up the bar menu just to do something with her hands, then decided it might make her look bored. Or hungry. God.

Instead, she took out her cell and used it to check for messages on her home answering machine. There weren't any, of course, since she'd only walked out the door twenty minutes earlier. But there were two hangups, a couple minutes apart.

She was frowning over that when she heard him speak.

"Bad news?"

"No." Both flustered and pleased, she disconnected, then dropped the phone into her purse. "Nothing important."

"Am I late?"

"No. I'm irritatingly prompt." It surprised her that he sat beside her on the little sofa rather than across the table in the chair. "Habit."

"Did I mention you smell great?"

"Yes, you did. I never asked what you were doing in the Gap."

"Some business, which I've managed to extend a few more days. Due to local attractions."

"Really." She wasn't nervous anymore, and wondered why she had been. "We have a number of them. There are some wonderful trails through the mountains if you like to hike."

"Do you?" He brushed his fingers over the back of her hand. "Like to hike."

"I don't make much time for it. The store keeps me busy. And your business?"

"Fills the day," he said, and glanced up when the waitress stopped by their table.

"What can I get you?"

She was new, and not someone Laine recognized. "Bombay martini, straight up, two olives. Iced."

"That sounds perfect. Make it two. Did you grow up here?" he asked Laine.

"No, but I imagine it would be nice to grow up here. Small-town enough without being Mayberry, close enough to the city without being crowded. And I like the mountains."

She remembered this part of the first-date ritual. It hadn't been *that* long. "Do you still live in Savannah?"

"New York primarily, but I travel a lot."

"For?"

"Business, pleasure. Insurance, but don't worry, I'm not selling."

The waitress brought the glasses and shakers on a tray and poured the drinks at the table. She set down a silver bowl of sugared nuts, then slipped discreetly away.

Laine lifted hers, smiled over the rim. "To your mother."

"She'd like that." He tapped his glass to hers. "How'd you come to running an antique store?"

"I wanted a place of my own. I always liked old things, the continuity of them. I don't mind paperwork, but I didn't want to work in an office all day." Comfortable now, she settled back with her drink, shifting her body so they could continue the flirtatious eye contact along with the small talk. "I like buying and selling, and seeing what people buy and sell. So I put all that together and opened Remember When. What kind of insurance?"

"Corporate, mainly. Boring. Family in the area?"

Okay, she thought, doesn't want to talk about his work, particularly. "My parents live in New Mexico. They moved there several years ago."

"Brothers, sisters?"

"Only child. You?"

"I've got one of each. Two nephews and a niece out of them."

"That's nice," she said and meant it. "I always envy families, all the noise and traumas and companionship. Competition."

"We've got plenty of that. So, if you didn't grow up here, where did you?"

"We moved around a lot. My father's work."

"I hear that." He sampled a nut, kept it casual. "What does he do?"

"He . . . he was in sales." How else to describe it in polite company. "He could sell anything to anyone."

He caught it, the hint of pride in her voice, the contrast of the shadow in her eyes. "But not anymore?"

She didn't speak for a moment, using a sip of her drink as cover until she worked out her thoughts. Simple was best, she reminded herself. "My parents opened a little restaurant in Taos. A kind of working retirement. With work the main feature. And they're giddy as kids about it."

"You miss them."

"I do, but I didn't want what they wanted. So here I am. I love the Gap. It's my place. Do you have one?"

"Maybe. But I haven't found it yet."

The waitress stopped by. "Another round?"

Laine shook her head. "I'm driving."

He asked for the check, then took Laine's hand. "I made reservations in the dining room here, in case you changed your mind. Change your mind, Laine, and have dinner with me."

He had such wonderful eyes, and that warm bourbon-on-the-rocks voice she loved listening to. Where was the harm?

"All right. I'd love to."

He told himself it was business and pleasure and there was never anything wrong with combining the two as long as you remembered your priorities. He knew how to steer conversations, elicit information. And if he was interested in her on a personal level, it didn't interfere with the work.

It wouldn't interfere with the work.

He was no longer sure she was neck-deep. And his change of mind had nothing, absolutely nothing to do with the fact that he was attracted to her. It just didn't play the way it should have. Her mother tucked up with husband number two in New Mexico, Laine tucked up in Maryland. And Big Jack nobody knew just where.

He couldn't see how they triangulated at this point. And he read people well, well enough to know she wasn't marking time with her shop. She loved it, and had forged genuine connections with the community.

But it didn't explain Willy's visit, or his death. It didn't explain why she'd made no mention of knowing him to the police. Not that innocent parties were always straight with the cops.

Weighing down the other side of the scale, she was careful to edit her background, and had a smooth way of blending her father and stepfather so the casual listener would assume they were the same man.

No mention of divorce when they spoke of family. And that told him she knew how to hide what she wanted to hide.

Though he regretted it, he pushed Willy's ghost into the conversation. "I heard about the accident right outside your place." Her knuckles, he noted, whitened for a moment on her spoon, but it was the only sign of internal distress before she continued to stir her after-dinner coffee.

"Yes, it was awful. He must not have seen the car—with the rain."

"He was in your shop?"

"Yes, right before. Just browsing. I barely spoke to him as I had several other customers, and Jenny, my full-time clerk, had the day off. It was nobody's fault. Just a terrible accident."

"He wasn't a local?"

She looked directly into his eyes. "He was never in my

shop before. I suppose he might've come in just to get out of the rain for a few minutes. It was a nasty day."

"Tell me about it. I was driving in it. Seems I got into town only a couple hours after it happened. Heard different versions of it every place I stopped the rest of the day. In one of them, I think it was at the gas pump, he was an international jewel thief on the lam."

Her eyes softened with what he could only judge as affection. "International jewel thief," she murmured. "No, he certainly wasn't that. People say the oddest things, don't they?"

"I guess they do." For the first time since he'd taken the job, he believed that Laine Tavish aka Elaine O'Hara had absolutely no clue what her father, William Young and a so far unidentified third party had pulled off six weeks before.

He walked her out to her car and tried to think how he could, and might have to, use her as a lever. What he could tell her, and what he wouldn't if and when the time came.

It wasn't what he wanted to think about with the chill of the early spring evening blowing at her hair, sending her scent around him.

"Chilly yet," he commented.

"It can stay cool at night right up into June, or turn on a dime and bake you before May's out." He'd be gone before the nights grew warm. It would be smart to remember that. It would be sensible.

She was so damn tired of being sensible.

"I had a nice time. Thanks." She turned, slid her hands up his chest, linked them around his neck and pulled his mouth down to hers.

That's what she wanted, and screw being sensible. She wanted that punch, that rush, that immediate flash in the blood that comes from a single dangerous act. She lived safe. The second half of her life had been nothing if not safe.

This was better. This hot and shocking clash of lips, of tongue, of teeth was better than safe. It pumped life into her, and made her remember what it was to just take.

How could she have forgotten what a thrill it was to leap and look later?

He'd known she'd surprise him. The minute he'd clamped eyes on her, he'd known. But he hadn't expected her to stagger him. It wasn't a come-on kiss, or a silky flirtation, but a full-on, sexual blast that rocked him back and shot the libido into overdrive.

One minute she had that compact and curvy body plastered to his like they were a couple of shipwreck survivors, then there was a little cat-in-cream purr in her throat and she was pulling away slowly—an elastic and endless move that he was too dazed to stop.

She rubbed her lips together. Sexy, wet lips. And smiled.

"Good night, Max."

"Hold it, hold it, hold it." He slapped a hand on her car door before she could open it. Then just left it there as he wasn't confident of his balance.

She was still smiling—soft lips, sleepy eyes. She had the power now, all of it, and they both knew it. How the hell had that happened?

"You're going to send me up there." He nodded toward the hotel, the general direction of his room. "Alone? That's just mean."

"I know." Her head angled a bit to the side as she studied him. "I don't want to, but I have to. That's just going to have to hold us both."

"Let's have breakfast. No, a midnight snack. Screw it, let's go have a brandy now."

She laughed. "You don't want a brandy."

"No. It was a thinly disguised euphemism for wild and crazy sex. Come inside, Laine." He ran a hand over her hair. "Where it's warm."

"I really, really can't, and it's a damn shame." She opened the car door, glancing over her shoulder, deliberately provocative, as she slid inside. "Henry's waiting for me."

His head snapped back as if she'd sucker punched him. "Whoa."

Suppressing a bubble of laughter, she slammed the door, waited just a beat, then rolled down the window. "Henry's my dog. Thanks for dinner, Max. Good night."

She was laughing as she drove away, and couldn't remember the last time she'd felt so alive. They'd be seeing each other again, she was absolutely sure of it. Then they'd see . . . well, what they'd see.

She turned the radio up to blast and sang along with Sheryl Crow as she drove, just a bit too fast. The recklessness felt good, a sexy fit. Lusty little chills danced over her skin as she bumped up her lane and parked in the secluded dark outside her house. There was a nice kicky breeze whisking along through the barely budded trees and a pretty half-moon that added its light to the old amber glass lantern she'd left glowing on the porch.

For a moment, she sat in the car, in the music and moonlight, and replayed every move and touch and taste of that brain-draining kiss.

Oh yeah, she was definitely going to get another taste of Max Gannon, transplanted Georgia boy with the tiger eyes.

She was still singing as she strolled up her path. She unlocked her front door, tossed her keys into their bowl, slid her cell phone into the recharger, then all but skipped into the living room.

The heady sexual buzz flipped into shock. Her couch was turned over, its cushions shredded. The cherry wood armoire she used as an entertainment center stood wide open, and empty. The trio of African violets she'd rooted from leaves and babied into lush plants had been dumped out of their pots, and the soil scattered. Tables had been overturned, drawers emptied, and framed prints she'd arranged on the walls were tossed on the floor.

For a moment she stood, frozen in the inertia of denial. Not possible. Not her house, not her things, not her world. She broke through it with a single thought.

"Henry!"

Terrified, she bolted for the kitchen, ignoring the debris of her possessions that littered the hall, the mess of glass-ware and staples that covered the kitchen floor.

Tears of relief stung her eyes as she heard the frantic answering barks as she charged toward the mudroom door. The instant she flung open the door she was covered by trembling, frightened dog. She went down with him, her shoes skidding on spilled sugar, to clutch him against her as he struggled to crawl into her lap.

They were all right, she told herself over the frantic pounding of her heart. That's what mattered most. They were okay.

"They didn't hurt you. They didn't hurt you," she crooned to him while tears tracked down her cheeks, while she ran her hands over his fur to check for injuries. "Thank God they didn't hurt you."

He whimpered, then bathed her face as they tried to calm each other down.

"We have to call the police." Shivering herself, she pressed her face into his fur. "We're going to call the police, then see how bad it is."

It was bad. In the few hours she'd been gone, someone had come into her home, stolen her property and left a manic rubble in his wake. Small treasures broken, valuables gone, her personal things touched and examined then taken or discarded. It bruised her heart, shattered her sense of safety.

Then it just pissed her off.

She'd worked her way up to anger before Vince arrived. She preferred anger. There was something powerful about the rage that was building inside her, something more useful than her initial shock and fear.

"You're okay?" It was Vince's first question as he took her arms, gave them a quick, bolstering rub.

"I'm not hurt, if that's what you mean. They were gone before I got home. Henry was in the mudroom. He couldn't get out, so they left him alone. Jenny. I left Jenny here, Vince. If she'd still been here when—"

"She wasn't. She's fine. Let's deal with what is."

"You're right. Okay, you're right." She drew a deep breath. "I got home about ten-thirty. Unlocked the front door, walked in, saw the living room." She gestured.

"Door was locked?"

"Yes."

"Broken window here." He nodded to the front facing window. "Looks like that's how they got in. Got your stereo and components, I see."

"The television in the media room upstairs, the little portable I used in the kitchen. Jewelry. I've just taken an overview, but it looks like they took electronics and small valuables. I've got a couple of good Deco bronzes, several other nice pieces, but they left those. Some of the jewelry they took is the real deal, some of it junk." She shrugged.

"Cash?"

"A couple hundred that I kept in my desk drawer. Oh, and the computer I used here at home."

"Made a goddamn mess out of it, too. Who knew you'd be out tonight?"

"Jenny, the man I met for drinks—we ended up having dinner, too. He's at the Wayfarer. Max Gannon."

"Jenny said you just met him, in the shop."

Heat tingled its way up her neck. "It was just a drink and a meal, Vince."

"Just saying. We're going to go through everything. Bunch of cops tromping around in here, you might want to go to our place, stay the night."

"No, but thanks. I'll stick."

"Yeah. Jenny said you would." He gave her shoulder a pat with his big hand and walked to the door as he heard the radio car pull up. "We'll do what we do. You might want to start working up a list of what's missing."

She spent the time in the sitting room upstairs with Henry curled tight at her feet. She wrote down what she'd already seen was missing, answered questions as Vince or one of the other cops stopped in. She wanted coffee, but since what she'd stocked was on her kitchen floor, she settled for tea. And drank a potful.

She knew her feelings of violation, fear, anger were all classic reactions, just as the sheen of disbelief that kept layering over them. It wasn't that crime was nonexistent in the

Gap. But this sort of break-in, the malicious destruction of it, certainly wasn't typical.

And to Laine, it seemed very, very personal.

It was after one in the morning before she was alone again. Vince offered to leave an officer outside, but she'd refused. Though she'd gratefully accepted his offer to board up the broken window.

She checked, then double-checked the locks, with Henry keeping close on her heels as she moved around the house. Anger was trickling back, wiping away the fatigue that had begun to drag at her while the police worked. She used it, and the resulting energy, to set her kitchen to rights.

She filled a waste can with broken crockery and glassware, and tried not to mourn the lost pieces of colorful Fiestaware she'd collected so carefully. She swept sugar, coffee, flour, salt, loose tea, then mopped the biscuit-colored tiles.

Energy was leaking out of her system by the time she trudged upstairs. One look at her bed—the mattress stripped and dragged onto the floor, the turned-out drawers of her lovely mahogany bureau, the gaping holes in the old apothecary chest she'd used as a jewelry case, brought the grief back.

But she wouldn't be driven out of her own room, out of her own home. Gritting her teeth, she hauled the mattress back into place. Then got out fresh sheets, made the bed. She rehung clothes that had been pulled out of her closet, folded more and tucked them neatly into drawers.

It was after three before she crawled into bed, and breaking her own rule, she patted the mattress and called Henry up to sleep beside her.

She reached for the light but hesitated, then drew her

hand away. If it was cowardice and a foolish security blanket to sleep with a light on, she could live with that.

She was insured, she reminded herself. Nothing had been taken, or broken, that couldn't be replaced. They were just things—and she made her living, didn't she, buying and selling things?

She burrowed under the blankets with the dog staring soulfully into her eyes. "Just things, Henry. Things don't matter all that much."

She closed her eyes, let out a long sigh. She was just drifting off when Willy's face floated into her mind.

He knows where you are now.

She sat straight up in bed, her breath coming in short pants. What did it mean? *Who* did it mean?

Willy shows up one day, out of the blue, after nearly twenty years, and ends up dead on the doorstep of her shop. Then her house is burgled and vandalized.

It had to be connected. How could it not be? she asked herself. But who was looking for what? She didn't have anything.

CHAPTER

4

Half-dressed, his hair still dripping from his morning shower, Max answered the knock on his hotel room door with one and only one thought on his mind: coffee.

The disappointment was one thing. A man learned to live with disappointments. Hadn't he slept alone? Finding a cop at his door was another. It meant nimbling up the brain without the God-given and inalienable right of caffeine.

He sized up the local heat—big, fit, suspicious—and tried on a cooperative if puzzled smile. "Morning. That doesn't look like a room service uniform, so I'm guessing you're not here to deliver my coffee and eggs."

"I'm Chief Burger, Mr. Gannon. Can I have a minute of your time?"

"Sure." He stepped back, glanced at the room. The bed was unmade, and steam from the shower was still drifting into the room through the open bathroom door.

The desk looked like the hotel room desk of a busy businessman—laptop, file folders and disks, his PDA, his cell phone—and that was fine. He'd taken the precaution, as he always did, of closing down all files and stashing any questionable paperwork.

"Ah . . ." Max gestured vaguely to the chair. "Have a seat," he invited and walked to the closet to pull out a shirt. "Is there some problem?"

Vince didn't sit; he didn't smile. "You're acquainted with Laine Tavish."

"Yeah." A lot of little warning bells went off and echoed with questions, but Max just pulled on the shirt. "Remember When. I bought a present for my mother at her place yesterday." He put a shadow of concern in his voice. "Something wrong with my credit card?"

"Not that I'm aware of. Miss Tavish's residence was broken into last night."

"Is she all right? Was she hurt?" He didn't have to feign concern now as those alarm bells shot through him. The hands that had been busily buttoning his shirt dropped to his side. "Where is she?"

"She wasn't on the premises at the time of the break-in. Her statement indicates she was with you."

"We had dinner. Damn it." As coffee was no longer paramount on his list, Max cursed at the knock. "Hold on a minute." He opened the door to the cute little blonde who stood by the room service cart.

"Morning, Mr. Gannon. Ready for breakfast?"

"Yeah, thanks. Just . . . put it anywhere."

She caught sight of Vince as she rolled in the cart. "Oh, hi, Chief."

"Sherry. How you doing?"

"Oh . . . you know." She angled the cart and tried not to

look overly curious as she shot glances at both men. "I can go down, get another cup if you want coffee, Chief."

"Don't you worry about it, Sherry. I had two before I left the house."

"Just call down if you change your mind." She pulled the warming cover off a plate, revealing an omelette and a side of bacon. "Um . . ." She held out the leather folder to Max, waited while he signed the bill. "Hope you enjoy your breakfast, Mr. Gannon."

She walked out, casting one last look over her shoulder before she shut the door.

"Go ahead," Vince invited. "No point letting those eggs get cold. They make a nice omelette here."

"What kind of break-in was it? Burglary?"

"Looked that way. Why was Miss Tavish with you last night?"

Max sat, decided to pour the coffee. "Socializing. I asked her to have a drink with me. She agreed. I hoped to be able to extend that to dinner, and since she was agreeable to that after we had a drink—down in the lounge here—we went into the dining room."

"You always make dates with women when you buy presents for your mother?"

"If it worked that well, I'd be buying my mama a lot more presents." Max lifted his cup, drank and met Vince's eyes over the rim. "Laine's a very attractive, very interesting woman. I wanted to see her, socially. I asked. I'm sorry she's got trouble."

"Somebody got in and out of her place during the time she was in town here, socializing with you."

"Yeah, I get that." Max decided he might as well eat, and forked up some omelette. "So you're wondering if I go around hitting on pretty women in shops, then setting them up for a burglary while I charm them over dinner. That's a stretch, Chief, since I never set eyes on Laine before yesterday, don't—as yet—know her residence or if she's got something worth stealing in it. Be smarter, wouldn't it, to hit the shop? She's got a lot of nice merchandise in it."

Vince simply watched Max eat, said nothing. "Couple of good thick glasses over there," Max said after a moment, "if you want some of this coffee after all."

"I'll pass. What's your business in Angel's Gap, Mr. Gannon?"

"I'm with Reliance Insurance, and I'm here doing some fieldwork."

"What kind of fieldwork?"

"Chief Burger, you can contact Aaron Slaker, CEO of Reliance, and verify my association with the company. He's based in New York. But I'm not at liberty to discuss the details of my work without my client's permission."

"That doesn't sound like insurance work to me."

"There's all kinds of insurance." Max opened a little jar of strawberry jam and spread some on a triangle of toast.

"You got identification?"

"Sure." Max rose, walked over to the dresser and took his driver's license out of his wallet. He passed it to Vince, then took his seat again.

"You don't sound like New York City."

"Just can't drum the Georgia out of the boy." He was just irritated enough to exaggerate his drawl and make it a challenge. "I don't steal, Chief. I just wanted to have dinner with a pretty woman. You go ahead and call Slaker."

Vince dropped the license beside Max's plate. "I'll do that." He started for the door, turned with his hand on the knob. "How long do you plan to be in town, Mr. Gannon?"

"Till the job's done." He scooped up more egg. "Chief? You were right. They do a really good omelette here."

Even when the door shut behind Vince, Max sat and ate. And considered. A cop being a cop, Burger would run him, and the run would turn up his four years on the force. And his investigator's license. Small towns being small towns, that little tidbit would get back to Laine before too long.

He'd decide how to play that when it had to be played. Meanwhile there was the matter of the break-in. The timing was just a little too good to be serendipity. And it told him he wasn't the only one who thought the very attractive Miss Tavish had something to hide.

It was all a matter of who was going to find it first.

"Don't worry about anything," Jenny assured Laine. "Angie and I can handle things here. Are you sure you don't want to just close the store for the day? Vince said your place is a wreck. I could come over and help you out."

Laine switched the phone to her other ear, scanning her home office and thinking about the very pregnant Jenny dragging chairs and tables into place. "No, but thanks. I'd feel better knowing you and Angie have the shop. There's a shipment coming in this morning, a pretty big one from the auction in Baltimore."

And, damn it, she wanted to be there, getting her hands on all those lovely things. Admiring them, cataloguing them, arranging them. A good deal of the enjoyment came from setting up new stock in her place, and the rest came from watching it walk out the door again.

"I need you to log in the new stock, Jen. I've already done the pricing, that's in the file. There's a Clarice Cliff lotus jug, with a tulip design. You want to call Mrs. Gunt and let her know we have it. The price we agreed on is seven hundred, but she'll want to negotiate. Six seventy-five is firm. Okay?"

"Gotcha."

"Oh, and—"

"Laine, relax. It's not my first day on the job. I'll take care of things here, and if anything comes up I can't handle, I'll call you."

"I know." Absently, Laine reached down to pet the dog, who was all but glued to her side. "Too much on my mind."

"Small wonder. I hate the thought of you handling that mess on your own. You sure you don't want me to come? I could bop over at lunchtime. Angie can handle the shop for an hour. I'll bring you something to eat. Something loaded with fat and wasted calories."

Angie *could* handle the shop, Laine considered. She was good and getting better. But Laine knew herself. She'd get more done if she worked alone without conversation or distraction.

"That's okay. I'll be all right once I get started. I'll probably be in this afternoon."

"Take a nap instead."

"Maybe. I'll talk to you later." When she hung up, Laine stuck the little portable phone in the back pocket of her baggy jeans. She knew herself well enough to be sure she'd find half a dozen reasons to call the shop during the day. Might as well keep a phone handy.

But for now, she needed to focus on the matter at hand.

" 'Hide the pooch,' " she murmured. Since the only pooch she had was Henry, she had to assume Willy had been delirious. Whatever he'd come to tell her, to ask of her, to give her, hadn't been done. He'd thought someone was after him, and unless he'd changed his ways, which was highly unlikely, he'd probably been right.

A cop, skip tracer, a partner in crime who hadn't liked the cut? Any or all of the above was a possibility. But the state of her house told her the last option was the most likely.

Now whoever had been looking for him was looking at her.

She could tell Vince . . . what? Absolutely nothing. Everything she'd built here was dug into the foundation that she was Laine Tavish, a nice, ordinary woman with a nice, ordinary life with nice, ordinary parents who ran a barbecue place in New Mexico.

Elaine O'Hara, daughter of Big Jack of the charming and wily ways—and yard-long yellow sheet—didn't fit into the pretty, pastoral landscape of Angel's Gap. Nobody was going to come into Elaine O'Hara's place to buy a teapot or a piecrust table.

Jack O'Hara's daughter couldn't be trusted.

Hell, she didn't trust Jack O'Hara's daughter herself. Big Jack's daughter was the type who had drinks in a bar with a strange man and ended up knocking said man on his excellent ass with a steamy, soul-deep kiss. Jack's daughter took big, bad chances that had big, bad consequences.

Laine Tavish lived normal, thought things through and didn't make waves.

She'd let the O'Hara out for one brief evening, and look what it had gotten her. An exciting, sexy interlude, sure, and a hell of a mess at the end of it.

"It just goes to show," she murmured to Henry, who demonstrated his accord by thumping his tail.

Time to put things back in order. She wasn't giving up who she was, what she'd accomplished, what she planned to accomplish, because some second-rate thief believed she had part of his last take.

Had to be second-rate, she thought as she gathered up the loose stuffing from the once pretty silk throw pillows she'd picked out for the George II daybed. Uncle Willy never traveled in the big leagues. And neither, despite all his talk, all his dreams, had Big Jack.

So, they'd trashed her place, come up empty and took easily fenced items in lieu.

That, Laine thought, would be that.

Of course, they'd probably left prints all over the damn place. She rolled her eyes, sat on the floor and started stacking scattered paperwork. Dim bulbs were a specialty when Uncle Willy was involved in a job. It was likely whoever'd broken in, searched, stolen, would have a record. Vince would trace that, identify them, and it was well within the realm of possibility that they'd get picked up.

It was also in that realm that they'd be stupid enough to tell the cops why they broke in. If that came down, she'd claim mistaken identity.

She'd be shocked, outraged, baffled. Acting the part—whatever part was necessary—was second nature. There was enough of Big Jack in her veins that running a con wouldn't be a stretch of her skills.

What was she doing now, Laine Tavish of Angel's Gap, but running a lifetime con?

Because the thought depressed her, she pushed it aside and immersed herself in refiling her paperwork. Immersed enough that she nearly jumped straight off the floor when she heard the knock on the front door.

Henry bolted out of his mid-morning snooze and sent out a furious spate of throaty, threatening barks—even as he slunk behind Laine and tried to hide his bulk in the crook of her arm.

"My big, brave hero." She nuzzled him. "It's probably the window guy. No eating the window guy, right?"

As a testament to his great love and devotion, Henry went with her. He made growling noises and stayed one safe pace behind.

She was wary enough herself after the break-in to peek out the window before unlocking the door. Her brain, and her blood, did a little snap and sizzle when she saw Max.

Instinctively she looked down, in disgust, at her oldest jeans, her bare feet, the ancient gray sweatshirt. She'd yanked her hair back in a short tail that morning and hadn't bothered with makeup.

"Not exactly the look I wanted to present to the man I considered getting naked with at the first reasonable opportunity," she said to Henry. "But what're you gonna do?"

She pulled open the door and ordered herself to be casual. "Max. This is a surprise. How'd you find me?"

"I asked. You okay? I heard about . . ." He trailed off, his gaze tracking down to her knees. "Henry? Well, that's about the homeliest dog I've ever seen." A big grin split his face when he said it, and it was hard to take offense as he crouched down to dog level and aimed the grin at the dog.

"Hey, big guy, how's it going?"

Most, in Laine's experience, were at least initially intimidated by the dog. He *was* big, he *was* ugly, and when he was growling in his throat, he sounded dangerous. But Max was already holding a hand out, offering it for a sniff. "That's some bad face you've got there, Henry."

Obviously torn between terror and delight, Henry inched his snout forward, took some testing whiffs. His tail whapped the back of Laine's knees before he collapsed, rolled and exposed his belly for a rub.

"He has no pride," Laine stated.

"Doesn't need any." Max became the newest love of Henry's life by giving the soft belly a vigorous rub. "Nothing like a dog, is there?"

First there'd been lust, she thought, naturally enough. Then interest and several layers of attraction. She'd been prepared—or had been trying to prepare—to shuffle all those impulses aside and be sensible.

Now, seeing him with her dog, she felt the warming around the heart that signaled—uh-oh—personal affection. Add that to lust and attraction and a woman, even a sensible woman, was sunk. "No, there really isn't."

"Always had a dog at home. Can't keep one in New York, not the way I travel around. Doesn't seem right." His hand slid up to rub Henry's throat and send the dog into ecstasy.

Laine very nearly moaned.

"That's the downside of city living for me," Max added. "How'd they get around him?"

"I'm sorry?"

He gave Henry a last thumping pat, then straightened. "I heard about the break-in. Big dog like this should've given them some trouble."

Down, girl, Laine ordered herself. "Afraid not. One, he was shut in the mudroom. That's his place when I'm out. And second, well . . ." She looked down at Henry, who was slavishly licking Max's hand. "He doesn't exactly have a warrior's heart."

"You okay?"

"As good as it gets, I suppose, the morning after you

come home and find somebody's trashed your house and stolen your property."

"You're pretty secluded back here. I don't guess anyone saw anything."

"I doubt it. Vince, the police chief, will ask, but I'm the only house back on this lane."

"Yeah, I met the chief. Another reason I came by was to make sure you didn't think I asked you to dinner to get you out of the house so this could happen."

"Well, of course not. Why would . . ." She followed the dots. "Vince. I hope he didn't make you uncomfortable."

"It's his job. And now I see I've put the same suspicion in your head."

"No, not . . ." But she was trying it on. "Not really. It's just been a very strange week. I think I've dealt with Vince twice on a professional level since I moved here. Now it's been twice in a matter of days. He must've come by your hotel room this morning. I'm sorry."

"Just routine. But coming home and finding your house has been burgled isn't." He reached out, touched her cheek. "I was worried about you."

The warmth pumped up a few degrees. She told herself it wasn't a good fit—Willy Young and Max Gannon in league. And that if Max was of the ilk, she'd know.

Like, she believed, recognized like.

"I'm okay. Jenny and Angie will work the shop today while I put the house back into shape." She gestured toward the living room. "I've barely made a dent. Good thing I like to shop, because that'll be stage two."

He stepped around her, looking into the room himself.

It could be taken for a spate of vandalism accompanying a burglary. But to Max's eyes it looked like what it was: a fast, nasty search. And if they'd gotten what they were after, he didn't think Laine would be calmly clearing up the debris and talking about shopping.

Nobody was that cool.

On the tail of that thought, he imagined her coming home alone, in the dark, and opening her house to this. Small wonder she had shadows under her eyes and the pale look of a woman who'd spent a sleepless night.

"They did a number on you," he murmured.

"Not the usual thing in the Gap. When I lived in Philadelphia, I worked with a woman who went home one night, found her apartment broken into. They cleaned her out *and* spray-painted obscenities on the walls."

He looked back at her. "So it could be worse?"

"It can always be worse. Listen, I've put the kitchen back together and made a quick morning run to the store so there's coffee. You want?"

"I always want." He walked to her. She looked so fresh. All that bright hair pulled back from that pretty face, her eyes only bluer with the shadows haunting them. She smelled like soap, just soap. The innocent charm of freckles was sprinkled over her nose.

"Laine, I'm not looking to get in your way, but . . . let me help you."

"Help me what?"

He wasn't sure, but he knew he meant it, that the offer was unqualified. He looked at her, and he wanted to help. "For a start, I can help you put your house back together."

"You don't have to do that. You must have work—"

"Let me help." He cut off her protest simply by taking her hand. "I've got time, and the fact is, if I went on my way, I'd worry about you and I'd never get anything done anyway."

"That's awfully sweet." And she knew she was a goner. "That's really very sweet."

"And there's this one other thing." He took a step forward, into her, which put her back up against the wall. Still, when his mouth came down, the kiss was slow and smooth, almost dreamy. She felt her knees unlock and go halfway to dissolve before he lifted his head. "If I didn't do that, I'd be thinking about doing it. Figured we'd get more done if I got it out of the way first."

"Good." She ran her tongue over her bottom lip. "Finished?"

"Not hardly."

"That's good, too. Coffee," she decided before they started rolling around on the floor of the disordered room instead of setting it to rights. "I'll just get that coffee."

She walked back toward the kitchen, with the dog prancing happily beside her. It helped, for the moment, to keep busy. Grinding beans, measuring coffee into the French press. He'd gotten her nerves up again, she realized. He was just leaning against the counter, watching her. That long body relaxed, but those eyes focused. Something about him made her want to rub up against him like a cat begging to be stroked.

"I have to say something."

"Okay."

She got down two of the mugs that had survived the kitchen rampage. "I don't usually . . . Hold on, let me figure out how to say this without sounding incredibly stupid and ordinary."

"I don't think you could sound either. Ever."

"Boy, you really push the right buttons. All right." She turned to him while the coffee steeped. "It's not my habit to make dates, even casual ones, with a man I've just met. With a customer. In fact, you're the first."

"I've always liked being first."

"Who doesn't? And while I enjoy the company of men, and the benefits thereof, I also don't, as a rule, wrap myself around one after dinner like sumac around an oak."

He was certain he'd remember the moment she had for a long time. It would probably come back to him on his deathbed as a major highlight of his life and times. "Would I be the first there, too?"

"At that level."

"Better and better."

"You want cream? Sugar?"

"Just black's good."

"Okay then, to continue. I also don't—and this has been a pretty hard-and-fast rule of thumb—contemplate sleeping with a man I've only known for twenty-four hours, give or take."

He was scratching Henry between the ears, but he never took his eyes off her face. "You know what they say about rules."

"Yes, and though I agree with what they say, I don't break them lightly. I'm a firm believer in the need for structure, Max, in rules and lines. So the fact that I'm considering breaking a rule, crossing a line, makes me nervous. It'd be smarter, safer, more sensible if we backed away a bit, at least until we get to know each other better. Until we give things a chance to develop at a more reasonable and rational pace."

"Smarter," he agreed. "Safer. Sensible."

"You have no idea how hard I've worked to live by those three attributes." She laughed a little, then poured the coffee. "And the problem here is I've never been as attracted to anyone as I am to you."

"Maybe I'm a little looser when it comes to rules and lines, and not as worried about being sensible in certain areas." He took the mug she offered, then set it on the counter. "But I know I've never looked at another woman and wanted her the way I want you."

"That's not going to help me be smart." She picked up her coffee, stepped back. "But I need some order. Let me put my house back together, as best I can, and we'll see where things go."

"Hard to argue with that. We share some of these domestic chores, we ought to get to know each other."

"Well, it's one way." He'd be a distraction, she concluded. A lot more of a distraction than Jenny and a lunchtime Big Mac.

But what the hell.

"Since I've got some muscle on hand, let's start with the living room. The sofa's pretty heavy."

In Remember When, business was brisk. Or at least browsing was. It hadn't taken long for word to get out about Laine's latest trouble, or to bring out the curious to pump for more details. By one, with the new shipments logged, tagged and displayed, sales rung up and gossip exchanged in abundance, Jenny pressed a hand to the ache in her lower back.

"I'm going to take lunch at home where I can put my feet up for an hour. Will you be all right on your own?"

"Sure." Angie held up a protein bar and a bottled, low-fat Frappucino. "Got my lunch right here."

"You don't know how sad it makes me, Ange, to hear you call that lunch."

"Weighed in at one-nineteen this morning."

"Bitch."

While Angie laughed, Jenny got her purse from behind the counter and her sweater from the hook. "I'm going to nuke leftover pasta primavera and finish it off with a brownie."

"Now who's the bitch?" She gave Jenny's belly a pat, hoping as always to catch the baby kicking. "How's it going in there?"

"Night owl." She stuck a loose bobby pin back in her messy topknot. "I swear the kid wakes up and starts tap dancing every night about eleven, and keeps it up for hours."

"You love it."

"I do." Smiling now, Jenny tugged on the sweater. "Every minute of it. Best time of my life. Be back in an hour."

"Got it covered. Hey, should I call Laine? Just check on her?"

"I'll do it from home," Jenny called back as she walked to the door. Before she reached it, it opened. She recognized the couple, searched around in her mental files for the name. "Nice to see you. Dale and Melissa, right?"

"Good memory." The woman, thirtyish, gym-fit and stylish, smiled at her.

"And as I recall, you were interested in the rosewood armoire."

"Right again. I see it's still here." Even as she spoke, she walked to it, ran her hand over the carving on the door. "It keeps calling my name."

"It's such a beautiful piece." Angie strolled around the counter. "One of my favorites." The truth was she preferred the modern and streamlined, but she knew how to pitch. "We just got another rosewood piece today. It's a gorgeous little davenport. Victorian. I think they're made for each other."

"Uh-oh." Laughing, Melissa squeezed her husband's arm. "I guess I have to take a look at least."

"I'll show you."

"I was just on my way out, if you don't need me . . ."

"We're fine." Angie waved Jenny away. "Isn't it beautiful?" she said, aiming her pitch at Melissa as she ran a fingertip down the glossy writing slope. "It's in wonderful condition. Laine has such a good eye. She found this in Baltimore a few weeks ago. It arrived only this morning."

"It's wonderful." Leaning down, Melissa began opening and closing the small side drawers. "Really wonderful. I thought a davenport was a kind of couch."

"Yeah, but this kind of little desk is called that, too. Don't ask me why; that's Laine's territory."

"I really love it, whatever it's called. Dale?"

He was fingering the price tag and sent her a look. "I've got to think about getting both, Melissa. It's a pretty big chunk."

"Maybe we can chip it down a little."

"We can work on that," Angie told her.

"Let me take another look at the armoire." She walked back over, opened the doors.

Knowing how to pace a sale, Angie hung back while Dale joined his wife and they began a whispered consultation.

The doors were closed again, opened again, drawers were pulled out.

"Do we get what's inside, too?" Dale called out.

"I'm sorry?"

"Box in here." He took out the package, shook it. "Is it like the prize in the cereal box?"

"Not this time." With an easy laugh, Angie crossed over to take the box. "We had a big shipment come in this morning," she began. "And we were pretty busy on top of it. Jenny must've gotten distracted and set this in there."

Or had she? Things had been hopping for an hour or two. Either way, Angie considered it a lucky break the drawer had been opened before the piece was missed.

"We're just going to talk this over for a few minutes," Melissa told her.

"Take your time." Leaving them to it, Angie went back to the counter. She unwrapped the package and studied the silly ceramic dog. Cute, she thought, but she didn't understand why anyone paid good money for animal pieces.

She found soft, fuzzy stuffed animals more companionable.

This was probably Doulton or Derby or one of those things Laine was still trying to teach her.

Since, from little snatches of conversation, Melissa seemed to be wearing Dale down all on her own, Angie gave them a little more space by walking the statue over to one of a few displays of figurines and bric-a-brac to try to identify the type and era.

It was like a game to her. She'd find it in the file, of course, but that would be cheating. Identifying pieces in the shop was very like identifying character types in the bar. If you spent enough time at it, it got so you knew who was who and what was what.

"Miss?"

"Angie." She turned, grinned.

"If we took both, what sort of a price could you give us?"

"Well . . ." Delighted with the prospect of greeting Jenny with news of a double, she set the ceramic dog down and went over to bargain with the customers.

In the excitement of closing the deal, arranging for delivery, ringing up the sale, she didn't give the little dog another thought.

Max learned quite a bit about Laine over the next few hours. She was organized, practical and precise. More linear-minded than what he'd expected from someone of her background. She looked at a task, saw it from beginning to end, then followed it through the steps to completion. No detours, no distractions.

And she was a nester. His mother had the same bent, just loved feathering that nest with pretty little—what did his father call them?—gimcracks. And like his mother, Laine knew exactly where she preferred every one of them.

But unlike his mother, Laine didn't appear to have a sentimental, almost intimate attachment to her things. He'd once seen his mother weep buckets over a broken vase, and he himself had felt the mighty heat of her wrath when he'd shattered an old decorative bowl.

Laine swept up shards of this, pieces of that, dumped

broken bits into a trash can with barely a wince. Her focus was on returning order to her space. He had to respect that.

Though it was a puzzlement to him how the daughter of a drifter and a grifter executed a one-eighty to become a small-town homebody, the fact that puzzles were his business made it, and her, only more interesting.

He liked being in her nest, being in her company. It was a given that the sizzle between them was going to complicate things along the way, but it was tough not to enjoy it.

He liked her voice, the fact that it managed to be both throaty and smooth. He liked that she looked sexy in a sweatshirt. He liked her freckles.

He admired her resilience in the face of what would have devastated most people. And he admired and appreciated her flat-out honesty about her reaction to him and what was brewing between them.

The fact was, under other circumstances, he could see himself diving headfirst into a relationship with her, burning his bridges, casting caution to the wind or any number of clichés. Even given the circumstances, he was poised to make that dive. He couldn't quite figure out if that was a plus or a minus.

But side benefit or obstacle to the goal, it was time to get back in the game.

"You lost a lot of stuff," he commented.

"I can always get more stuff." But she felt a little tug of sorrow at the wide chip in the Derby jug she'd kept on the dining room server. "I got into the business because I like to collect all manner of things. Then I realized I didn't need to own them so much as be around them, see them, touch."

She ran her finger down the damaged jug. "And it's just

as rewarding, more in some ways, to buy and sell, and see interesting pieces go to interesting people."

"Don't dull people ever buy interesting pieces?"

She laughed at that. "Yes, they do. Which is why it's important not to become too attached to what you plan to sell. And I love to sell. Kaching."

"How do you know what to buy in the first place?"

"Some's instinct, some's experience. Some is just a gamble."

"You like to gamble?"

She slid a glance over and up. "As a matter of fact."

Oh yeah, he thought, he was poised and rolling up to his toes on the edge of the cliff. "Want to blow this joint and fly to Vegas?"

She arched her eyebrows. "And if I said sure, why not?"

"I'd book the flight."

"You know," she said after a moment's study, "I believe you would. I think I like that." The O'Hara in her was already on her way to the airport. "But unfortunately, I can't take you up on it." And that was the Tavish. "How about a rain check?"

"You got it. Open-ended." He watched her place a few pieces that had survived the break-in. Candlesticks, an enormous pottery bowl, a long flat dish. He had a feeling she'd put them precisely where they'd been before. There would be comfort in that. And defiance.

"You know, looking around at all this, it doesn't seem like a simple break-in. If that can be simple when it's your place. It sure doesn't strike me as a standard grab-and-run. It feels more personal."

"Well, that goes a long way to relieving my mind."

"Sorry. Wasn't thinking. Actually, you don't seem particularly spooked."

"I slept with the light on last night," she admitted. "Like that would make a difference. It doesn't do any good to be spooked. Doesn't change anything or fix anything."

"An alarm system wouldn't hurt. Something a little more high-tech than the canine variety," he added, looking down at where Henry snored under the dining room table.

"No. I thought about that for about five minutes. An alarm system wouldn't make me feel safe. It'd just make me feel like I had something to worry about. I'm not going to be afraid in my own home."

"Let me just push this button a little more before we let it go. Do you think this could've been somebody you know? Do you have any enemies?"

"No, and no," she answered with a careless shrug as she scooted the ladder-back chairs back to the table. But she heard Willy's words in her head: *He knows where you are.*

Who knew?

Daddy?

"Now I've got you worried." He tipped her face up with a finger under her chin. "I can see it."

"No, not worried. Disconcerted, maybe, at the idea that I could have enemies. Ordinary shopkeepers in small Maryland towns shouldn't have enemies."

He rubbed his thumb along her jaw. "You're not ordinary."

She let her lips curve as his came down to meet them. He had no idea, she thought, how hard she'd worked for nearly half her life to *be* ordinary.

His hands were sliding over her hips when her phone rang. "You hear bells?" he asked.

She drew back with a little laugh and pulled the phone out of her pocket. "Hello? Hi, Angie." As she listened, she shifted the chipped jug a half inch on the server. "*Both* pieces? That's wonderful. What did . . . ? Uh-huh. No, you did exactly right. It's called a davenport because a small desk was designed for a Captain Davenport back in the 1800s and it stuck, I guess. Yes, I'm fine. Really, and yes, this certainly perks me up. Thanks, Angie. I'll talk to you later."

"I thought a davenport was a couch," Max said when she stuck the phone back in her pocket.

"It is, or a small sofa that often converts into a bed. It's also a small desk with a boxlike form with an upper section that slides or turns to provide knee space."

"Huh. The things you learn."

"I could teach you all sorts of things." Enjoying herself, she walked her fingers up his chest. "Want me to show you the difference between a canterbury and a commode?"

"Can't wait."

She took his hand, drew him toward her little library, where she could give a short lesson in antiques while they put the room back in order.

When the tall, distinguished gentleman with the trim pewter mustache walked into Remember When, Jenny was contemplating what she might fix for dinner. Since it seemed she was hungry *all* the time, thinking about food was nearly as satisfying as eating it.

After Angie's big sale, the pace had slowed. She'd had a few browsers, and Mrs. Gunt had come on the run to see the lotus jug and snap it up. But for the next hour, she and Angie had been puttering, and the day took on a lazy tone that had her giving Angie an early out.

She looked over at the sound of the door, pleased that a customer would temporarily take her mind off pork chops and mashed potatoes.

"Good afternoon. Can I help you?"

"I think I'll just look around, if that's all right. What an interesting place. Yours?"

"No. The owner's not in today. Browse all you like. If you have any questions or need any help, just let me know."

"I'll do that."

He was wearing a suit nearly the same color as his mustache and the thick, well-cut head of hair. The suit, and subtle stripe of the tie, made her think money. His voice was just clipped enough to have her assuming North.

Her saleswoman's instinct told her he wouldn't mind a little conversation as he wandered. "Are you visiting Angel's Gap?"

"I have business in the area." He smiled, and it deepened the hollows of his cheeks, turned his eyes into a warm blue and made distinguished just a little sexy. "Such a friendly town."

"Yes, it is."

"And so scenic. Good for business, I'd think. I have a shop of my own." He leaned over to study the display of heirloom jewelry. "Estate jewelry," he said, tapping the glass. "The buying and selling. Very nice pieces here. Unexpected, really, outside a metropolitan area."

"Thank you. Laine's very particular about what we sell here."

"Laine?"

"Laine Tavish, the owner."

"I wonder if I haven't heard that name. Possibly even met her at one of the auctions. It's a relatively small pool we swim in."

"You might have. If you're staying in town for a while, you could come back in. She's usually here."

"I'll be sure to do that. Tell me, do you sell loose stones as well?"

"Stones?"

At Jenny's blank look he angled his head. "I often buy stones—gemstones—to replace ones lost from an antique setting, or to duplicate an estate piece for a client."

"Oh. No, we don't. Of course, the jewelry's just a small part of our stock."

"So I see." He turned, and those eyes scanned every inch of the main showroom. "An eclectic mix, styles, periods. Does Ms. Tavish do all the buying?"

"Yes, she does. We're lucky to have someone like Laine in the Gap. The store's developed a good reputation, and we're listed in several guides to the area, and antique and collectible magazines."

He wandered off, walking in the direction of a table set with porcelain figurines and small bronzes. "So, she's not a local then."

"You're not a local in the Gap unless your grandfather was born here. But no, Laine moved here a few years ago."

"Tavish, Tavish . . ." He angled back around, narrowing his eyes, stroking his mustache. "Is she a tall, rather lanky woman with very short blond hair? Wears little black glasses?"

"No, Laine's a redhead."

"Ah well, hardly matters. This is a lovely piece." He picked up an elegant china cat. "Do you ship?"

"We certainly do. I'd be happy to . . . Oh, hi, honey," she said when Vince walked in. "My husband," she said to the customer with a wink. "I don't call all the cops honey."

"I was heading by, thought I'd stop in to see if Laine was here. Check on her."

"No, I don't think she's coming in today after all. Got her hands full. Laine's house was broken into last night," she said.

"God, how awful." The man lifted a hand to the knot of his tie, and the dark blue stone in his pinkie ring winked. "Was anyone hurt?"

"No, she wasn't home. Sorry, Vince, this is Mr. . . . I never did get your name."

"It's Alexander, Miles Alexander." He offered a hand to Vince.

"Vince Burger. Do you know Laine?"

"Actually, we were just trying to determine that. I sell estate jewelry and wondered if I've met Ms. Tavish along the circuit. I'm sorry to hear about her trouble. I'm very interested in the cat," he said to Jenny, "but I'm going to be late for my afternoon appointment. I'll come back, and hopefully meet Ms. Tavish. Thanks for your time, Mrs. Burger."

"Jenny. Come back anytime," she added as he walked to the door.

When they were alone in the shop, Jenny poked Vince in the belly. "You looked at him like he was a suspect."

"No, I didn't." He gave her a return, and very gentle, poke in her belly. "I'm just curious, that's all, when I see a guy in a slick-looking suit hanging around the shop the day after Laine's house is broken into."

"Yeah, he looked like a rampaging burglar all right."

"Okay, what's a rampaging burglar look like?"

"Not like that."

*His name was Alex Crew, though he had proper iden-*tification in the name of Miles Alexander—and several other aliases. Now he walked briskly along the sloping

sidewalk. He had to walk off his anger, his quietly bub-
bling rage that Laine Tavish hadn't been where he'd wanted
to find her.

He despised being foiled, on any level.

Still, the walk was part business. He needed to get the
lay of the land on foot, though he had a detailed map of
Angel's Gap in his head. He didn't enjoy small towns, or
the burgeoning green view of the surrounding mountains.
He was a man for the city, its pace, its opportunities.

Its abundance of marks.

For rest and relaxation, he enjoyed the tropics, with their
balmy breezes, moon-washed nights and rich tourists.

This place was full of hicks, like the pregnant sales-
clerk—probably on her fourth kid by now—and her ex–
high-school football hero turned town cop husband. Guy
looked like the type who sat around on Saturday nights
with his buddies and talked about the glory days over a six-
pack. Or sat in the woods waiting for a deer to come by so
he could shoot it and feel like a hero again.

Crew deplored such men and the women who kept their
dinner warm at night.

His father had been such a man.

No imagination, no vision, no palate for the taste of larceny. His old man wouldn't have taken the time of day if
it wasn't marked on his time sheet. And what had it gotten
him but a worn-out and complaining wife, a hot box of a
row house in Camden and an early grave.

To Crew's mind, his father had been a pathetic waste
of life.

He'd always wanted more, and had started taking it
when he crawled through his first second-story window at
twelve. He boosted his first car at fourteen, but his ambitions had always run to bigger, shinier games.

He liked stealing from the rich, but there was nothing of the Robin Hood in him. He liked it simply because the rich had better things, and having them, taking them, made him feel like he was part of the cream.

He killed his first man at twenty-two, and though it had been unplanned—bad clams had sent the mark home early from the ballet—he had no aversion to stealing a life. Particularly if there was a good profit in it.

He was forty-eight years old, had a taste for French wine and Italian suits. He had a home in Westchester from which his wife had fled—taking his young son—just prior to their divorce. He also kept a luxurious apartment off Central Park where he entertained lavishly when the mood struck, a weekend home in the Hamptons and a seaside home on Grand Cayman. All of the deeds were in different names.

He'd done very well for himself by taking what belonged to others and, if he said so himself, had become a kind of connoisseur. He was selective in what he stole now, and had been for more than a decade. Art and gems were his specialties, with an occasional foray into rare stamps.

He'd had a few arrests along the way, but only one conviction—a smudge he blamed entirely on his incompetent and overpriced lawyer.

The man had paid for it, as Crew had beaten him to bloody death with a lead pipe three months after his release. But to Crew's mind those scales were hardly balanced. He'd spent twenty-six months inside, deprived of his freedom, debased and humiliated.

The idiot lawyer's death was hardly compensation.

But that had been more than twenty years ago. Though he'd been picked up for questioning a time or two since, there'd been no other arrests. The single benefit of those months in prison had been the endless time to think, to evaluate, to consider.

It wasn't enough to steal. It was essential to steal well, and to live well. So he'd studied, developed his brain and his personas. To steal successfully from the rich, it was best to become one of them. To acquire knowledge and taste, unlike the dregs who rotted behind bars.

To gain entrée into society, to perhaps take a well-heeled wife at some point. Success, to his mind, wasn't climbing in second-story windows, but in directing others to do so. Others who could be manipulated, then disposed of as necessary. Because, whatever they took, at his direction, by all rights belonged exclusively to him.

He was smart, he was patient, and he was ruthless.

If he'd made a mistake along the way, it was nothing that couldn't and wouldn't be rectified. He *always* rectified his mistakes. The idiot lawyer, the foolish woman who'd objected to his bilking her of a few hundred thousand dollars, any number of slow-minded underlings he'd employed or associated with in the course of his career.

Big Jack O'Hara and his ridiculous sidekick Willy had been mistakes.

A misjudgment, Crew corrected as he turned the corner and started back to the hotel. They hadn't been quite as stupid as he'd assumed when he'd used them to plan out and execute the job of his lifetime. His grail, his quest. *His.*

How they had slipped through the trap he'd laid and gotten away with their cut before it sprang was a puzzle to him. For more than a month they'd managed to elude him. And neither had attempted to turn the take into cash—that was another surprise.

But he'd kept his nose to the ground and eventually picked up O'Hara's scent. Yet it hadn't been Jack he'd managed to track from New York to the Maryland mountains, but the foolish weasel Willy.

He shouldn't have let the little bastard see him, Crew thought now. But goddamn small towns. He hadn't expected to all but run into the man on the street. Any more than he'd expected Willy to bolt and run, a scared rabbit hopping right out and under the wheels of an oncoming car.

He'd been tempted to march through the rain, up to the bleeding mess and kick it. Millions of dollars at stake, and the idiot doesn't remember to look both ways before rushing into the street.

Then she'd come running out of that store. The pretty redhead with the shocked face. He'd seen that face before. Oh, he'd never met her, but he'd seen that face. Big Jack had photographs, and he'd loved to take them out and show them off once he had a couple of beers under his belt.

My daughter. Isn't she a beauty? Smart as a whip, too. College-educated, my Lainie.

Smart enough, Crew thought, to tuck herself into the straight life in a small town so she could fence goods, transport them, turn them over. It was a damn good con.

If Jack thought he could pass what belonged to Alex Crew to his daughter, and retire rich to Rio as he often liked to talk of doing, he was going to be surprised.

He was going to get back what belonged to him. Everything that belonged to him. And father and daughter were going to pay a heavy price.

He stepped into the lobby of the Wayfarer and had to force himself to suppress a shudder. He considered the accommodations barely tolerable. He took the stairs to his suite, put out the DO NOT DISTURB sign as he wanted to sit in the quiet while he planned his next move.

He needed to make contact with Laine Tavish, and

should probably do so as Miles Alexander, estate jewelry broker. He studied himself in the mirror and nodded. Alexander was a fresh alias, as was the silver hair and mustache. O'Hara knew him as Martin Lyle or Gerald Benson, and would have described him as clean-shaven, with close-cropped salt-and-pepper hair.

A flirtation might be an entrée, and he did enjoy female companionship. The mutual interest in estate jewelry had been a good touch. Better to take a few days, get a feel for her before he made another move.

She hadn't hidden the cache at her house, nor had there been any safe-deposit or locker key to be found. Otherwise he and the two thugs he'd hired for the job would have found them.

It might've been rash to burgle her place in such a messy fashion, but he'd been angry and so sure she had what belonged to him. He still believed she did, or knew where to find it. The best approach was to keep it friendly, perhaps romantic.

She was here, Willy was here—even if he was dead. Could Jack O'Hara be far behind?

Satisfied with the simplicity of the plan, Crew sat in front of his laptop. He brought up several sites on estate jewelry and began to study.

Laine woke in lamplight and stared blankly around her bedroom.

What time was it? What day was it? She scooped her hair back as she pushed herself up to peer at the clock. Eight-fifteen. It couldn't be A.M. because it was dark, so what was she doing in bed at eight at night?

On the bed, she corrected, with her chenille throw

tucked around her. And Henry snoring on the floor beside the bed.

She yawned, stretched, then snapped back.

Max!

Oh my God. He'd been helping her clear out the worst of the guest room, and they'd talked about going out to dinner. Or ordering in.

What had happened then? She searched her bleary brain. He'd taken the trash downstairs—outside—and she'd come into her bedroom to freshen up and change.

She'd just sat down on the bed for a minute.

All right, she'd stretched out on the bed for a minute. Shut her eyes. Just trying to regroup.

And now she was waking up nearly three hours later. Alone.

He'd covered her up, she thought with a sappy smile as she brushed a hand over the throw. And had turned on the light so she wouldn't wake in the dark.

She started to toss the throw aside and get up, and saw the note lying on the pillow beside her.

You looked too pretty and too tired for me to play Prince Charming to your Sleeping Beauty. I locked up, and your fierce hound is guarding you. Get a good night's sleep. I'll call you tomorrow. Better, I'll come by and see you.

Max

"Could he be more perfect?" she asked the still snoring Henry. Lying back, she pressed the note to her breast. "You should immediately suspect perfection, but oh boy, I'm enjoying this. I'm so tired of being suspicious and cautious, and alone."

She lay there another moment, smiling to herself. Sleeping Beauty wasn't sleepy anymore. In fact, she couldn't have been more awake or alert.

"You know how long it's been since I've done something really reckless?" She drew a deep breath, let it out. "Neither do I, that's how long it's been. It's time to gamble."

She sprang up, dashed into the bathroom to start the shower. On second thought, she decided, a bubble bath was more suited to the occasion she had in mind. There was time for one, and while it ran she'd look through her choices and pick something to wear most suited for seducing Max Gannon.

She used a warm freesia scent in the tub, then spent a full twenty minutes on her makeup. It took her nearly that long to decide whether to leave her hair down or put it up. She opted for up because he hadn't seen it that way yet, and fashioned a loose updo that would tumble at the slightest provocation.

This time, she went for the obvious and the little black dress. She was grateful for the shopping spree months before with the not-yet-pregnant Jenny that had netted them both some incredible lingerie.

Then, remembering that Jenny credited her current condition to that lingerie, Laine added more condoms to the ones she'd already tucked in her purse. It brought the total up to half a dozen, a number she giddily decided was both cautious and optimistic.

She slipped a tissue-thin black cashmere cardigan, a ridiculous indulgence she didn't get to wear nearly often enough, over the dress.

Taking one last study in the mirror, she turned to every angle. "If he turns you down," she stated, "there's no hope for mankind."

She whistled for the dog to follow her downstairs. After a dash into the kitchen to grab a bottle of wine, she took Henry's leash from the hook by the back door.

"Wanna go for a ride?" she asked, a question that always sent Henry into leaps and dashes of wild glee and shuddering excitement. "You're going to Jenny's. You're going to have a sleepover, and please, God, so am I. If I don't find an outlet for all this heat, I'm going to spontaneously combust."

He raced to the car and back three times by the time she reached it and opened the door for him. He leaped in and sat grinning in the passenger seat while she strapped the seat belt over him.

"I'm not even nervous. I can't believe I'm not nervous when I haven't done this in . . . well, no point thinking of that," she added as she got behind the wheel. "If I think of that, I *will be nervous*. I really like him. It's crazy because I hardly know him, but I really like him, Henry."

Henry barked, either in understanding or in joy as she started down the lane.

"It probably can't come to anything," she continued. "I mean, he lives in New York and I live here. But it doesn't have to come to anything, right? It doesn't have to mean undying love or lifetime commitment. It can just be lust and respect and affection and . . . lust. There's a whole lot of lust going on here, and there's nothing wrong with that.

"And I'm going to shut up before I find a way to talk myself out of this."

It was nearly ten by the time she pulled up in Jenny's driveway. Late, she thought. Sort of late to go knocking on a guy's hotel room door.

But just what was the proper time to go knocking on a guy's hotel room door?

Jenny was already coming out of the front door and down the walk. Laine released Henry's seat belt and waited for her friend to open the passenger door.

"Hi, Henry! There's my best guy, there he is. Vince is waiting for you."

"I owe you," Laine said as Henry raced madly for the house.

"Do not. Late date, huh?"

"Don't ask, don't tell."

Jenny leaned in as far as her belly would allow. "Are you kidding me?"

"Yes. I'll tell you everything tomorrow. Just do me one more favor?"

"Sure, what?"

"Pray, really hard, that there's something to tell."

"You got it, but the fabulous way you look, those prayers are already answered."

"Okay. Here goes."

"Go get 'em, honey." Jenny closed the door and stepped back, rubbing her belly as Laine drove away. "The guy's toast," she murmured, and went inside to play with Henry.

CHAPTER

6

It occurred to Laine that she looked like a woman on her way to an assignation. The little black dress, the sexy shoes, the bottle of wine tucked into the crook of her arm.

But that was okay. She *was* a woman on her way, she hoped, to an assignation. The man involved just didn't know it yet. And if she ran into someone she knew, so what? She was an adult, she was single and unencumbered. She was entitled to a night of healthy, no-strings sex.

But she was relieved when she crossed the lobby of the Wayfarer without seeing a familiar face. She pressed the Up button on the elevator and caught herself doing a relaxation breathing technique she'd learned in a yoga class.

She stopped.

She didn't want to relax. She could relax tomorrow. Tonight she wanted that live-wire sizzle in the blood, the tingling stomach muscles, the dance of chills and heat along the skin.

She stepped into the car when the doors opened and pressed the button for Max's floor. As her elevator doors closed, the doors on the one beside hers opened.

Alex Crew stepped out.

At his desk, with the TV muttering in the background for company, Max reviewed his notes and wrote up his daily report. He left out a few things, it was true. There was no point in documenting that he'd played with the dog, kissed Laine, or that he'd tucked a blanket over her then stood watching her sleep.

None of that was salient information.

He did detail the extent of the damage to her property, her actions and reactions and his opinions on what he observed to be her current lifestyle.

Simple, small-town, successful. Knowledgeable about her profession, cozily dug into her hillside home and the community.

But where had she gotten the funds to buy that home, to start up her business? The business loan and the mortgage he'd accessed—not in a strictly legal manner—didn't quite add up. She'd put down sizable deposits—more than it logically seemed possible for a young woman who'd earned a steady but unremarkable salary since college.

And still not an exorbitant amount, he reflected. Nothing showy. Nothing that hinted there was a great big money tree somewhere dripping with millions.

She drove a good, middle-of-the-road car. American made and three years old. She had some nice pieces of art and furnishings in her home, but she was in the business, so it wasn't remarkable.

Her wardrobe, what he'd seen, showed good classic taste. But it, too, wasn't exorbitant, and fit very neatly into the image of the single, successful antique merchant.

Everything about her fit that image, down to the ground.

She didn't live rich. She didn't look like an operator, and he could usually spot one. What was the point of buying a house in the woods, getting an ugly dog, opening a Main Steet, U.S.A., business if it wasn't what you wanted?

A woman with her attributes could be anywhere, doing anything. Therefore, it followed that she was doing exactly what she wanted to do.

And *that* just didn't add up either.

He was messed up about her, that was the problem. He tipped back in his chair, stared up at the ceiling. Every time he looked at her, his brain went soft on him. There was something about that face, the voice, Jesus, the *smell* of her, that was making a sap out of him.

Maybe he couldn't see her as an operator because he didn't want to see her that way. He hadn't been this twisted up in a woman since . . . Actually, he'd never been this twisted up in a woman.

Practically then, professionally then, he should back off a bit on the personal contact. Whether or not she appeared to be his best conduit to Jack O'Hara, he couldn't use her if he couldn't get over her.

He could make an excuse, leave town for a few days. He could establish a base nearby where he could observe and record. And use his contacts and connections, as well as his own hacker skills, to dig deeper into the life and times of Elaine O'Hara aka Laine Tavish.

When he knew more, he'd decide how to handle her and come back. But meanwhile, he'd have to maintain some objective distance. No more dinners for two, no more spending the day with her at home, no more physical contact that couldn't lead to anything but complications.

He would check out in the morning, give her a quick call to tell her he'd been called back to New York and would be in touch. Keep the lines open, but ease back on the personal front.

A man couldn't do his job efficiently if he was wandering around in a sexual haze.

Satisfied with the plan, Max got up. He'd pack most of his things tonight, maybe go down afterward for a nightcap, then try to sleep off the feelings for her that were building much too quickly and much too inappropriately inside him.

The knock on the door distracted him. They'd already done the turndown, little chocolate mints on the pillows included. He half expected to see an envelope sliding under the door. Though he preferred all communications via e-mail, his clients often insisted on a hard copy fax for instructions.

When nothing appeared, he walked over, glanced through the peep. And came within a breath of swallowing his own tongue.

What the hell was she doing at his door? And what was she wearing?

Jesus Christ.

He backed up, rubbed a hand over his face, his heart. Professional instinct kicked in enough to have him hurrying back to the desk, shutting down his files, burying any hard paperwork, then doing a quick visual sweep for anything that might blow his cover.

He'd get her downstairs to the lounge, that's what he'd do. Get her down, in a public place, tell her he'd been called back, have a quick drink with her.

And move out. Move along. Move away.

He dragged a hand through his hair a couple of times, shook off the nerves. He worked up what he considered an easy, mildly surprised, mildly pleased expression and opened the door.

The full impact of her hadn't come through the peephole. Now the tongue he'd nearly swallowed rolled out again and all but plopped at his feet.

He couldn't quite focus on what she was wearing other than noticing it was black, it was short, and it displayed more curves than a Formula One race. Her legs were longer than he'd imagined, and ended in very high, very thin black heels.

All that fiery hair was scooped up somehow or other, and her eyes seemed bluer, brighter than ever. She'd slicked something dark and glossy and tantalizingly wet over her lips.

God help him.

"I woke up."

"You did. You certainly did."

"Can I come in?"

"Ah. Um." It was as coherent as he could manage, so he just stepped back. And when she walked by him, the scent of her wrapped around his glands, and squeezed.

"I didn't get a chance to thank you, so I thought I would."

"Thank you. Thank me," he corrected, and felt like an imbecile.

She smiled and, holding up the bottle of wine, wagged it slowly side to side. "How do you feel about Merlot?"

"I feel pretty good about it."

It took all her willpower not to laugh. Was there anything that made a woman feel more of a woman than having a man stare at her as if he'd been bewitched? She took a step toward him and was wonderfully flattered when he took one in retreat. "Good enough to share?" she asked him.

"Share?"

"The wine."

"Oh." He'd had a couple of concussions in his day. They often gave the victim the same fuzzy, out-of-body sensation he was experiencing now. "Sure." He took the bottle she held out. "Sure. Sure."

"Well then."

"Well?" There seemed to be some sort of time lag between his brain and his mouth. "Oh, right. Ah, corkscrew." He glanced toward the minibar, but she reached in her purse.

"Try this." She offered him a corkscrew. One half of the handle was a naked woman, head to torso. The other was all leg.

"Cute," he managed.

"Kitschy," she corrected. "I have a small collection. Nice room," she added. "A lot of bed." She wandered to the window, eased the drapes apart a few inches. "I bet the view's wonderful."

"Oh yeah."

Perfectly aware his gaze was on her, she continued to look out the window and slowly peeled off the thin sweater. She heard the abrupt clunk of the wine bottle against wood and was satisfied the dress had done its job. From his viewpoint, there wasn't much of it, just a lot of her naked back framed by a bit of snug black.

She wandered away, toward the bed, and plucked one of the mints from the pillow. "Mmm, chocolate. Do you mind?"

The best he could do was a slow shake of his head. The cork came out of the bottle with a surprised pop and the words "Oh my God" rushed into his mind as she unwrapped the little mint, bit slowly into it.

She gave a sexy little moan, licked her lips. "I heard somewhere that money talks but chocolate sings. I like that." She walked to him, held the second half of the mint to his lips. "I'll share, too."

"You're killing me."

"Let's have some wine then, so you can die happy." She sat on the edge of the bed, crossed her legs. "Did I interrupt your work?"

"Reports. I'll get back to it." *When I find my sanity,* he decided. He poured wine, handed her a glass. And watched her watch him as she took the first, slow sip.

"It's been a while since anyone's tucked me in. I didn't mean to fall asleep on you, Max."

"You had a rough night, a hard day."

"Not as hard a day as I'd expected, thanks to you."

"Laine—"

"Let me thank you. It was easier doing what needed to be done with you there. I like spending time with you." She took another, longer sip. "I like wanting you, and speculating that you want me."

"Wanting you's squeezing the breath out of my throat, cutting off the oxygen to my brain. That wasn't the plan."

"Ever want to say screw the plan and go with impulse?"

"All the time."

She did laugh now, downed the wine and rose to pour

another glass. After another sip, she walked to the door. "I don't. Or rarely do. But you have to respect the exceptions that make the rule."

She opened the door, hung the DO NOT DISTURB sign on the outside knob. She closed the door, locked it, leaned back against it. "If you don't like where this is going, better speak up."

He took a deep gulp of wine himself. "I have absolutely nothing to say."

"That's good because I was prepared to get rough."

He imagined the grin that split his face was big, and stupid. He didn't give a damn. "Really?"

She started back toward him. "I wasn't sure I'd be able to fight fair."

"That dress isn't fighting fair."

"Oh?" She took a last sip of wine, then set the glass aside. "Then I should just take it off."

"Let me. Please." He trailed a fingertip along the milky white skin edged with black. "Let me."

"Help yourself."

He forgot about practicality, professionalism. He forgot about the emotional and physical distance he'd decided would best suit his needs. He forgot about everything but the reality of her, the water-soft texture of her skin, the heady scent, the hot, ripe taste of her mouth when he gripped her hips, pulled her close and kissed her.

She enveloped him—those textures, that scent, that taste until they were—she was—everything he could want or need or imagine.

It was a mistake. Taking her now, like this, was a mistake and edged very close to the forbidden. Knowing that only added an irresistible element of danger to the whole.

He tugged the dress away from her shoulder, set his

teeth on flesh. And when her head fell back, he worked his way back toward the little purr in her throat.

"Something to be said about plans though," he murmured, and bared her other shoulder. "I've got all sorts of plans for you."

"I was hoping." She fumbled her hand back to where she'd dropped her purse on the bed. "You're going to need this," she said, and pulled out a condom.

"At some point, we're also going to need a defibrillator and a fire extinguisher."

"Promises, promises."

He grinned. "I could go seriously crazy over you." He laid his lips on hers again, rubbed. "Is this one of those peel-out-of-it deals? The dress, I mean."

"Pretty much."

"Hot damn, a personal favorite." He worked slowly, drawing out the process with his mouth on hers until they were both ready to shudder. Then he drew back, took her hand so she could step out of the dress that pooled at her feet. And just looked at her.

She wore some sort of fascinating female construction of silk and lace that flirted over her breasts so they had little choice but to rise up, threaten to spill out. The black silk skimmed down her torso, nipping in her waist, molding over her hips to end in flirty little garters that held up sheer black stockings.

"I'm trying to think of something memorable to say, but it's really hard when all the blood's drained out of my head."

"Give it a shot."

"Wow."

"That's what I was shooting for." She reached out and began to unbutton his shirt. "I like the way you look at me. I did right from the first time. I especially like the way you're looking at me now."

"I see you even when I'm not looking. That's a first for me, and a little unnerving."

"Maybe some people are supposed to see each other. Maybe that's why this is happening so fast. I don't care why." She drew his shirt away, ran her hands up his chest, then locked them around his neck. "I don't care," she repeated and crushed her lips to his.

She only knew she wanted to go on feeling this way, to have these jolts of excitement shocking her system, to tremble with the sizzling flood of anticipation. To know the power of having a man's, *this* man's, complete attention and desire.

She wanted to be reckless, to take exactly what she wanted in greedy gulps for once in her life, and to think only of the moment, of the pleasure, of the passion.

When he spun her around, she arched back against him, lifting her arms to hook them around his neck, and gave his hands the freedom to run over her. Over lace, silk, flesh. He fed at her neck, at the curve of her shoulder while he touched her, aroused her. Her breath caught, released on a moan when his hand slid between her thighs. She pressed hers against his, rocked her hips and rose up on that hot wave of pleasure.

He imagined himself swinging her up, laying her on the bed to take the next stage with something approaching romance and finesse. But somehow they were tangled together on the neatly turned-down sheets in a desperate struggle to touch, to taste.

Her hair had spilled down, bright fire against the white. The scent of it, of her skin, dazed his senses until he wondered if he would ever take another breath without drawing her in.

"Do things to me." Her mouth was wild hunger on his. "Do everything to me."

He was lost in a storm of needs and greed, drowning in the heat of them even as he feasted on her, and she on him. As she moved under him, over him, surrounded him, he was rougher than he meant to be in a desperate search for more.

Her lungs were screaming, her heart galloping to the point of pain. Her skin was so hot it seemed it might melt off her bones. And God, it was glorious.

His hands were so strong, his mouth so ravenous. She could revel in the sensation of being taken over, body and mind. He tugged and pulled at snaps, impossibly tiny hooks, made her laugh breathlessly when he fumbled and cursed. Made her gasp in shock when he drove into her and shot her over the edge.

It was she who demanded it all, now, now, *now*! And arched and opened, who cried out when he plunged inside her. Her vision blurred, her galloping heart stopped. Then everything, everything was clear as crystal, her heartbeat raging, her body racing as they took each other.

She could see his face, the lines and hollows, the shadow of the beard not shaved since morning, and his eyes, tiger eyes focused on hers. Then going darker, going opaque an instant before he buried his face in her hair and emptied into her.

Her body was drenched, saturated with pleasure, and her mind calm as a summer lake. She was trapped under his body, and delighted with herself and him. She could hear the ragged sound of his breathing. There was such satisfaction in knowing she'd caused that. Toying with his hair, she closed her eyes and let herself drift.

"You okay down there?" he murmured.

"I'm wonderful down here, thanks. You okay up there?"

"I may be paralyzed, but I'm feeling pretty good about it." He turned his head so his lips brushed the side of her neck. "Laine."

Eyes still closed, she smiled. "Max."

"I have to say . . . I have to say," he repeated as much for himself as her, "this is something I never expected when I . . . took this assignment."

"I like surprises. I stopped liking them along the way, but I'm remembering why I always liked surprises. It's because they just happen."

"If surprises deal with finding you at my door wearing a sexy black dress, I freaking love them."

"If I did it again, it wouldn't be a surprise, it would be a repeat."

"I can live with that. Where's Henry?"

"Henry?"

He pushed onto his elbows to look down at her. "You didn't leave him at home, did you? After what happened last night."

It wasn't heat flashing now, but a slow and lovely warmth sliding. He was worried about a dog. Her dog. Any man who'd worry about a dog when he was naked in bed with a woman shot straight to the top of her list of all-time heroes. She dragged his face down to hers so she could rain kisses over it.

"No, I didn't leave him alone. I took him to Jenny's. How can you be so perfect? I'm always looking for the flaws in everything, but you're just . . ." She pressed her lips to his in a long, noisy kiss. "Absolutely perfect."

"I'm not." He didn't care for the twinge of guilt. It was a sensation he overcame or avoided. Worse, there was worry tangled with it. What would she think, how would she react when she found out just what his flaws were?

"I'm selfish and single-minded," he told her. "I—"

"Selfish men don't wander into antique stores looking for a gift for their mother, just because."

The twinge became a pang. "That was impulse."

"See, a surprise. Didn't I just say I love surprises? Don't try to convince me you're not perfect. I'm too happy with you right now to think anything else. Uh-oh, now I've got you thinking." She ran her hands down his back, gave his butt a friendly pat. "Is she trying to turn this into more than fun and games?"

"That's not what I was thinking. And it already is more than fun and games."

"Oh." Her heart tripped, but she kept her eyes steady on his. "Is it?"

"That's what I wasn't expecting, Laine." He lowered his head, touched his lips to hers. "Makes things a little more complicated."

"I don't mind complications, Max." She framed his face with her hands. "We can worry about what this is, or isn't, what it's going to be, tomorrow, or we can enjoy it. And each other. The one thing I know is when I woke up at home tonight, I was happy because I knew I wanted to be with you. I haven't felt that way in a long time."

"Happy?"

"Satisfied, content, productive and happy enough. But not dance-around-the-house happy. So about the only thing you could tell me that would make this too complicated for me is that you've got a wife and a couple of kids in Brooklyn."

"I don't. They're in Queens."

She pinched him, hard, then wrestled him over onto his back. "Ha ha. Very funny."

"It's my ex-wife who lives in Brooklyn."

She straddled him, tossed her hair back. "You've been busy."

"Well, you collect corkscrews. Some guys collect women. My current mistress is in Atlanta, but I'm thinking of branching out. You could be my Maryland tootsie."

"Tootsie? It's always been one of my driving ambitions to be someone's tootsie. Where do I sign up?"

He sat up, wrapping his arms around her and just holding on. Complications, he thought. He couldn't begin to list them. So he'd just have to deal with them. So would she. But not tonight. Tonight he was going to take her at her word and just enjoy.

"Are you going to stay awhile? Stay awhile, Laine."

"I thought you'd never ask."

"Don't go." The moment the words were out of Max's mouth, he realized he'd never said them to a woman before. Maybe it was sleep deprivation, sexual exhaustion. Maybe it was just her.

"It's after three in the morning."

"Exactly. So come on back to bed. We'll just spoon up here and snooze for a couple hours, then order breakfast."

"That sounds wonderful, but I'll need another one of those rain checks." She wiggled into the dress, forgoing underwear. And erased all thoughts of snoozing from his mind.

"Then just come back to bed."

"I have to go." She chuckled, dancing out of reach when he made a grab for her. "I need to go home, catch a couple hours' sleep, change, run back into town and pick up Henry, take him home, then go back into town to the shop."

"If you stay here, you could pick up Henry on the way home and save yourself a trip."

"And provide the gossip mill with enough grist to run it until next Christmas." She was small-town enough, in the woman she'd created, to be concerned about such things. "A woman strolls out of a hotel in the morning wearing this sort of dress, eyebrows raise. Especially in the Gap."

"I'll lend you a shirt."

"I'm going." She stuffed her lingerie into her purse. "But if you'd like to have dinner with me tonight . . ."

"Name the time and place."

"Eight, my place. I'll cook."

"Cook?" His eyes blinked slowly, twice, then seemed to glaze. "Food?"

"No, I thought I'd cook up an insidious plot against the government. Of course food." She turned to the mirror, pulled a tiny brush out of her bulging purse and swooped it through her hair. "What do you like?"

He just stared at her. "Food?"

"I'll think of something." Satisfied she was as good as she was going to get, she dropped the brush back into the purse and crossed to him. She leaned over the bed, gave him a light kiss. "See you later."

He stayed where he was after she'd closed the door behind her. Stayed, staring at the door with the taste of her lingering on his lips.

None of it made any sense. Not what had happened between them, not what he felt for her, not who she was.

Because his reading of her wasn't off. He was *never* this far off, and it had nothing to do with glands.

If Laine Tavish was mixed up in a multimillion-dollar heist, he'd eat his own investigator's license.

It didn't explain why William Young had come to see her. It didn't explain why he was dead. It didn't explain why her house had been ransacked.

But there were explanations, and he'd ferret them out. He was good at it. Once he had, once he'd cleared her, satisfied his client, done the job, he'd tell her everything.

She'd probably be a little upset.

Get real, Gannon, he thought, she'd be completely pissed. But he'd bring her around.

He was good at bringing people around, too.

The best way to work through the mess he'd gotten into was to proceed with logic. Logically, Jack O'Hara's daughter Elaine had severed ties with him, changed her name, adjusted her background and started a life for herself. Everything pointed in that direction, including his own instincts.

That didn't mean Big Jack, Willy or any of their associates were unaware of her and her location. Didn't mean there wasn't occasional contact, or the attempt to contact.

And okay, her finances still struck him as dicey, but he'd work on that. A few thousand here or there to put a down payment on a house or start up a business was nothing. Not compared to a share of $28 million and change.

Willy may have tracked her down to ask her for help, a place to hide out, to deliver a message from her father. Whatever the purpose, he was dead as Moses now and couldn't be asked. And would never cash in on his share either, Max mused.

Didn't that up the stakes considerably?

Laine didn't have anything at the house worth worrying about. There was no question of that. Even if whoever'd broken in had missed something, she wouldn't have left the house unattended for the night to play heat the sheets if she had something hidden there.

Logically, she didn't have anything. She'd been in Angel's Gap when the jewels were stolen. For Christ's sake, she'd barely finished her first decade when she was shuffled out of Big Jack's aegis and influence.

Regardless, to clear her, to cross her name off all lists, he had to cover all the bases. He had to take a good look around her shop.

The sooner he did it, the sooner they could move on. He checked the time, judged he had a good three hours before daylight.

Might as well get started.

CHAPTER

7

It amazed him that anyone who shared DNA with a thief would secure their own business with standard locks and a rinky-dink alarm system any twelve-year-old with a Swiss Army knife and a little imagination could circumvent.

Really, if this . . . thing of theirs turned into an actual relationship, he was going to have a serious sit-down with Laine about home and business security. Maybe a store in a town of this type and size didn't require riot bars, gates or surveillance cameras, but she hadn't even bothered with security lights, in or out. As for the door, it was pathetic. If he'd *been* a thief who didn't worry about finesse, a couple of good kicks would've done the job.

Her current excuse for a system made the nighttime B&E embarrassingly easy. He bypassed the alarm and picked the locks on the back door in case some insomniac decided to take a predawn stroll down Market Street. And he'd walked from the hotel, taking his time, circling the block on foot. Just because something was easy didn't mean you could afford to be careless about procedure.

The town was quiet enough so he could hear the rumble of a furnace when it kicked on inside a building. And the long, mournful whistle of a freight train that rose eerily out of the silence. There were no winos, no junkies, no homeless, no hookers or street people populating the night in what would be considered downtown Angel's Gap.

You had to wonder if you were actually in America or if you'd somehow stumbled into a postcard printed up by the local chamber of commerce.

It was, Max decided, mildly creepy.

The streetlights along the steep sidewalk were old-fashioned lantern style, and every one of them glowed. All the display windows in the storefronts were sheer glass. As with Remember When, there were no gates, no security bars.

Hadn't anyone ever thrown a brick through one and helped themselves before hotfooting it away? Or kicked in a door for a quick looting party?

It just didn't seem right.

He thought of New York at three twenty-seven A.M. There'd be action, or trouble, if you were inclined for either. There'd be both pedestrian and vehicular traffic and the stores would all be chained down for the night.

So was there more crime there on a per capita basis just because it was expected?

It was an interesting theory, and he'd have to give some thought to it when he had a little downtime.

But for now, alarm and locks dispatched, he eased open the rear door of Remember When.

In and out in an hour, tops, he promised himself. Then back to the hotel to catch a little sleep. When New York opened, he'd contact his client and report that all evidence pointed to the fact that Laine Tavish was not, knowingly, involved.

That would clear him, from his point of view, to explain things to her. Once he'd done that, and talked her out of being pissed off, he'd pick her brain. He had a feeling she'd be an excellent source in tracking Big Jack and the diamonds.

And in collecting his finder's fee.

Max shut the door quietly behind him. Reached down to switch on his penlight.

But instead of the narrow beam coming on, lights exploded inside his head.

He woke in dead dark with his head banging with all the gusto and violence of his young nephew slamming pot lids together. He managed to roll over to what he thought was his back. The way his head was pounding and spinning, he couldn't be sure.

He lifted a hand to check if that head was still face front and felt the warm wet running.

And that pushed temper through the pain. It was bad enough to get ambushed and knocked out, but it was a hell of another thing if he had to go to the damn ER and get stitches.

He couldn't quite clear his brain, but he pushed himself to a sitting position. Since the head he was now reasonably certain was still on the correct way seemed in danger of falling off his shoulders, he lowered it to his hands until he felt more secure.

He needed to get up, turn on a light. Take stock of himself and what the hell had happened. He wiped at the blood, opened his aching eyes and scowled at the open rear door.

Whoever'd hit him from behind was long gone. He started to get to his feet with the idea of taking a quick look around the place before following suit.

And the rear doorway was suddenly filled with cop.

Max took a long look at Vince Burger, and at the police-issue pointing in his direction and said, "Well, shit."

"Look, you can pop me for the B and E. It'll sting. I'll get around it, but it'll sting. But—"

"I did pop you for the B and E." Vince kicked back in his desk chair and smiled humorlessly at Max, who sat cuffed to a visitor's chair in the office of the station house.

Didn't look so big city and cocky now, Vince thought, with the bandage on his temple and the sizable lump on his forehead.

"Then there's attempted burglary—"

"I wasn't stealing anything, damn it, and you know it."

"Oh, so you just break into stores in the middle of the night to browse around. Like window shopping but on the inside." He lifted an evidence bag, gave it a shake that rattled Max's burglar tools and personal data assistant. "And you carry these around in case you have to do some small home repairs?"

"Look—"

"I can pop you on possession of burglary tools."

"That's a goddamn PDA. Everybody's got a PDA."

"I don't."

"Surprise, surprise," Max said sourly. "I had reasons for being inside Laine's shop."

"You break into all the shops and homes of women you date?"

"I never broke into her house, and it's pretty damn elementary, Watson, that whoever was in the store ahead of me, whoever coldcocked me was the one who did. You're protective of her, I get that, but—"

"Damn right." The good old boy's eyes went hard as cinders. "She's a friend of mine. She's a good friend of mine, and I don't like some New York asshole messing with my friends."

"I'm a Georgia asshole, actually. I just live in New York. I'm conducting an investigation for a client. A private investigation."

"So you say, but I didn't find any license on you."

"You didn't find any wallet either," Max snapped back, "because whoever knocked me out helped himself to it. Goddamn it, Burger—"

"Don't swear in my office."

At wits' end, Max leaned his head back, closed his eyes. "I didn't ask for a lawyer, but I'm going to beg you, I may even work up some tears along with it, for some fricking aspirin."

Vince opened a desk drawer, took out a bottle. Maybe he slammed the drawer just for the satisfaction of seeing Max wince, but he heaved himself up and poured a cup of water.

"You know I'm what I say I am." Max took the pills, downed them with the water and prayed for them to break Olympic records swimming into his bloodstream. "You've run me. You know I'm a licensed investigator. You know I used to be a cop. And while you're wasting time and getting your jollies busting my balls, whoever was in her place has gone back to ground. You need—"

"You don't want to tell me what I need to do." The voice was mild enough to have Max respecting the cold fury under it—particularly since he was cuffed to a chair. "You told Laine all that? About the used to be a cop, going private, working on a case here in the Gap?"

Just his luck, Max decided, to run foul of the Norman Rockwell version of a hard-ass town cop. "Is this about my relationship with Laine or about me being inside the shop?"

"Six of one to me. What's the case you're working on?"

"I'm not giving you any details on that until I talk to my client." And his client was unlikely to be pleased he'd been busted slithering around the fine points of the law. Not that he'd slithered, but that he'd gotten caught. But that was another problem.

"Look, someone was in that shop when I walked in, and that same person tore up Laine's house. Laine's the one we need to be concerned about right now. You need to send a deputy out to her place and make sure—"

"Telling me how to do my job isn't going to make me feel any more kindly toward you."

"I don't care if you want to ask me out to the prom. Laine needs protection."

"You've been doing a good job of that." Vince settled his weight on the edge of the desk, like, Max thought with a sinking heart, a man settling in for a nice, long chat. "Funny how you show up from New York right after I end up with a guy from New York in the morgue."

"Yeah, I'm still laughing about that one. Eight million people in New York, give or take," Max said coolly. "Seems reasonable a few of them would pass through here from time to time."

"Guess I'm not feeling real reasonable. Here's what I

see. Some guy walks out of Laine's shop, gets spooked and runs into the street, ends up dead. You show up, talk Laine into having dinner with you, and while you're moving on her, her house gets burgled and vandalized. Next thing you know, you're inside her shop at three-thirty in the morning carrying burglar tools. What are you looking for, Gannon?"

"Inner peace."

"Good luck with that," Vince said as they heard the quick march of footsteps down the hall.

Laine swung into the room. She wore sweats, and her hair was pulled back into a tail that left her face unframed. There were smudges from lack of sleep under her eyes, and those eyes were full of baffled concern.

"What's going on? Jerry came by the house, told me there was trouble at the shop and that I had to come right in and talk to you. What kind of trouble? What's—" She spotted the handcuffs and stopped short as she stared at them, then slowly lifted her gaze to Max's face. "What is this?"

"Laine—"

"You're going to want to sit quiet a minute," Vince warned Max. "You had a break-in at the store," Vince told her. "Far as I could see there wasn't any damage. You'll have to take a look yourself to see if anything was taken."

"I see." She wanted to sit, but only braced a hand on the back of a chair. "No, I don't. Why have you got Max cuffed?"

"I got an anonymous call that there was a burglary in progress at the location of your store. When I got there, I found him. Inside. He had a nice set of lock picks in his possession."

She took a breath—air in, air out—and shifted her gaze to Max's face. "You broke into my shop?"

"No. Well, yes, technically. But after someone else did. Someone who bashed me on the head, then called in the tip so I'd get rousted for this."

She studied the bandage on his temple, but the concern had already chilled out of her eyes. "That doesn't explain what you were doing there in the middle of the night." *After I left your bed,* she thought. *After I spent the night in your bed.*

"I can explain. I need to talk to you privately. Ten minutes. Give me ten minutes."

"I'd like to hear it. Can I talk to him alone, Vince?"

"I wouldn't recommend it."

"I'm a licensed investigator. He knows it." Max jerked a thumb at Vince. "I have a case and a client, and I'm pursuing leads. I'm not free to say any more."

"Then you'd be wasting all our time," Vince pointed out.

"Ten minutes, Laine."

An investigator. A case. In the time it took her to absorb the blow, she'd added her father into the mix. Hurt, anger and resignation rolled through her in a messy trio, but none of it showed. "I'd appreciate the time, Vince. It's personal."

"Figured as much." Vince pushed to his feet. "As a favor to you, then. I'll be right outside the door. Watch yourself," he added to Max, "or you're going to have a few new bruises to go with the old ones."

Max waited until the door clicked shut. "You've got very protective friends."

"How much of the ten minutes do you want to waste on irrelevant observations?"

"Could you sit down?"

"I could, but I won't." She walked over to Vince's Mr. Coffee machine. She needed something to do with her hands before she surrendered to impulse and pounded them into Max's face. "What game are you running, Max?"

"I'm working for Reliance Insurance, and I'm skirting a line telling you that before I clear it with my client."

"Really? But breaking into my shop after spending several hours having sex with me isn't a line you're worried about, apparently."

"I didn't know. I didn't expect . . ." Fuck it, he thought. "I can apologize, but it wouldn't make any difference to you, and wouldn't excuse the way this happened."

"Well, there we are." She drank coffee, bitter and black. "We're on the same page on something, after all."

"You can be pissed off at me if you want—"

"Why, thanks. I believe I will."

"But you've got to get past it. Laine, you're in trouble."

She lifted her eyebrows, stared deliberately at the handcuffs. "*I'm* in trouble?"

"How many people know you're Elaine O'Hara?"

She didn't bat an eyelash. He hadn't expected her to be quite that good.

"You'd be one, apparently. I don't choose to use that name. I changed to my stepfather's name a long time ago. And I fail to see how this is any of your business." She sipped at the coffee. "Why don't we get back to the part where, about an hour after we were sliding around naked on each other, you were arrested for breaking into my place of business."

Guilt swept over his face but gave her little satisfaction. "One doesn't have anything to do with the other."

With a nod, she set the coffee down. "With answers like that we don't need our allotted ten minutes."

"William Young died outside your store," Max said as she took a step toward the door. "Died, according to witness reports, all but in your arms. You must've recognized him."

Her facade cracked minutely, and the grief eked through. Then she shored it up again. "This sounds more like an interrogation than an explanation. I'm not interested in answering the questions of a man who lied to me, who used me. So you can start telling me what you're doing here and what you want, or I'll bring Vince back in and we'll get started on pressing charges."

He took a moment. It was all he needed to confirm in his mind that she'd do exactly that. Shove him aside, lock the door, walk away. It was all he needed to understand he'd toss the job aside before he'd let that happen.

"I broke into your shop tonight so I could clear you, so I could report to my client this morning that you weren't involved, and so I could tell you the truth."

"Involved in what? The truth about what?"

"Sit down for a damn minute. I'm tired of craning my neck."

She sat. "There. Comfy?"

"Six weeks ago, diamonds appraised at and insured by Reliance for twenty-eight point four million dollars were stolen from the offices of the International Jewelry Exchange in New York City. Two days later, the body of Jerome Myers, a gem merchant with offices in that location, was found in a New Jersey construction site. Through the investigation it's been determined this merchant was the inside man. It's also been determined he had a connection and an association with William Young and Jack O'Hara."

"Wait a minute, wait a minute. You're saying you believe my father was involved in a heist with a take of over twenty-eight million? *Million*? That he had something to do with a murder? The first is ridiculous, the second impossible. Jack O'Hara dreamed big, but he's small-time. And he never hurt anyone, not that way."

"Things change."

"Not that much."

"The cops don't have enough to charge Jack or Willy, though they'd sure like to talk to them. Since Willy's not going to be talking to anybody, that leaves Big Jack. Insurance companies get really irritated when they have to pay out big-ass claims."

"And that's where you come in."

"I've got more of a free hand than the cops. And a bigger expense account."

"And a bigger payoff," she added. "What's your take?"

"Five percent of the recovered amount."

"So in this case, you bring back the twenty-eight-plus, you tuck away . . ." Her eyes narrowed as she did the math. "A tidy one million, four hundred and twenty thousand in your piggy bank. Not bad."

"I earn it. I've put a lot of hours in on this. I know Jack and Willy were in it, just like I know there was a third party."

"Me?" She'd have laughed if she hadn't been so angry. "So I, what, broke out my black catsuit and watch cap, bopped up to New York, stole millions in jewels, cut out my share, then came home to feed my dog?"

"No. Not that you wouldn't look hot in a catsuit. Alex Crew. The name ring any bells?"

"No."

"Both the merchant and your father were seen with him prior to the heist. He's not small-time, though this would be his biggest effort. In the interest of time, let's just say he's not a nice guy, and if he's looking at you, you're in trouble."

"Why would he look at me?"

"Because you're Jack's daughter and Willy died minutes after talking to you. What did he tell you, Laine?"

"He didn't tell me anything. For God's sake, I was a kid the last time I saw him. I didn't recognize him until . . . I didn't know who he was when he came in. You're chasing the wrong tail, Max. Jack O'Hara wouldn't begin to know how to organize or execute a job like this—and if by some miracle he had a part in it, he'd be long gone with his share. That's more money than he'd know what to do with."

"Then why was Willy here? What spooked him? Why were your home and business broken into? Whoever got in your house was looking for something. They were probably doing the same, or about to, when I interrupted them in the shop. You're too smart not to follow the dots."

"If anyone's looking at me, it's probably because you led them here. I don't have anything. I haven't spoken to my father in over five years, and I haven't seen him in longer than that. I've made a nice life here, and I'm going to keep right on living it. I'm not going to let you, my father or some mythical third party screw that up."

She got to her feet. "I'll get you out of the cuffs, and out of this jam with Vince. In return you leave me the hell alone."

"Laine—"

"Just shut up." She rubbed a hand over her face, her first sign of fatigue. "I broke my own rule and followed impulse with you. Serves me right."

She went to the door, gave Vince a weary smile. "I'm sorry about all this trouble. I'd like you to let Max go."

"Because?"

"It's been a stupid misunderstanding, Vince, and largely my own fault. Max tried to convince me I needed a better security system at the store, and I argued that I didn't. We had a little tiff about it, and he broke in to prove me wrong."

"Honey." Vince lifted one of his big hands and patted her cheek. "That's just bullshit."

"I'd like you to write it up that way, if you have to write it up at all. And let him go. There's no point in charging him when he'll use his investigator's license, his rich client and their fancy lawyers to get it tossed anyway."

"I need to know what this is about, Laine."

"I know you do." The sturdy foundation of her new life shook a bit. "Give me a little time, will you, to sort it all through. I'm so damn tired right now, I can barely think straight."

"All right. Whatever it is, I'm on your side."

"I hope so."

She walked out without another look, without another word for Max.

She wasn't going to break. She'd worked too hard, she'd come too far to break over a good-looking man with a dreamy southern accent. A charmer, Laine thought as she paced around her house.

She *knew* better than to fall for a charmer. What was her father but a charming, smooth-talking cheat?

Typical, she thought in disgust. Typical, typical and so embarrassingly predictable for her to fall for the same type. Max Gannon might do his lying and cheating on the legal side, but it was still lying and cheating.

Now everything she'd worked for was at risk. If she

didn't come clean with Vince, he'd never really trust her again. Once she came clean . . . how could he trust her again?

Screwed either way, she thought.

She could pack up, move on, start over. That's what Big Jack did when things got rough. So she was damned if she'd do the same. This was her home, her place, her life. She wouldn't give it up because some nosy PI from the big city tramped over it and left her smudged.

And heartbroken, she admitted. Under the anger and anxiety, her heart was broken. She'd let herself *be* herself with him. She'd taken the big risk, and trusted him with herself.

He'd let her down. The men who mattered most to her always did.

She flopped down on the couch, which caused Henry to bump his nose against her arm in hopes of a good petting.

"Not now, Henry. Not now."

Something in her tone had him whimpering in what sounded like sympathy before he turned a couple of circles and settled down on the floor beside her.

Lesson learned, she told herself. From now on the only man in her life was Henry. And it was time to close down the pity party and *think*.

She stared up at the ceiling.

Twenty-eight million in gems? Ridiculous, impossible, even laughable. Big, blustering Jack and sweet, harmless Willy pulling off the big score? Millions? And out of a New York landmark? No possible way. At least not if you went by history and skill and background.

But if you threw the believable out the window, you were left with the fantastic.

What if Max was right? What if the fantastic had happened, and he was right? Despite all the years between, she felt a quicksilver thrill at the possibility.

Diamonds. The sexiest of takes. Millions. The perfect number. It would have been the job of a lifetime. The mother of all jobs. If Jack had . . .

No, it still didn't play.

The affection inside her that wouldn't die for her father might let her fantasize that he'd finally, finally, hit it big. But nothing and no one would convince her Jack O'Hara had any part in a killing. A liar, a cheat, a thief with a very flexible conscience—okay, those attributes fit him like a glove. But to cause anyone physical harm? Not possible.

He'd never carried a weapon. The fact was, he was phobic about guns. She still remembered the story of how he'd done his first stretch, before she was born. He'd hit a cat while driving away from a B&E and not only stopped to check, but took the injured cat to a vet. The local cops spotted the car—stolen, of course—in the lot.

The cat recovered and lived a long, happy life. Big Jack did two to five.

No, he wouldn't have had any part in the murder of Jerome Myers.

But the con could be conned, couldn't he? Had he gotten roped into something that was bigger and badder than he'd believed? Had someone dangled a shiny carrot and had him hopping along after it?

That she could believe.

So he'd sent Willy to tell her something, or give her something, but he'd died before he could do either.

But he'd tried to warn her. *He knows where you are now.*

Had he meant Max? Had he seen Max and panicked, ran into the street?

Hide the pooch? What the hell had he meant? Could Willy have placed some kind of dog figurine in the store? Laine tried to visualize the store after Willy's visit. She had personally arranged all the displays, and she couldn't think of a single thing out of place. And neither Jenny nor Angie had mentioned any strange items.

Maybe he'd meant "pouch." Maybe she'd misunderstood. You could put gems in a pouch. But he hadn't given her a pouch, and if he'd had a bag of gems hidden on him, or in his things, the authorities would have found it.

And this was all just stupid conjecture, based on the word of a man who'd lied to her.

She let out a huge breath. How could she pretend to hold honesty in such pompous hands when she was living a lie herself?

She had to tell Vince and Jenny everything. She supposed it went against her early childhood training to volunteer information to a cop, but she could overcome it. All she had to do was figure out how to tell them.

"Let's take a walk, Henry."

The words acted like an incantation and popped the snoozing dog up as if his legs were springs. He bounced all the way to the front door. A walk would clear the cobwebs, she decided, give her time to sort out the best way to tell her friends.

She opened the front door so Henry could fly out like a cannonball. And saw Max's car parked at the end of her lane. He was behind the wheel, eyes shielded with dark glasses. But they must have been open and trained on the house, as he stepped out of the car even before she'd shut the front door.

"What the hell are you doing here?"

"I said you're in trouble. Maybe I brought some of that

trouble along with me, maybe it was already here. But either way, I'm keeping an eye on you, whether you like it or not."

"I learned how to take care of myself about the same time I learned how to run a three-card monte scam. So the only watchdog I need is Henry."

As Henry was currently trying to climb a tree in pursuit of a squirrel, Max merely gave the dog a baleful stare. "I'm sticking."

"If you think you're going to collect your five percent by staking out my house, you're going to be disappointed."

"I don't think you had anything to do with it. I did," he added when she sneered and turned away to walk. "When I first made you, I figured you had to have some piece of it. I did some checking on you, and things didn't add up right on either side, but I stopped looking at you for the job."

"Thanks so very much. If that's so, why were you breaking into my shop?"

"My client wants facts, not feelings, though they give me a nice retainer largely based on my instinct track record. I've been through your house with you," he said when her head turned sharply. "A woman's hiding any portion of damn near thirty million in diamonds on the premises, she doesn't let some guy help her sweep her floors and take out the trash. Next step was to take a look around the shop, verify there was nothing there that linked you."

"Missed a step, Max. I believe it has to do with a lot of naked bouncing on your hotel room bed."

"Okay, let's run this. You see a halo?" He pointed a finger at the top of his head.

She felt a little bubble that might have been humor in her throat and ruthlessly swallowed it. "No," she said after a narrow-eyed stare. "But wait . . . are those little horns?"

"Okay, give me a flat yes or no. A guy opens his hotel room door to an incredible-looking woman, a woman he's got all kinds of feelings for messing around in his head— and other parts of the body. The woman indicates—no, let's get it right—the woman states without qualification that she'd enjoy an evening of intimate physical contact. Does said guy close the door in her face?"

She stopped by a skinny stream running briskly from the spring rains. "No. Now you give me one. Does a woman, upon learning that the guy she had this intimate physical contact with set her up, and lied about his purpose and his interest, then have the right to kick his lying ass black and blue?"

"Yeah, she does." He took off the sunglasses, hooked one arm of them in the front pocket of his jeans. They both recognized the gesture for what it was.

Look at me. You have to see what I'm saying as much as hear it. Because it matters.

"She does, Laine, even when that interest twisted around, changed into something he'd never dealt with before and bit him on that ass. I think I fell in love with you last night."

"That's a hell of a thing to say to me."

"It's a hell of a thing to hear myself say to you. But I'm saying it. Actually, I think I tripped somewhere between hauling out your trash and vacuuming your sitting room, then I swung my arms around, working on my balance, and fell flat between rounds of intimate physical contact."

"And I should believe that because?"

"You shouldn't. You should kick my ass, dust your hands off and walk away. I'm hoping you won't."

"You've got a knack for saying the right thing at the

right time. That's a damn handy skill—and suspect to me."
She turned away a moment, rubbed her arms warm.

"When it comes to the job I'll say whatever I need to
say to get it done. This isn't about the job. I hurt you, and
I'm sorry, but that was the job. I don't see how I could've
played it any different."

She let out a half laugh. "No, I don't suppose so."

"I'm in love with you. Hit me like a damn brick upside
the head, and I still can't see straight. I don't know how I
could've played that any different either, but it gives you
all the cards, Laine. You can finish the hand, or toss it in
and walk away."

Up to her, she thought. Isn't that what she wanted? To
make her own choices, take her own chances. But what he
hadn't said, and they were both smart enough to know it,
was that holding all the cards didn't mean you wouldn't
lose your shirt.

Tavish would cut her losses and fold. But O'Hara, she'd
want the chance to scoop up that big, juicy pot.

"I spent the first part of my life adoring a man who
couldn't spit out the truth if it was dancing the tango on his
tongue. Jack O'Hara."

She blew out a breath. "He's just no damn good, but,
Jesus, he makes you believe there's a pot of gold at the
end of the rainbow. He makes you believe it because *he*
believes it."

She dropped her hands, turned to face Max. "I spent
the next part with a woman who was trying to get over him.
Trying more for me than herself, which it took me a while
to figure out. She finally succeeded. The next part I spent
with a very decent man I love very much standing in as my
father. A good, loving man who will never give the same

shine to my heart as that born liar can. I don't know what that makes me. But I've spent the last part of my life trying to be responsible and ordinary and comfortable. I've done a good job of it. You've messed that up for me, Max."

"I know it."

"If you lie to me again, I won't bother to kick your ass. I'll just dust my hands and walk away."

"Fair enough."

"I don't have the diamonds you're after, and I don't know anything about them. I don't know where my father is, how to contact him or why Willy came to see me."

"Okay."

"But if I figure it out, if what I figure leads you to that five percent, I get half."

He stared at her a minute, then his grin moved slowly over his face. "Yeah, pretty damn sure I fell for you."

"We'll see about that. You can come in. I need to call Vince and Jenny, ask them to come out so I can confess my sins. Then we'll see if I still have friends, and a place in this town."

She worried over it. Not just what to say, how to say it, but *where* to say it. Laine started to set up in the kitchen with coffee and the coffee cake she had in the freezer. But that was too informal, she decided, and too friendly when friendship was at stake.

Vince was a cop, she reminded herself. And Jenny a cop's wife. However tight they'd become over the past few years, the bonds of that relationship could unravel when she told them about her past. When she told them she'd lied to them right from the start.

The living room was better—and hold the coffee cake.

While she agonized if that was the proper setting, she got out her little hand vac and started on the sofa.

"Laine, what the hell are you doing?"

"Planting apple trees. What does it look like I'm doing? I'm getting the dog hair off the furniture."

"Okay."

He stuck his hands in his pockets, pulled them out, dragged them through his hair as she vacuumed, plumped pillows she'd restuffed, fussed with the angle of the chenille throw.

"You're making me nervous."

"Well, excuse me." She stepped back, inspected the results. Though she'd shoved most of the stuffing back in the cushions, arranged them damaged side down, the sofa still looked sad and pitiful. "I have the chief of police and my closest friend coming by so I can tell them basically everything they think they know about me is a big, juicy lie; I've had two break-ins in the same number of days; my father's suspected of taking part in a twenty-eight-million-dollar burglary, with murder on the side; and my couch looks like it was attacked by rabid ferrets. But I'm really sorry I'm making you nervous."

"You forgot the part where you had a sexual marathon with the investigator assigned to the case."

She tapped the vacuum against her palm. "Is that supposed to be funny? Is that supposed to be some warped attempt to amuse me?"

"Pretty much. Don't hit me with that thing, Laine. I've already got a mild concussion. Probably. And relax. Changing your name and editing your background isn't a criminal offense."

"That's not the point. I lied to them every day. Do you know why so many scams work? Because after the marks realize they've been taken, they're too embarrassed to do anything about it. Someone's made a fool out of them, and that's just as tough a hit as losing money. More, a lot of the time."

He took the hand vac and set it on the table, so he could

touch her. So he could cup his hands on her shoulders, slide them up until his thumbs brushed her cheeks.

"You weren't looking to make fools out of them, and they're not your friends because of your all-American-girl background."

"I could run a bait and switch by the time I was seven. Some all-American girl. I should change." She looked down at the sweats she'd pulled on when the deputy had come by the house to wake her. "Should I change?"

"No." Now he laid his hands on her shoulders, rubbing until she lifted her head and met his eyes. "You should stay just the way you are."

"What do you think you're falling for, Max? The small-town shopkeeper, the reformed grifter, the damsel in distress? Which one of those trips up a guy like you?"

"I think it's the sharp redhead who knows how to handle herself, and gives in to the occasional impulse." He lowered his head to press his lips to her forehead. He felt her breath hitch, a sob that threatened and was controlled. "There are a lot of sides to her. She loves her dog, worries about her friends, she's a little anal on the organization front, and I've heard she cooks. She's practical, efficient and tough-minded—and she's amazing in bed."

"Those are a lot of opinions on short acquaintance."

"I'm a quick study. My mama always said, 'Max, when you meet the woman, you'll go down like you've been poleaxed.' "

A smile twitched at her lips. "What the hell does that mean?"

"Hell if I know, but Marlene's never wrong. I met the woman."

He drew her in, and she let herself take the warmth

and comfort of him, the sturdiness of being held against a strong man. Then she made herself pull away.

She didn't know if love meant leaning on someone else, but in her experience, that sort of indulgence often sent the leaner and the leanee down to the mat.

"I can't think about it. I can't think about it, or what I feel about it. I just need to take the next step and see where I land."

"That's okay."

She heard Henry's crazed barking, and a moment later the sound of tires crushing gravel. There was a quick dip in her belly, but she kept her shoulders straight. "They're here." She shook her head before Max could speak. "No, I have to gear up. I have to handle this."

She walked to the door, opened it and watched Jenny play with Henry.

Jenny looked over. "Must be true love," she called out, then started toward the house. "Getting me out of bed and over here before eight in the morning must be a sign of true friendship."

"I'm sorry it's so early."

"Just tell me you have food."

"I . . . I have a coffee cake, but—"

"Sounds great. What are you having?" She gave her big, barking laugh, then shut it down when she saw Max. "I don't know what I think about you being here. If you're some big-city detective, why didn't you say so?"

"Jenny." Laine laid a hand on her friend's arm. "It's complicated. Why don't you and Vince go in the living room and sit down?"

"Why don't we just sit in the kitchen? It's closer to the food." And rubbing circles on her belly, Jenny started back.

"Okay then." Laine took a deep breath, closed the door behind Vince. "Okay."

She followed them back. "This might be a little confusing," she began, talking as she set out the pot of herbal tea she'd made for Jenny. "I want to apologize first off. Just say I'm sorry, right off the bat."

She poured coffee, cut slices of cake. "I haven't been honest with you, with anyone."

"Sweetie." Jenny stepped over to where Laine stood meticulously arranging the cake on a garnet glass dessert plate. "Are you in trouble?"

"I guess I am."

"Then we'll fix it. Right, Vince?"

Vince was watching Laine. "Why don't you sit down, Jen. Let her say what she needs to."

"We'll fix it," Jenny said again, but she sat, bored through Max with a steely stare. "Is this your fault?"

"It's not," Laine said quickly. "It's really not. My name's not Laine Tavish. It is . . . I changed it, legally, and I've used it since I was eighteen, but it's not the name I was born with. That's Elaine O'Hara. My father's name is Jack O'Hara, and if Vince was to do a background check on him, he'd find my father has a long and varied sheet. It's mostly theft, and cons. Scams."

Jenny's eyes went round and wide. "He doesn't run a barbecue place in New Mexico?"

"Rob Tavish, my stepfather, does. My father got popped—" Laine cut herself off, sighed. How quickly it comes back. "Jack was arrested and sent to prison for a real-estate scam when I was eleven. It wasn't the first time he'd been caught, but this time my mother had had enough. She was, I realized later, worried for me. I just worshiped my father, and I was doing considerably well, considering my age, at following in his footsteps."

"You ran con games?"

There was as much fascination as shock in Jenny's tone, and it made Laine smile a little. "Mostly I was just the beard, but yes, I did. Picking pockets was turning into my specialty. I had good hands, and people don't look at a little girl when they realize their wallet's been lifted."

"Holy cow," was all Jenny could say.

"I liked it. It was exciting, and it was easy. My father . . . well, he made it such a *game*. It never occurred to me that when I took some man's wallet, he might not be able to pay the rent that month. Or when we bilked some couple out of a few thousand in a bogus real-estate deal, that might've been their life savings, or a college fund. It was fun, and they were marks."

"And you were ten," Max added. "Give the kid a break."

"You could say that's what happened. I got a break. The direction I was heading in convinced my mother to change her life, and mine. She divorced my father and moved away, changed her name, got a straight job waiting tables. We moved around a lot the first few years. Not to shake my father loose—she wouldn't have done that to him. She let him know where we were, as long as he kept his word and didn't try to pull me back into the game. He kept his word. I don't know which of the three of us was more surprised by that, but he kept his word. We moved around to keep the cops from rousting us every time . . ."

She trailed off, managed a sickly smile in Vince's direction. "Sorry, but when you've got a rep for scams and theft, even by association, the locals tend to look you over. She wanted a fresh start, that's all. And a clean slate for me. It wasn't easy for her. She loved Jack, too. And I didn't help. I liked the game and didn't appreciate having it called, or being separated from my father."

She topped off cups of coffee, though she'd yet to touch her own. "But she worked so hard, and I started to see something in her, the pride and the satisfaction she got from earning her way. The straight way. And after a while, we weren't moving every time we turned around anymore. We weren't packing up in the middle of the night and slipping out of apartments or hotel rooms. And she kept her promises. Big Jack was long on the promises but came up short on keeping them. When my mother said she was going to do something, she did it."

No one spoke when she went to the refrigerator and took out a pitcher of water with lemon slices. She poured a glass, drank to wet her dry throat.

"Anyway, things changed. She met Rob Tavish, and things changed again, for the better. He's a wonderful man, crazy about her, and he was good to me. Sweet and kind and fun. I took his name. I made myself Laine Tavish because Laine Tavish was normal and responsible. She could have a place of her own, and a business of her own, and a life of her own. Maybe it wouldn't have all those wild ups she'd ridden on during the first part of her life, but it wouldn't have all those scary downs either. That seemed just fine. So anytime you asked me about my background, or growing up, I fabricated whatever seemed to fit Laine Tavish. I'm sorry. That's all. I'm sorry."

There was a long moment of silence. "Okay, wow." Jenny goggled at Laine. "I'm going to have a lot of follow-up comments and questions after my head stops spinning, but the first thing I have to ask is how all this—and there's a lot of this—applies to you being in trouble."

"There's probably a quote somewhere about not being able to escape the past, or cover it over. William Young." She saw Vince nod slowly and knew he was putting some of it together.

"The man who was killed when he ran out into the street," Jenny prompted.

"Yes. He used to run with my father. They were close as brothers, and hell, he lived with us half the time. I called him Uncle Willy. I didn't recognize him when he came in. I swear that, Vince. It's been years since I've seen him, and it just didn't click. It wasn't until after the accident and he . . . God, he was dying."

She drank more water, but this time her hand trembled lightly. "He looked so sad when I didn't recognize him, when I basically brushed him off. Then he was lying there, bleeding. Dying. He sang part of this stupid song he and my father used to do as a duet. 'Bye Bye Blackbird.' Something they'd start singing when we were loading up to skip out of a hotel. I realized who he was, and it was too late. I didn't tell you, and that's probably some sort of offense, but I didn't tell you I knew him."

"Why did he come to see you?"

"He didn't get much of a chance to tell me. I didn't give him much of a chance," she corrected.

"It's a waste of time to beat yourself up over that." Max said it briskly, and had her swallowing tears.

"Maybe. Looking back, I know he was nervous, edgy, tired. He gave me his card—just as I told you—with a phone number written on it. I really thought he was in the market to sell something. After, I realized he wanted to talk to me about something."

She stared into her empty glass, set it aside. "I think my father must've sent him. One of Willy's best skills was blending. He was a small, nondescript sort of man. Jack's big and redheaded and stands out, so I think Jack sent him to tell me something or give me something. But he didn't have a chance to do either. He only said . . . he said, 'He knows where you are now,' and for me to hide the pouch. I think he said 'pouch,' it's the only thing that makes sense. Except it sounded like 'pooch,' but that's just silly."

"What?" Max snapped the word like a whip. "You're just getting around to telling me?"

In contrast, Laine's voice was mild as milk. "That's right, and I really don't believe you're in any position to criticize timing. Insurance, my ass."

"It *is* insurance, goddamnit. Where's the pouch? What did you do with it?"

Heat flamed into her cheeks, not from embarrassment but temper. "He didn't give me a pouch, or anything else. I don't have your stupid diamonds. He was delirious, he was *dying*." Despite all her determination, her eyes filled and her voice broke. "He was dying right in front of me, and it was too late."

"Leave her alone." A mama bear protecting her cub, Jenny rounded on Max before she shifted to wrap her arms around Laine. "You just leave her alone."

While Vince patted Laine's shoulder in a show of support, his gaze was keen on Max's face. "What diamonds?"

"The twenty-eight point four million in diamonds stolen from the International Jewelry Exchange in New York six weeks ago. The diamonds my client, Reliance, insured and would very much like to recover. The diamonds my investigation has led me to believe were stolen by Jack O'Hara, William Young and a third party I believe is one Alex Crew."

"Holy shit," Jenny whispered.

"I don't know anything about them," Laine said wearily. "I don't have them, I've never seen them, I don't know where they are. I'll take a polygraph."

"But somebody thinks you have them, or access to them."

Grateful for the support, Laine rested her head on Jenny's shoulder and nodded at Vince. "Apparently. You can search the house, Vince. You and Max. You can search the shop. I'll authorize you full access to my phone records, bank records, anything you want. I'm only asking you to keep it quiet so I can just live my life."

"Do you know where your father is?"

"I don't have a clue."

"What do you know about this Alex Crew?"

"I've never heard of him. I'm still having a hard time believing Jack O'Hara was part of anything with this scope. He was loose change compared to this."

"If you had to get ahold of your father, what would you do?"

"It's never come up." Because they stung and burned, she rubbed her eyes. "I honestly don't know. He's contacted me a few times over the years. Right after I graduated from college, I got a FedEx letter. Inside was a first-class ticket to Barbados, and vouchers for a week's stay at a suite in a luxury hotel. I knew it was from him, and almost didn't go. But hey, Barbados. He met me there. We had a great time. It's impossible not to have a great time with Jack. He was proud of me—the whole college-graduate thing. He never held any hard feelings toward my mother or me for stepping out of his life. He popped up a couple more times. The last was before I moved here, when I was living in Philadelphia."

"The New York business isn't mine," Vince said. "But your break-ins are—and William Young is."

"He'd never hurt Willy, if that's what you're thinking. Not over ten times as much money. And he'd never come into my home and tear it up this way. He wouldn't do that to me. To anyone, for that matter. He loves me, in his way, he loves me. And it's just not his style."

"What do you know about this Crew?" Vince asked Max.

"Enough to say Jack and Willy fell in with bad companions. The inside man on the New York job was a gem merchant. He was shot, execution style. His body was found in his burned-out car in New Jersey."

His gaze flicked to Laine. "We can link O'Hara to Myers, the gem merchant. But neither O'Hara's nor Young's history runs to violent crimes, or any sort of armed offense. Can't say the same for Crew—though he's never been convicted of murder, he's suspected of a few. He's smooth, and smart. Smart enough to know these stones are hot, hot enough to wait until they've cooled off some before trying to liquidate them or transport them out of the country. It could be somebody got greedy or impatient."

"If this is Alex Crew, and he's trying to get to the stones or my father through me, he's doomed to disappointment."

"That doesn't mean he's going to stop trying," Max pointed out. "If so, he's been in the area, and may still be in the area. He copped my wallet, so he knows who I am and why I'm here." Absently, Max fingered the bandage on his temple. "He'll have to think about that for a while. I've got copies of photographs. He likes to play with faces, change his looks, but if he's been around town, maybe one of you will recognize him."

"I'll want copies for my men," Vince put in. "Cooperating with the New York authorities on a suspect believed to be in the vicinity. I'll keep Laine out of it as long as I can."

"Good enough."

"Thanks, Vince. Thank you." Laine lifted her hands, let them fall.

"Did you think we were going to be mad at you?" Jenny asked her. "Did you think this was going to affect our friendship?"

"Yes, I did."

"That's a little bit insulting, but I'm cutting you a break because you look really tired. What about him?" She jerked her chin up toward Max. "Are you forgiving him?"

"I guess I have to, considering the circumstances."

"All right, I'll forgive him, too. God, I just realized, I've been too preoccupied with all this to eat. Just let me make up for that." She took a slice of cake, bit in, then spoke around it. "I think you should come stay with Vince and me until this is all cleared up."

"I love you, Jenny." Because she felt the tears threaten again, she rose so she could turn her back and get them under control under the guise of getting more coffee. "And I appreciate the offer, but I need to be here, and I'll be fine. Max will be staying with me."

She turned back just in time to see the surprise wing over his face. She only smiled as she brought the pot over to top off cups. "Isn't that right, Max?"

"Yeah. Sure. I'll look out for her," he told Jenny.

"Since you're the one with the mild concussion, why don't we just leave it that you'll be staying here. I need to go up and change for work. I have to open the shop."

"What you need to do," Jenny disagreed, "is go upstairs

and crawl into bed for a few hours. You can keep the shop closed one day."

"I think the cops—public and private—would both say I need to keep it business as usual."

"You do that. We'll be keeping a close eye on the shop and your house until we run this all down. I want those pictures," Vince said to Max.

"I'll bring them by."

Laine walked them to the door.

"I'm going to have tons of questions. We need to have a girls' night," Jenny decided, "so I can pump you. Did you ever do that shell thing? You know, the switcheroo?"

"Jenny." Vince cast his eyes at the sky.

"Well, I want to *know,* for God's sake. Tell me later. How about the one with the three cards?" she called out as Vince pulled her toward the car. "Later, but I want specific details."

"She's something." Max watched Vince load his wife into the car.

"Yeah, she's something else again. She's the luckiest thing that ever happened to me." She waited until the car was out of sight before she closed the door. "Well, that went better than I deserved."

"You're doing better at forgiving me than you are at forgiving yourself."

"You were doing a job. I respect the work ethic." She gave a little shrug, turned toward the stairs. "I need to pull myself together and get into town."

"Laine? I figured we were going to go a few rounds when I told you I was going to stay out here. Instead, you tell me I'm staying out here. Why is that?"

She leaned against the railing. "There are a few reasons. First, I'm not a sniveling coward, but I'm not brainless and brave. I have no intention of staying out here alone, so far from town, when someone who wishes me no good may come back. I'm not risking myself or my dog over someone else's rocks."

"Sensible."

"So, I get me a big-city PI who I assume, despite current evidence, can handle himself."

He scowled at that and shifted his feet. "I can handle myself just fine."

"Good to know. Next, since I have a stake in seeing these gems are recovered, I prefer you at hand so I know exactly what you're doing about it. I can use seven hundred thousand dollars, just like the next guy."

"Practical."

"Last, I liked the sex and don't see why I should deprive myself of more of it. Easier to get you into bed if you're staying here."

Since he didn't seem to be able to come up with a term for that one, she smiled. "I'm going up to shower."

"Okay," he managed after she'd strolled upstairs. "That explains that."

Thirty minutes later, she came back down looking fresh as the spring morning in a short green jacket and pants. Her hair was scooped back at the temples with silver combs and left to fall straight toward her shoulders in that bright flood.

She walked up to Max and handed him a brass key ring. "Front and back doors," she told him. "If and when you get home before me, I'd appreciate you letting Henry out, giving him some play time."

"No problem."

"If and when I cook, you do the dishes."

"Deal."

"I like a tidy house and have no intention of picking up after you."

"I was raised right. Thank Marlene."

"That should do it for now. I've got to go."

"Hold it, those are your rules. Now here are mine: Take this number." He pressed a card into her hand. "That's my cell. You call me when you leave for home. If you're not coming straight home for any reason, you let me know that, too."

"All right." She slipped the card into her pocket.

"You call that number if anything happens, anything that bothers you. I don't care how minor it seems, I want to hear about it."

"So, if I get one of those calls from a telemarketer, I let you know."

"I'm serious, Laine."

"All right, all right. Anything else? I'm running very late."

"If you hear from your father, you tell me. You tell me, Laine," he repeated when he saw her face. "Divided loyalties aren't going to do him any good."

"I won't help you put him in prison. I won't do that, Max."

"I'm not a cop. I don't put people in prison. All I want is to recover the gems, collect my fee. And keep us all healthy while I'm at it."

"You promise me you won't turn him in, no matter what, and I'll promise to tell you if I hear from him."

"Done." He held out a hand, shook hers. Then gave it a yank so she'd tumble into his arms. "Now kiss me goodbye."

"All right."

She took a good grip on his hips, rose on her toes and met his mouth with hers. She took it slow, rocking into him, changing the angle to tease, using her teeth to challenge. She felt his hands tunnel through her hair, fingers tangling. When the heat rose inside her, when she felt it pumping off him, she slid her hands around, gave his butt a squeeze.

Her own pulse was tripping, but she enjoyed the sensation of being in control and turned her head so her lips were close to his ear.

"That oughta hold me," she whispered, then drew away.

"Now I'll kiss you goodbye."

She laughed and slapped a hand on his chest. "I don't think so. Mark your place, then you can kiss me hello. I should be home by seven."

"I'll be here."

He went out with her, followed her into town and peeled off to go to his hotel.

He stopped by the desk to ask the clerk to make up his bill for checkout.

She scanned his face. "Oh, Mr. Gannon, are you all right? Were you in an accident?"

"It was pretty much on purpose, but I'm fine, thanks. I'll be back down in a few minutes."

He got in the elevator. He'd already decided to work on his notes and reports once he'd set up at Laine's. Might as well make himself comfortable. A man who traveled as often as he did knew how to pack quickly and with the least amount of fuss. He swung the strap of his garment bag over one shoulder, the strap of his laptop case over the other, and was walking out of the room fifteen minutes after he'd walked in.

Back at the desk, he glanced over his bill, signed the credit slip.

"I hope you enjoyed your stay."

"I did." He made a note of her name tag. "One thing before I head out, Marti." Bending, he pulled a file out of his laptop case, flipped through for the photos of Jack O'Hara, William Young and Alex Crew. He laid them faceup on the desk. "Have you seen any of these men?"

"Oh." She blinked at him. "Why?"

"Because I'm looking for them." To this he added a thousand-watt smile. "How about it?"

"Oh," she repeated, but this time she looked down at the photos. "I don't think so. Sorry."

"That's okay. Anybody in the back? Maybe they could come out for a minute, take a look?"

"Sure, I guess. Mike's here. If you'll just wait a minute."

He ran the same routine with the second clerk, minus the flirtatious smile, and garnered the same results.

After stowing his bags in the trunk of his car, he made the rounds. First stop, he took the photos to Vince, waited while copies were made. Then he hit the other hotels, motels, B and B's within a ten-mile radius.

Three hours later, the most tangible thing he had to show for his efforts was a raging headache. He popped four extra-strength ibuprofen like candy, then got a take-out sandwich at a sub shop.

Back at Laine's he generously split the cold cut sub with a grateful Henry and hoped that would be their little secret. With the headache down to an ugly throb he decided to spend the rest of the day unpacking, setting up some sort of work space and reviewing his notes.

He spent about ten seconds debating where to put his clothes. The lady had said she wanted him in bed, so it was only fair his clothes be handy.

He opened her closet, poked through the clothes. Imagined her in some of them, imagined her out of all of them. He noted that she apparently shared his mother's odd devotion to shoes.

After another short debate, he concluded that he was entitled to reasonable drawer space. Because rearranging her underwear made him feel like a pervert, he made a stack of his own in a drawer with a colorful army of neatly folded sweaters and shirts.

With Henry clipping after him, he surveyed Laine's home office, then her sitting room, then the guest room. The fancy little writing desk in the guest room wouldn't have been his first choice, but it was the best space available.

He set up. He typed up his notes, a progress report, read them both over and did some editing. He checked his e-mail, his voice mail, and answered what needed answering.

Then he sat at the pretty little desk, stared up at the ceiling and let theories ramble through his mind.

He knows where you are now.

So, who was he? Her father. If Willy knew where Laine was, odds were so did Big Jack. But from what Laine had said, Jack had kept tabs on her off and on all along. So the phrase didn't work. He knows where you are *now*. The arrow in Max's mind pointed to Alex Crew.

There was no violence in O'Hara's history, but there was in Crew's. O'Hara didn't look good for the two taps to the back of the diamond merchant's head. And no reason, going by that history, for Willy to run scared of his old pal Jack O'Hara.

More likely, much more likely, he'd run from the third man, the man Max was convinced was Alex Crew. And following that, Crew was in the Gap.

But that didn't tell Max where Willy had put the stones.

He'd wanted to get them to Laine. Why in the hell would Willy, or her father, want to put Laine in front of a man like Crew?

He batted it around in his head, getting nowhere. Uncomfortable in the desk chair, he moved to stretch out on the bed. He closed his eyes, told himself a nap would refresh his brain.

And dropped into sleep like a stone.

It was his turn to wake with a blanket tucked around him. As was his habit, he came out of sleep the same way he went into it. Fast and complete.

He checked his watch and winced when he saw he'd been under for a solid two hours. But it was still shy of seven, and he'd expected to be up and around before Laine got back.

He rolled out of bed, popped a couple more pills for the lingering headache, then headed down to find her.

He was several paces from the kitchen when the scent reached out, hooked seductive fingers in his senses and drew him the rest of the way.

And wasn't she the prettiest damn thing, he thought, standing there in her neat shirt and pants with a dishcloth hooked in the waistband while she stirred something that simmered in a pan on the stove. She was using a long-handled wooden spoon, keeping rhythm with it, and her hips, to the tune that bounced out of a mini CD player on the counter.

He recognized Marshall Tucker and figured they'd mesh well enough in the music area.

The dog was sprawled on the floor, gnawing at a hank of rope that had seen considerable action already from the look of it. There were cheerful yellow daffodils in a speckled blue vase on the table. An array of fresh vegetables were grouped beside a butcher-block cutting board on the counter.

He'd never been much on homey scenes—or so he'd believed. But this one hit him right in the center. A man, he decided, could walk into this for the next forty or fifty years and feel just fine about it.

Henry gave two thumps of his tail then rose to prance over and knock the mangled rope against Max's thigh.

Tapping the spoon on the side of the pot, Laine turned and looked at him. "Have a nice nap?"

"I did, but waking up's even better." To placate Henry, he reached down to give the rope a tug, and found himself engaged in a spirited tug-of-war.

"Now you've done it. He can keep that up for days."

Max wrenched the rope free, gave it a long, low toss down the hallway. Scrambling over tile then hardwood, Henry set out in mad pursuit. "You're home earlier than I expected."

She watched him walk to her, her eyebrows raising as he maneuvered her around until her back was against the counter. He laid a hand on either side, caging her, then leaned in and went to work on her mouth.

She started to anchor her hands on his hips, but they went limp on her. Instead she went into slow dissolve, her body shimmering under the lazy assault. Her pulse went thick; her brain sputtered. By the time she managed to open her eyes, he was leaning back and grinning at her.

"Hello, Laine."

"Hello, Max."

Still watching her, he reached down to give the rope Henry had cheerfully returned another tug. "Something smells really good." He leaned down to sniff at her neck. "Besides you."

"I thought we'd have some chicken with fettuccine in a light cream sauce."

He glanced toward the pot, and the creamy simmering sauce. "You're not toying with me, are you?"

"Why, yes, I am, but not about that. There's a bottle of pinot noir chilling in the fridge. Why don't you open it, pour us a glass."

"I can do that." He backed up, went another round with Henry, won the rope and tossed it again. "You're actually cooking," he said as he retrieved the wine.

"I like to cook now and then. Since it's just me most of the time, I don't bother to fuss very much. This is a nice change."

"Glad I could help." He took the corkscrew she offered, studied the little silver pig mounted on the top. "You do collect them."

"Just one of those things." She set two amber-toned wineglasses on the counter. It pleased her to see the way he switched between sommelier duties and playing with the dog. To give him a break, she squatted down to get a tin from a base cabinet.

"Henry! Want a treat!"

The dog deserted the rope instantly to go into a crazed display of leaping, trembling, barking. Max could have sworn he saw tears of desperation in the dog's eyes as Laine held up a Milk-Bone biscuit.

"Only good dogs get treats," she said primly, and Henry plopped his butt on the floor and shuddered with the effort of control. When she gave the biscuit a toss, Henry nipped it out of the air the way a veteran right fielder snags a pop-up. He raced away with it like a thief.

"What, you lace them with coke?"

"His name is Henry, and he's a Milk-Bone addict. That'll keep him busy for five minutes." She pulled out a skillet. "I need to sauté the chicken."

"Sauté the chicken." He moaned it. "Oh boy."

"You really are easy."

"That doesn't insult me." He waited while she got a package of chicken breasts from the refrigerator and began slicing them into strips. "Can you talk and do that?"

"I can. I'm very skilled."

"Cool. So, how was business?"

She picked up the wine he'd set beside her, sipped. "Do you want to know how things went today in the world of retail, or if I saw anything suspicious?"

"Both."

"We did very well today, as it happens. I sold a very nice Sheraton sideboard, among other things. It didn't appear that anything in the shop, or my office, or the storeroom was disturbed—except for a little blood on the floor in the back room, which I assume is yours." She drizzled oil in the skillet, then glanced at him. "How's your head?"

"Better."

"Good. And I saw no suspicious characters other than Mrs. Franquist, who comes in once or twice a month to crab about my prices. So how was your day?"

"Busy, until naptime." He filled her in while she laid

the chicken strips in the heated oil, then started prepping the salad.

"I guess there are a lot of days like that, where you go around asking a lot of questions and not really getting any answers."

"A no is still an answer."

"I suppose it is. Why does a nice boy from Savannah go to New York to be a private detective?"

"First he decides to be a cop because he likes figuring things out and making them right. At least as right as they can be made. But it's not a good fit. He doesn't play well with others."

She smiled a little as she went back to the salad. "Doesn't he?"

"Not so much. And all those rules, they start itching. Like a collar that's too tight. He figures out what he really likes to do is look under rocks, but he likes to pick the rocks. To do that, you've got to go private. To do that and live well . . . I like living well, by the way."

"Naturally." She poured some wine in with the chicken, lowered the heat, covered the pan.

"So to live well, you've got to be good at picking those rocks, and finding people who live even better than you to pay you to poke at all the nasty business going on under them." He snitched a chunk of carrot to snack on. "Southern boy moves north, Yankees a lot of time figure he moves slow, thinks slow, acts slow."

She glanced up from whisking salad dressing ingredients together in a small stainless steel bowl. "Their mistakes."

"Yeah, and my advantage. Anyway, I got interested in computer security—cyber work. Nearly went in that direction, but you don't get out enough. So I just throw that little talent in the mix. Reliance liked my work, put me on retainer. We do pretty well by each other all in all."

"Your talents extend to table setting?"

"A skill I learned at my mama's knee."

"Dishes there, flatware there, napkins in that drawer."

"Check."

She put water on for the pasta while he went to work. After checking the chicken, adjusting the heat, she picked up her wine again. "Max, I've thought about this a lot today."

"Figured you would."

"I believe you'll do right by my father for a couple of reasons. You care about me, and he's not your goal. Recovering the stones is."

"That's a couple of them."

"And there's another. You're a good man. Not shiny and bright," she said when he paused to look at her. "Which would just be irritating to someone like me, because I'd keep seeing my own reflection bounced off someone like that, and I'd always come up short. But a good man, who might bend the truth when it suits, but keeps his word when he gives it. It settles my mind on a lot of levels knowing that."

"I won't make a promise to you that I can't keep."

"You see, that's just the right thing to say."

While Laine and Max ate pasta in the kitchen, Alex Crew dined on rare steak accompanied by a decent cabernet in the rustic cabin he'd rented in the state park.

He didn't care for rustic, but he did appreciate the privacy. His room at the Wayfarer in Angel's Gap had abruptly become too warm to suit him.

Maxfield Gannon, he mused, studying Max's investigator's license while he ate. Either a free agent out for a bounty, or a private working for the insurance company. Either way, the man was an irritant.

Killing him would have been a mistake—though he'd spent a tempting and satisfying moment considering it as he'd stood over the unconscious detective, fuming over the interruption.

But even a yahoo police force such as those fumbling around that pitiful little town would be riled to action by murder. Better for his purposes if they continued to bumble about giving parking tickets and rousting the local youth.

Better, he mused as he sipped his wine, and easier by far to have taken the irritant's identification, to have placed an anonymous call. It pleased him to think of this Maxfield Gannon trying to explain to the local law just what he'd been doing inside a closed store at three-thirty in the morning. It should have knotted things up nicely for a space of time. And no doubt it sent a very clear message to Jack O'Hara through his daughter.

But it was annoying just the same. He hadn't been able to take the time to search the premises, and he'd had to change his accommodations. That was very inconvenient.

He took out a small leather-bound notebook and made a list of these additional debits. When he caught up with O'Hara—and of course he would—he wanted to be able to detail all these offenses clearly while he tortured the location of the remaining diamonds out of him.

The way the list was mounting up, he was going to have to hurt O'Hara quite a bit. It was something to look forward to.

He could add O'Hara's daughter and the PI to his payment-due list as well. It was a bonus, in the grand scheme, for a man who equated inflicting pain with power.

He'd been quick and merciful with Myers, the greedy and idiotic gem buyer he'd employed as an inside man. But then Myers hadn't done anything more than be stupid enough to believe he was entitled to a quarter of the take. And greedy enough to meet him alone, in a closed construction site, in the middle of the night when promised a bigger cut.

Really, the man hadn't deserved to live if you thought about it.

In any case, he'd been a loose end that required snipping. The trail would have led to him eventually. He'd have bragged to someone, or would have thrown money around, squandering it on tasteless cars or women or God knew what that class of people considered desirable.

He'd blubbered and begged and sobbed like a baby when Crew held the gun to his head. Distasteful display, really, but what could one expect?

He'd also handed over the key to the mailbox locker where he'd stashed the Raggedy Andy doll with a bag of gems in its belly.

Genius, really, he had to give O'Hara credit for that little touch. Tucking millions of dollars' worth of gems into innocuous objects, objects no one would look at twice. So when the alarms went off, the building locked down, the cops swarmed, no one would consider all those pretty stones were still inside, tucked into something as innocent as a child's doll. Then it was just a matter of retrieving the extraordinary within the ordinary while the search went on elsewhere.

Yes, he could give Jack credit for that amusing detail, but that didn't negate all the debits.

They could hardly be trusted to hold millions of dollars' worth of gems for the year they'd agreed to. How could he possibly trust thieves to keep their word?

After all, he'd had no intention of keeping his.

Besides, he wanted it all. Had always intended to take it all. The others had merely been tools. When a tool had served its purpose, you discarded it. Better, you destroyed it.

But they'd deceived him, slipped through his fingers and taken half the prize with them. And cost him weeks of time and effort. He had to worry that they'd be caught pulling one of the pitiful scams Big Jack was so fond of, and end up confessing to the heist and losing half his property.

They should be dead now. The fact that one of them continued to live, to breathe, to walk, to hide, was a personal insult. He never tolerated insults.

His plan had been simple and clean. Myers first, execution style to make it seem as if one of his gambling debts had caught up with him. Then O'Hara and Young, bumbling idiots. They should have been where he'd *told* them to be, but they were too *stupid* to follow instructions.

If they had, he'd have contacted them as he'd planned, planted seeds of worry over Myers's demise and arranged for a meeting in a quiet, secluded location not unlike the one he was dining in now.

There, he could have dealt with them both with little effort as neither had the stomach to so much as carry a weapon. He'd have left enough evidence to link them to the New York job, and set the scene to look, even to the most moronic cop, like a matter of thieves falling out.

But they'd vanished on him. Scuttled his careful planning by attempting to go underground. Over a month now, it had taken over a month to finally pick up the trail and track Willy back to New York, only to miss him by inches and be forced to spend more time, more effort, more money to chase him to Maryland.

Then lose him to a traffic accident.

Shaking his head, Crew cut another bite of bloody steak. He'd never be able to collect directly from Willy now, so that account would be transferred to Big Jack—and the rest.

How to do it was the question, and the possibilities entertained him through the rest of his meal.

Did he go after the girl directly at this point, sweat her father's location and the whereabouts of the gems out of her? But if Willy had died before giving her any salient information, that would be a wasted effort.

Then there was this Maxfield Gannon to factor in. It might be wise to do a bit of research there, find out just what sort of man he was. One amenable to a bribe, perhaps? Obviously, he knew something about the girl or he wouldn't have been sneaking into her shop.

Or, and the thought struck him like an arrow in the heart, she had already cut a deal with Gannon. And that would be too bad, he thought, slapping his fist on the table again and again. That would be too bad for all involved.

He wasn't going to settle for half. It was not acceptable. Therefore, he would find a way to get back the rest of his property.

The girl was the key. What she knew or didn't know was undetermined. But there was one simple fact: She was Jack's daughter, and the apple of his larcenous eye.

She was bait.

Considering this, he leaned back, tidily dabbed his mouth with his napkin. Really, the food was better here than one might think, and the quiet was soothing.

Quiet. Private. A nice little woodland getaway. He began to smile as he indulged himself in another glass of wine. Quiet and private, with no neighbors nearby to disturb if one was to have a discussion with . . . associates. A discussion that might become a bit heated.

He looked around the cabin, at the country dark pressing against the windows.

It might do very well, he thought. It might do very well indeed.

It was very odd waking up with a man in your bed. A man took up considerable room, for one thing, and she wasn't used to worrying about how she looked the minute she opened her eyes in the morning.

She supposed she'd get over the last part, if she continued to wake up with this man in her bed for any length of time. And she could always get a bigger bed to compensate for the first part.

The question was, how did she feel about sharing her bed—and wasn't that just a metaphor for her life?—with this man for any length of time? She hadn't had time to think it through; hadn't taken time, she corrected.

Closing her eyes, she tried to imagine it was a month later. Her garden would be exploding, and she'd be thinking about summer clothes, about getting her outdoor furniture from the shed. Henry would be due for his annual vet appointment.

She'd be planning Jenny's baby shower.

Laine opened one eye, squinted at Max.

He was still there. His face was squashed into the pillow, his hair all cute and tousled.

So, she felt pretty good about having him there a month from now.

Try six months. She closed her eyes again and projected.

Coming up on Thanksgiving. In her usual organized fashion—she didn't care *what* Jenny said, it wasn't obsessive or disgusting—she'd have her Christmas shopping finished. She'd be planning holiday parties, and how she'd decorate the shop and the house.

She'd order a cord of wood and enjoy lighting a fire every evening. She'd stock a few bottles of good champagne so she and Max could . . .

Uh-oh, there he was.

She opened both eyes now and studied him. Yeah, there he was. Popping right up in her little projections, lying right there beside her sleeping while Henry, her pre-alarm clock, was beginning to stir.

She had a feeling if she added six months to that projection and made it a year, he was still going to be there.

He opened his eyes, a quick flash of that tawny brown, and had her yelping in surprise.

"I could hear you staring."

"I wasn't. I was thinking."

"I could hear that, too."

His arm shot out, hooked around her. She had a foolish little thrill tremble in her belly at the easy strength of him when he pulled her over and under him.

"I need to let Henry out."

"He can wait a minute." His mouth took hers so that thrill twisted into a throb.

"We're creatures of habit." Her breath caught. "Henry and me."

"Creatures of habit should always be in the market to develop another habit." He nuzzled her neck where her pulse pounded. "You're all warm and soft in the morning."

"Getting warmer and softer by the minute."

His lips curved against her skin, then he lifted his head to look into her eyes. "Let's see about that."

He scooped his hands under her hips, lifted them. And slid inside her. Those bright blue eyes blurred.

"Oh yeah." He watched her, watched her in the pale morning sunlight as he stroked. "You're absolutely right."

Henry whined and plopped his front paws on the side of the bed. He cocked his head as if trying to figure out why the two humans were still in there with their eyes closed when it was past time to let him out.

He barked once. A definite question mark.

"Okay, Henry, just a minute."

Max trailed his fingertips over Laine's arm. "Want me to do it?"

"You already did it. And thanks."

"Ha ha. Do you want me to let the dog out?"

"No, we have our little routine."

She got out of bed, which had Henry racing to the bedroom doorway, racing back, dancing in place while she got her robe out of the closet.

"Does the routine include coffee?" Max asked her.

"There is no routine without coffee."

"Praise God. I'm going to grab a shower, then I'll be down."

"Take your time. Are you sure you want to go out, Henry? Are you absolutely, positively sure?"

From the tone, and the dog's manic reaction, Max imagined the byplay was part of the morning ritual. He liked hearing the dog gallop up and down the steps, while Laine's laugh rolled.

He grinned all the way into the shower.

Downstairs, with Henry bouncing on all four legs, Laine unlocked the mudroom door. Per routine, she unlocked the outside door so Henry could fly through rather than wiggle through his doggie door, and so she could take a deep breath of morning air.

She admired her spring bulbs, bent down to sniff the hyacinths she'd planted in purples and pinks. Arms crossed, she stood and watched Henry make his morning circuit, lifting his leg on every tree in the near backyard. Eventually, he'd take a run into the woods, she knew, to see if he could scare up a few squirrels, flush some deer. But that little adventure would wait until he'd scrupulously marked his perimeter.

She listened to the birds chirp, and the bubble of her busy little stream. She was still warm from Max, still warm for him, and wondered how anyone could have a single worry on such a perfect and peaceful morning.

She stepped back in, closed the outside door. And was starting to hum when she walked back into the kitchen.

He stepped from behind the door and shot her heart into her throat. She was opening her mouth to scream when he laid a warning finger to his lips and had the sound sliding away.

It knocked the breath out of her so she stumbled back a step, hit the wall while her hand groped at her throat as if to decide whether to push the scream out or block it.

While he stood grinning at her, his finger still tapping on his lips, she sucked in a wheeze of breath and let it out with a single explosive whisper.

"Dad!"

"Surprise, Lainie." He whipped his hand from behind his back and held out a drooping clutch of spring violets. "How's my sweet baby girl?"

"Poleaxed" was a word Max had used. She now understood it perfectly. "What are you *doing* here? How did you—" She stopped herself before asking him how he'd gotten in. Ridiculous question seeing as lifting locks was one of his favorite pastimes. "Oh, Dad, what have you done?"

"Now, is that any way to greet your dear old dad after all this time?" He opened his arms wide. "Don't I get a hug?"

There was a twinkle in his eyes, eyes as blue as her own. His hair—his pride and joy—was stoplight red and combed into a luxurious mane around his wide, cheerful face. Freckles sprinkled over his nose and cheeks like ginger shaken on cream.

He wore a buffalo check flannel shirt in black and red, and jeans, both of which she imagined he'd selected as a nod to the area, and both of which appeared to have been slept in. The boots he'd paired with them looked painfully new.

He cocked his head and gave her a dreamy, puppy-dog smile.

Her heart had no defense against it. She leaped into his arms, locking herself around him as he squeezed tight and spun into a few giddy circles.

"That's my girl. That's my baby. My Princess Lainie of Haraland."

With her feet still a foot off the floor, she rested her head on his shoulder. "I'm not six anymore, Dad. Or eight, or ten."

"Still my girl, aren't you?"

He smelled like cinnamon sticks and had the build of a Yukon grizzly. "Yes, I guess I still am." She eased back, giving his shoulders a little nudge so he'd set her down. "How did you get here?"

"Trains, planes and automobiles. With the last of it on my own two feet. It's a place you've got here, sweetie pie. Scenic. But did you notice, it's in the woods?"

It made her smile. "No kidding? Good thing I like the woods."

"Must get that from your mother. How is she?"

"She's great." Laine didn't know why it always made her feel guilty when he asked, without rancor, with sincere interest. "How long have you been here?"

"Just got in last night. Since I arrived at your woodland paradise late, figured you to be in dreamland, I let myself in. Bunked on your couch, which I should tell you is in sorry shape." He pressed a hand to his lower back. "Be a lamb, sweetie, and make your daddy some coffee."

"I was just about . . ." She trailed off as the reminder of coffee cleared her head. *Max!* "I'm not alone." Panic trickled her throat. "There's someone upstairs in the shower."

"I gathered that from the car in your drive, the fancy piece with New York plates." He chucked her under the chin. "You're going to tell me, I hope, that you had a slumber party with an out-of-town girlfriend."

"I'm twenty-eight. I graduated from slumber parties with girlfriends to having sex with men."

"Please." Jack pressed a hand to his heart. "Let's just say you had a friend spend the night. This is the sort of thing a father needs to take in stages. Coffee, darling? That's a good girl."

"All right, all right, but there are things you need to know about . . . my overnight guest." She got out her bag of beans, poured some into her grinder.

"I already know the most important thing. He's not good enough for my baby. Nobody could be."

"This is so complicated. He's working for Reliance Insurance."

"So, he's got a straight job, a nine-to-fiver." Jack shrugged his broad shoulders. "I can forgive that one."

"Dad—"

"And we'll talk about this young man in just a bit." He

sniffed the air as she measured the coffee grounds into the filter. "Best scent in the world. While that's doing what it's doing, could you fetch me the package Willy left with you? I'll keep an eye on the pot."

She stared at him while all the thoughts, all the words, circled around in her head and coalesced into a single horrible certainty. He didn't know.

"Dad, I don't . . . He didn't . . ." She shook her head. "We'd better sit down."

"Don't tell me he hasn't been by yet." The faintest flicker of irritation crossed his face. "Man would get lost in his own bathroom without a map, but he's had more than enough time to get here. If he'd turn his damn cell phone on I'd have gotten in touch, told him there was a change in plans. I hate to tell you, Lainie, but your uncle Willy's getting old and absentminded."

No easy way, she thought as the coffee spilled into the pot. No easy way. "Dad, he's dead."

"I wouldn't go that far. Just forgetful."

"Dad." She gripped his arms, squeezing while she watched the indulgent smile fade from his face. "There was an accident. He was hit by a car. And he . . . he died. I'm sorry. I'm so sorry."

"That can't be. That's a mistake."

"He came into my shop a few days ago. I didn't recognize him." She ran her hands along his arms now because they'd begun to tremble. "It's been so long, I didn't recognize him. He gave me a number, asked me to call him. I thought he had something to sell, and I was busy so I didn't pay much attention. Then he left, and just after, just seconds after, it seemed, there were these horrible sounds."

Jack's eyes were filling, and hers did the same. "Oh, Dad. It was raining, and he ran into the street. I don't know why, but he ran out, and the car couldn't stop. I ran out, and I . . . I realized who he was but it was too late."

"Oh God. God. God." He did sit now, lowering into a chair, dropping his head into his hands. "He can't be gone. Not Willy."

He rocked himself for comfort while Laine wrapped her arms around him, pressed her cheek to his. "I sent him here. I told him to come because I thought it was . . . Ran out into the street?"

His head came up now. Tears tracked down his cheeks, and she knew he'd never been ashamed of them, or any big emotion. "He wasn't a child who goes running into the street."

"But he did. There were witnesses. The woman who hit him was devastated. There was nothing she could do."

"He ran. If he ran, there was a reason." He'd gone pale under the tears. "You need to get what he gave you. Get it and give it to me. Don't tell anyone. You never saw him before in your life, that's what you say."

"He didn't give me anything. Dad, I know about the stones. I know about the New York job."

His hands were on her shoulders now with a grip strong enough she knew there'd be bruises. "How do you know if he didn't give you anything?"

"The man who's upstairs. He works for Reliance. They insured the gems. He's an investigator."

"An insurance cop." He came straight out of the chair. "You've got a cop in your shower, for the sake of Jesus!"

"He tracked Willy here, and he connected him to me. To you and me. He only wants to recover the stones. He's not interested in turning you in. Just give me what you have, and I'll take care of this."

"You're sleeping with a cop? My own daughter?"

"I don't think this is the time to go into that. Dad, some-one broke into my house, into my shop because they're looking for the stones. I don't have them."

"It's that bastard Crew. That murdering bastard." His eyes were still wet and swimming, but there was fire behind them. "You don't know anything, do you hear me? You don't know anything, you haven't seen me. You haven't spoken to me. I'll take care of this, Laine."

"You can't take care of it. Dad, you're in terrible trouble. The stones aren't worth it."

"Half of twenty-eight million's worth quite a bit, and that's what I'll have to bargain with once I find out what Willy did with his. He didn't give you anything? Say anything?"

"He told me to hide the pouch, but he didn't give me one."

"Pouch? He took them out?"

"I just said he didn't give me a pouch. He was . . . fad-ing, and it was hard to understand him. At first I thought he said 'pooch.' "

"That's it." Some of the animation came back into his face. "His share is in the dog."

"The *dog*?" Genuine shock had her voice squeaking. "You fed diamonds to a dog?"

"Not a real dog. God almighty, Lainie, what do you take us for?"

She simply covered her face with her hands. "I don't know anymore. I just don't know."

"It's in a statue of a dog, little black-and-white dog. Cops probably have his things. Cops probably have it and don't know what they've got. I can work with that."

"Dad—"

"I don't want you to worry. No one's going to bother you

again. No one's going to touch my little girl. Just stay quiet about it, and I'll handle the rest." He gave her a hug, a kiss. "I'll just get my bag and be gone."

"You can't just go," she protested as she hurried after him. "Max says Crew is dangerous."

"Max is the insurance narc?"

"Yes." She glanced nervously toward the steps. "No, he's not a narc."

"Whatever, he's not wrong about Crew. Man doesn't think I know who he is," Jack muttered. "What he did. Figured I'd swallow his fake names and fairy story whole. Been in the game since I could talk, haven't I?" Jack slung a duffel over his shoulder. "I should never have gotten tangled with him, but well, twenty-eight million, give or take, makes for strange bedfellows. Now I've gotten Willy killed over it."

"You didn't. It's not your fault."

"I took the job knowing who Crew was though he called himself Martin Lyle. Knowing he was dangerous and planning a double cross all along, I took the job. Willy came with me. But I'll fix it. I won't let anything happen to you." He gave her a quick kiss on the top of her head, then moved to the front door.

"Wait. Just wait and talk to Max."

"I don't think so." He let out a snort at the idea. "And do us both a favor, princess." Now he tapped a finger to her lips. "I was never here."

She could hear him whistling "Bye Bye Blackbird" as he set off at a jog. He'd always moved well for a big man. Before she knew it, he'd rounded the curve of her lane and was gone.

As if he'd never been there.

She closed the door, rested her forehead against it. Everything ached: her head, her body, her heart. There'd been tears in his eyes still when he trotted away. Tears for Willy. He'd grieve, she knew. He'd blame himself. And in that state, he might do something stupid.

No, not stupid, she corrected and wandered into the kitchen to pace aimlessly. Reckless, foolish, but not stupid.

She couldn't have stopped him. Even if she'd begged, pleaded, even if she'd turned on the tears herself. He'd have carried the weight of them when he walked away, but he'd have walked.

Yes, he'd always moved well for a big man.

She heard Max coming toward the kitchen and hurriedly reached into the cupboard for mugs.

"Right on time," she said brightly. "Coffee's just up."

"Morning coffee's got to be one of life's best smells."

She turned then, stared at him as his words echoed her father's in her mind. His hair was still damp from the shower. Her shower. He'd smell like her soap. He'd slept in her bed. He'd been inside her.

She'd given him all that. But after a ten-minute visit from her father, she was holding back trust, and truth.

"My father was here." She blurted it out before she could question herself.

He set down the mug he'd just picked up. "What?"

"He just left. Minutes ago. And I realized I wasn't going to tell you, wasn't going to say anything. I was going to cover for him. It's conditioning, I guess. Or partly. I love him. I'm sorry."

"Jack O'Hara was here? He's been in the house, and you didn't tell me?"

"I'm telling you. I don't expect you to understand what

a step this is for me, but I'm telling you." She tried to pour coffee, but her hands were shaking. "Don't hurt him, Max. I couldn't stand it if you hurt him."

"Let's just back up a square here. Your father was here, in this house, and you cooked me dinner, went to bed with me. I'm upstairs making love to you and he's hiding out—"

"No! No! I didn't know he was here until this morning. I don't know when he got here, let himself in. He slept on the couch. I let Henry out, and when I walked into the kitchen again, there he was."

"Then what the hell are you apologizing to me for?"

"I wasn't going to tell you."

"For what, three minutes? Jesus Christ, Laine. You put that kind of honesty bar up for us, I'm going to keep rapping my head on it. Give me a break."

"I'm very confused."

"He's been your father for twenty-eight years. I've been the guy in love with you for about two days. I think I can cut you some slack. Okay?"

She let out a shuddering breath. "Okay."

"That's the end of the slack. What did he say, what did he want, where did he go?"

"He didn't know about Willy." Her lips trembled before she managed to press them together. "He cried."

"Sit down, Laine, I'll get the coffee. Sit down and take a minute."

She did what he asked as everything that had been aching was now shaking. She sat, stared at her hands while she listened to liquid hitting stoneware. "I think I might be in love with you, too. It's probably an awkward time to mention that."

"I like hearing it." He set the mug in front of her, then sat. "Whatever the time."

"I'm not playing you, Max. I need you to know that."

"Baby, I bet you're good at it. Considering. But you're not that good."

The cocky tone was just what was needed to dry up threatening tears. She looked at him then with a definite flash of amused arrogance. "Oh yeah, I am. I could swindle you out of your life savings, your heart, your pride, and make you believe it was your idea to hand them over with a bow on top. But since it looks like the only thing I'm interested in is your heart, I'd rather it really be your idea. Jack could never play it straight with my mother. He loved her. Still does, for that matter. But he could never play it straight, even with her. So they didn't make it. If you and I go into this, I want the odds in our favor."

"Then let's start by figuring out how to handle your father."

She nodded and picked up the coffee he'd brought her. She would be steady, and she would be straight. "He sent Willy here to give me a share of the take. For safekeeping, from what I can gather. You should know that if that had gone through, I'd have taken the stones, then passed them back to him. I'd have given him considerable grief about it, but I'd've done it."

"Blood's thick," Max acknowledged.

"From what I can gather, he got worried because Willy didn't call him—and his, Willy's, cell phone's been off. So he changed the plan, came here to pick up the dog."

"What dog?"

"See, it was a pooch, not a pouch. Or, the pouch is in the pooch. God, it sounds like a bad comedy routine. But I didn't get the pooch with the pouch, so my father figures the cops scooped it up with Willy's effects. And he believes Crew—he verified Crew, by the way—tracked Willy here, just like you did, and that's what spooked Willy and had him running into the street."

"There's not enough coffee in the world," Max murmured. "Go back to the dog."

"Oh, it's not an actual dog. It's a figurine of a dog. It's one of Jack's old gambits. Hide the take in something ordinary so it can be passed—and passed over by whoever's looking to get it back—until the heat's off. Once he hid a cache of rare coins inside my teddy bear. We strolled right out of the apartment building, chatted with the doorman and walked away with a hundred and twenty-five large inside Paddington."

"He took you on a job?"

His very real shock had her lowering her gaze to her coffee mug. "I didn't have what you'd call a standard childhood."

Max closed his eyes. "Where's he going, Laine?"

"I don't know." She reached out, covered his hand with hers until their eyes met. "I swear I don't know. He told me not to worry, that he'd take care of everything."

"Vince Burger has Willy's effects?"

"Don't tell him, Max, please don't. He'll have no choice but to arrest Jack if he shows up. I can't have any part in that. You and I, we don't have a chance if I have a part in that."

Thinking, he drummed his fingers on the table. "I searched Willy's motel room. Didn't see any dog figure." He brought the room back into his head, tried to see it section by section. "Don't remember anything like that, but it's possible I passed over it, thinking it was just part of the room's decor. 'Decor' being used in the loosest possible sense."

"That's why it works."

"All right. Can you talk Vince into letting you see Willy's effects?"

"Yes," she said without hesitation. "I can."

"Let's start there. Then we'll go to Plan B."

"What's Plan B?"

"Whatever comes next."

It was a little distressing how easy it all came back. Maybe it was easier, Laine thought, since she didn't have to talk to Vince. But she was, essentially, still deceiving a friend and lying to a cop.

She knew Sergeant McCoy casually, and when she realized she'd be dealing with him, quickly lined up all the facts she knew about him in her head. Married, Gap native, two children. She was nearly sure it was two, and that they were both grown. She thought there was a grand-child in the picture.

She added to those with observation and instinct.

Carrying an extra twenty pounds, so he liked to eat. Since there was a bakery Danish on a napkin on his desk, his wife was probably trying to get him to diet, and he had to sneak his fixes with store-bought.

He wore a wedding ring, his only jewelry, and his nails were clipped short. His hand was rough with calluses when it shook hers. He'd gotten to his feet to greet her and had done what he could to suck in his gut. She sent him a warm smile and noted the color that crept into his cheeks.

He'd be a pushover.

"Sergeant McCoy, it's nice to see you again."

"Miz Tavish."

"Laine, please. How's your wife?"

"She's fine. Just fine."

"And that grandbaby of yours?"

His teeth showed in a doting smile. "Not such a baby anymore. Boy's two now and running my daughter ragged."

"Such a fun age, isn't it? Taking him fishing yet?"

"Had him out to the river last weekend. Can't sit still long enough yet, but he'll learn."

"That'll be great fun. My granddaddy took me fishing a couple of times, but we had a serious difference of opinion when it came to worms."

McCoy let out an appreciative guffaw. "Tad, he loves the worms."

"That's a boy for you. Oh, I'm sorry. Sergeant, this is my friend Max Gannon."

"Yeah." McCoy studied the bruised temple. "Had you a little run-in the other night."

"It was all a misunderstanding," Laine said quickly. "Max came in with me this morning for a little moral support."

"Uh-huh." McCoy shook hands, because Max extended one, then glanced back at Laine. "Moral support?"

"I've never done this sort of thing before." She lifted her hands, looked fragile and frustrated. "Vince might have mentioned that I realized I knew William Young. The man who was killed in that awful accident outside my shop?"

"He didn't mention it."

"I just told him, and I guess it doesn't make any difference in the—in the procedure. It wasn't until after . . . until after that I remembered. He knew my father, when I was a child. I haven't seen him—William—since I was, oh, ten, I guess. I was so busy when he came into the shop."

Her eyes went shiny with distress. "I didn't recognize him, and I just didn't pay that much attention. He left me his card and asked me to call him when I had the chance.

Then nearly as soon as he walked out . . . I feel terrible that I didn't remember, that I brushed him off."

"That's all right now." McCoy dug a box of tissues out of a drawer and offered it.

"Thanks. Thank you. I want to do what I can for him now. I want to be able to tell my father I did what I could." Those things were true. It helped to work in truth. "He didn't have any family that I know of, so I'd like to make whatever arrangements need to be made for burial."

"The chief has his file, but I can check about that for you."

"I'd appreciate that very much. I wonder if, while I'm here, I could see his things. Is that possible?"

"I don't see why not. Why don't you have a seat?" He took her arm, gently, and led her to a chair. "Just sit down, and I'll go get them for you. Can't let you take anything."

"No, no, I understand."

As McCoy left the room, Max sat beside her. "Smooth as butter. How well you know this cop?"

"McCoy. I've met him a couple of times."

"Fishing?"

"Oh, that. He has a fishing magazine tucked under his case files on the desk, so it was a reasonable guess. I'm going to arrange for Uncle Willy's burial," she added. "Here, I think, in Angel's Gap, unless I can find out if there's somewhere else he'd rather . . ."

"I bet here would suit him fine."

He rose, as did she, when McCoy returned with a large carton. "He didn't have much. Looks like he was traveling light. Clothes, wallet, watch, five keys, key ring—"

"Oh, I think I gave him that key ring for Christmas one year." She reached out, sniffling, then closed it into her fist. "Can you imagine? He used it all these years. Oh, and I didn't even recognize him."

Clutching the keys, she sat, wept.

"Don't cry, Laine."

Max sent McCoy a look of pure male helplessness and patted Laine on the head.

"Sometimes they gotta." McCoy went back for the tissues. When he stepped back up, Laine reached out, took three, mopped at her face.

"I'm sorry. This is just *silly*. It's just that I'm remembering how sweet he was to me. Then we lost contact, you know how it is? My family moved away, and that was that."

Composing herself, she got to her feet again. "I'm fine. I'm sorry, I'll be fine." She took the manila envelope, dropped the keys back into it and slipped it back into the carton herself. "Can you just tell me the rest? I promise, that won't happen again."

"Don't you worry about it. You sure you want to deal with this now?"

"I do. Yes, thank you."

"There's a toiletry kit—razor, toothbrush, the usual. He was carrying four hundred twenty-six dollars and twelve cents. Had a rental car—a Taurus from Avis out of New York, road maps."

She was looking through the items as McCoy detailed them from his list.

"Cell phone—nothing programmed in the phone book for us to contact. Looks like there's a couple of voice messages. We'll see if we can track those."

They'd be from her father, she imagined, but only nodded.

"Watch is engraved," he added when Laine turned it over in her hand. " 'One for every minute.' I don't get it."

She gave McCoy a baffled smile. "Neither do I. Maybe

it was something romantic, from a woman he loved once. That would be nice. I'd like to think that. This was all?"

"Well, he was traveling." He took the watch from her. "Man doesn't take a lot of personal items with him when he's traveling. Vince'll be tracking down his home address. Don't worry about that. We haven't found any next of kin so far, and if we don't, seems like they'll release him to you. It's nice of you to want to bury an old friend of your father's."

"It's the least I can do. Thank you very much, Sergeant. You've been very kind and patient. If you or Vince would let me know if and when I can make the funeral arrangements, I'd appreciate it."

"We'll be in touch."

She took Max's hand as they walked out, and he felt the key press his palm. "That was slick," he commented. "I barely caught it."

"If I wasn't a little rusty, you wouldn't have caught it. It looks like a locker key. One of those rental lockers. You can't rent lockers at airports or train stations, bus stations, that sort of thing anymore, can you?"

"No. Too small for one of those garage-type storage lockers, and most of those are combination locks or key cards anyway. It might be from one of those mailbox places."

"We should be able to track it down. No dog though."

"No, no dog. We'll check the motel room, but I don't think it's there, either."

She stepped outside with him, took a fond look at the town she'd made her own. From this vantage point, high on the sloped street, she could see a slice of the river, and the houses carved into the rising hill on the other bank. The mountains climbed up behind, ringing their way around the sprawl of streets and buildings, the parks and bridges.

They formed a scenic wall covered with the green haze of trees beginning to leaf, and the white flash of blooming wild dogwoods.

The everydayers, as her father had dubbed normal people with normal lives, were about their business. Selling cars, buying groceries, vacuuming the rug, teaching history.

Gardens were planted, or being prepared for planting. She could see a couple of houses where the Easter decorations had yet to be dispatched, though it was nearly three weeks past. Colorful plastic eggs danced in low tree limbs, and inflatable rabbits squatted on spring-green grass.

She had rugs to vacuum and groceries to buy, a garden to tend. Despite the key in her hand, she supposed that made her an everydayer, too.

"I'm not going to pretend some of that didn't stir the juices. But when this is over, I'll be happy to retire again. Willy never could, my father never will."

She smiled as they walked to Max's car. "My father gave him that watch. The key ring was just a ploy, but my dad gave Willy that watch for his birthday one year. I think he might have actually bought it, but I can't be sure. But I was with him when he had it engraved. 'One for every minute.' "

"Meaning?"

"There's a sucker born every minute," she said, and slipped into the car.

It was the same clerk at the desk of the Red Roof, but Max could see the lack of recognition in his eyes. The simplest, quickest way into Willy's last room was to pay the standard freight.

"We want one-fifteen," Max told him.

The clerk studied the display of his computer, checked availability and shrugged. "No problem."

"We're sentimental." Laine added a sappy smile and snuggled next to Max.

Max handed over cash. "I need a receipt. We're not that sentimental."

With the key in hand, they drove around to Willy's section.

"He must've known where I live. My father did, so Willy did. I wish he'd just come to see me there. I can only think he knew somebody was right behind him—or was afraid someone was—and figured the shop was safer."

"He was only here one night. Hadn't unpacked." Max led the way to the door. "Looked like enough clothes for about a week. Suitcase was open, but he hadn't taken anything out but his bathroom kit. Could be he wanted to be ready to move again, fast."

"We were always ready to move again, fast. My mother could pack up our lives in twenty minutes flat, and lay it out again in a new place just as quick."

"She must be an interesting woman. Takes mine longer than that to decide what shoes to wear in the morning."

"Shoes aren't a decision to be made lightly." Understanding, she laid a hand on his arm. "You don't have to give me time to prepare myself, Max. I'm okay."

He opened the door. She stepped into a standard motel double. She knew such rooms made some people sad, but she'd always found them one of life's small adventures for their very anonymity.

In such rooms you could pretend you were anywhere. Going anywhere. That you were anyone.

"As a kid we'd stop off in places like this, going from one point to another. I loved it. I'd pretend I was a spy chasing down some nefarious Dr. Doom, or a princess traveling incognito. My father always made it such a wonderful game.

"He'd always get me candy and soft drinks from the vending machines, and my mother would pretend to disapprove. I guess, after a while, she wasn't pretending anymore."

She fingered the inexpensive bedspread. "Well, that's a long enough walk down Memory Lane. I don't see any dog in here."

Though he'd already done a search, and knew the police had been through the room, followed by housekeeping, Max went through the procedure again.

"Don't miss much, do you?" she said when he'd finished.

"Try not to. That key might be the best lead we've got. I'll check out the local storage facilities."

"And what you're not saying is he could've stashed it in a million of those kind of places from here to New York."

"I'll track it back. I'll find it."

"Yes, I believe you will. While you're doing that, I'll go back to work. I don't like leaving Jenny there alone very long, under the circumstances."

He tossed the room key on the bed. "I'll drop you off."

Once they were back in the car, she smoothed a hand over her pants. "You'd have disapproved, too. Of the motel rooms, the game. The life."

"I can see why it appealed to you when you were ten. And I can see why your mother got you out of it. She did what was right for you. One thing about your father . . ."

She braced herself for the criticism and promised herself not to take offense. "Yes?"

"A lot of men in . . . let's say, his line, they shake off wives and kids or anything that resembles responsibility. He didn't."

Her shoulders loosened, her stomach unknotted, and she turned to send Max a luminous smile. "No, he didn't."

"And not just because you were a really cute little red-headed beard with light fingers."

"That didn't hurt, but no, not just because of that. He loved us, in his unique Jack O'Hara way. Thanks."

"No problem. When we have kids, I'll buy them candy out of the vending machine, but we'll keep it to special occasions."

Her throat closed down so that she had to clear it in order to speak. "You do jump ahead," she stated.

"No point in dragging your feet once you've got your direction."

"Seems to me there's a lot of road between here and there. And a lot of curves and angles in it."

"So, we'll enjoy the ride. Let's round one of those curves now. I don't need to live in New York if that's something you're chewing on. I think this area's just fine for raising those three kids."

She didn't choke, but it was close. "Three?"

"Lucky number."

She turned her head to stare out the side window. "Well, you sailed right around that curve. Have you considered slowing down until we've known each other, oh, I don't know, a full week?"

"People get to know each other faster in certain situations. This would be one of them."

"Favorite childhood memory before the age of ten."

"Tough one." He considered a moment. "Learning to ride a two-wheeler. My father running alongside—with this big grin, and a lot of fear in his eyes I didn't recognize as such at the time. How it felt, this windy, stomach-dropping rush when I realized I was pedaling on my own. Yours?"

"Sitting on this big bed in the Ritz-Carlton in Seattle. It was a suite because we were really flush. Dad ordered this ridiculous room-service meal of shrimp cocktail and fried chicken because I liked them both, and caviar, which I hadn't yet acquired a taste for. There was pizza and hot fudge sundaes. An eight-year-old's fantasy meal. I was half sick from it, and sitting on the bed with probably a hundred in ones he'd given me to play with."

She waited a beat. "Not exactly from the same world, Max."

"We're in the same one now."

She looked back at him. He looked confident and tough, his clever hands on the wheel of the powerful car, his sun-streaked hair unruly from the breeze, those dangerous cat's eyes hidden behind tinted lenses.

Handsome, in control, sure of himself. And the butterfly bandage on his temple was a reminder he didn't always come out on top, but he didn't stay down.

Man of my dreams, she thought, *what am I going to do with you?*

"Hard to trip you up."

"I already took the big stumble, sweetheart, when I fell for you."

Laughing, she let her head fall back. "That's sappy, but somehow it works. I must still have a weakness for a guy with a quick line."

He pulled up in front of her shop. "I'll pick you up at closing." Leaning over, he gave her a light kiss. "Don't work too hard."

"This is all so strangely normal. A little pocket of ordinary in a big bunch of strange." She reached out, feathered her fingertips over his bandage. "Be careful, all right? Alex Crew knows who you are."

"I hope we run into each other soon. I owe him one."

The normal continued through most of the day. Laine waited on customers, packed merchandise to ship, unpacked shipments of items she'd ordered. It was the sort of day she usually loved, with plenty to do but none of it rushed. She was sending things off with people who enjoyed or admired them enough to pay for them, and finding things in the shipping boxes she'd enjoyed or admired enough to want in her shop.

Despite it, the day dragged.

She worried about her father and what reckless thing he might do while the grief was on him. She worried about Max and what could happen if Crew came after him.

She worried about her relationship with Max. Mentally examined, evaluated and dissected it until she was sick of herself.

"Looks like it's just you and me," Jenny said when a customer left the shop.

"Why don't you take a break? Put your feet up for a few minutes."

"Happy to. You do the same."

"I'm not pregnant. And I have paperwork."

"I am pregnant, and I won't sit until you sit. So if you don't sit down you're forcing a pregnant woman to stand on her feet and they're swollen."

"Your feet are swollen? Oh, Jenny—"

"Okay, not yet. But they *could* be. They probably will be, and it'll be your fault. So let's sit."

She nudged Laine toward a small, heart-backed divan. "I love this piece. I've thought about buying it a dozen times, then remember I have absolutely no place to put it."

"When you love a piece, you find a place."

"So you always say, but your house doesn't look like an antique warehouse." She ran her fingers over the satiny rose-on-rose stripes of the cushions. "Still, if it hasn't sold in another week, I'm going to cave."

"It'd look great in the little alcove off your living room."

"It would, but then I'd have to change the curtains, and get a little table."

"Naturally. And a nice little rug."

"Vince is going to kill me." She sighed, plopped her joined hands on the shelf of her belly. "Okay, time for you to unload."

"I've already unpacked the last shipment."

"Emotionally unload. And you knew what I meant."

"I wouldn't know where to start."

"Start with what pops to the surface first. You've got a lot bobbing around under there, Laine. I know you well enough to see it."

"You still think you know me after everything you've found out in the last couple of days?"

"Yeah, I do. So uncork it. What comes first?"

"Max thinks he's in love with me."

"Really?" It wasn't as easy for her to come to alert as it once had been, but Jenny dug her elbows into the cushions and pushed her heavy body straighter. "Did you intuit that, or did he say it? Right out say it?"

"Right out said it. You don't believe in love at first sight, do you?"

"Sure I do. It's all chemicals and stuff. There was this whole program on it on PBS. I think it was PBS. Maybe it was The Learning Channel. Anyway." She waved that part aside. "They've done all these studies on attraction and sex and relationships. Mostly, it boils down to chemicals, instincts, pheromones, then building on that. Besides, you know Vince and I met when I was in first grade. I went right home from school and told my mom that I was going to marry Vince Burger. Took us a while to get there. State law's pretty firm about six-year-olds getting hitched. But it sure was the right mix of chemicals from day one."

She never tired of picturing it—gregarious Jenny and slow-talking Vince. And she always saw them with their adult heads on sturdy little kids' bodies. "You've known each other all your lives."

"That's not the point. Minutes, days, years, sometimes it's just a click, click." Jenny snapped her fingers to emphasize. "Besides, why shouldn't he be in love with you? You're beautiful and smart and sexy. If I were a man I'd be all over you."

"That's . . . really sweet."

"And you've got this interesting and mysterious past on top of it. How do you feel about him?"

"All sort of loose and itchy and feebleminded."

"You know, I liked him right away."

"Jenny, you liked his ass right away."

"And your point would be?" She snickered, pleased when Laine laughed. "Okay, besides the ass, he's considerate. He bought his mother a gift. He's got that accent going for him, has a sexy job. Henry likes him, and Henry's a very good judge of character."

"That's true. That's very true."

"And he's not hung up with commitment phobia or he wouldn't have used the *l* word. Added to all that," she said softly, "he's on your side. That came across loud and clear. He's on your side, and that won him top points from the best-pal seats."

"So I should stop worrying."

"Depends. How is he in bed? Gladiator or poet?"

"Hmm." Thinking back, Laine ran her tongue over her bottom lip. "A poetic gladiator."

"Oh *God*!" With a little shudder, Jenny slumped back. "That's the best. Snap him up, girl."

"I might. I just might. If we manage to get through all this without screwing it up."

She glanced back as her door opened and the bells jingled. "I'll get this. Sit."

The couple was fortyish, and Laine pegged them as affluent tourists. The woman's jacket was a thin butter-colored suede, and the shoes and bag were Prada. Good jewelry. A nice, square-cut diamond paired with a channel-set wedding band.

The man wore a leather jacket that looked Italian in cut over nicely faded Levi's. When he turned to close the door behind him, Laine spotted the Rolex on his wrist.

They were both tanned and fit. Country club, she thought. Golf or tennis every Sunday.

"Good afternoon. Can I help you with anything?"

"We're just poking around," the woman answered with a smile, and a look in her eye that told Laine she didn't want to be guided or pressured.

"Help yourself. Just let me know if you need anything." To give them space, she walked to the counter, opened one of her auction catalogues.

She let their conversation wash over her. Definitely country club types, Laine thought. And made one of her little bets with herself that they'd drop five hundred minimum before heading out again.

If she was wrong, she had to put a dollar in the ginger jar in her office. As she was rarely wrong, the jar didn't see much action.

"Miss?"

Laine glanced over, then waved Jenny back before her friend could heft herself off the divan. She gave the female customer her merchant's smile and wandered over.

"What can you tell me about this piece?"

"Oh, that's a fun piece, isn't it? Chess table, circa 1850.

British. It's penwork and ivory-inlaid ebony. Excellent condition."

"It might work in our game room." She looked at her husband. "What do you think?"

"A little steep for a novelty piece."

All right, Laine thought. She was supposed to bargain with the husband while the wife looked around. No problem.

"You'll note the double spiral pedestal. Perfect condition. It's really one of a kind. It came from an estate on Long Island."

"What about this?"

Laine walked over to join his wife. "Late nineteenth century. Mahogany," she said as she ran a fingertip over the edge of the display table. "The top's hinged, the glass beveled." She lifted it gently. "Don't you just love the heart shape?"

"I really do."

Laine noted the signal the wife sent her husband. *I want both,* it said. *Make it work.*

She wandered off, and Laine gave Jenny the nod to answer any questions she might have over the collection of wineglasses she was eyeing.

She spent the next fifteen minutes letting the husband think he was cutting her price to the bone. She made the sale, he felt accomplished and the wife got the pieces she wanted.

Everybody wins, Laine thought as she wrote up the sale.

"Wait! Michael, look what I found." The woman hurried to the counter, flushed and laughing. "My sister loves this sort of thing. The sillier the better." She held up a ceramic black-and-white dog. "There's no price."

Laine stared at it, the practiced smile still curving her

lips while her pulse pounded in her ears. Casually, very casually, she reached out and took the statue. An icy finger pressed at the base of her spine.

"Silly's the word. I'm so sorry." Her voice sounded perfectly natural, with just a hint of laughter in it. "This isn't for sale. It's not part of the stock."

"But it was on the shelf, right back there."

"It belongs to a friend of mine. He must have set it down without thinking. I had no idea it was there." Before the woman could object, Laine set it on the shelf under the counter, out of sight. "I'm sure we can find something along the same lines that will suit your sister. And if we do, it's half off for the disappointment factor."

The half off stilled any protests. "Well, there was a cat figure. Siamese cat. More elegant than the dog, but still kitschy enough for Susan. I'll go take another look at it."

"Go right ahead. Now, Mr. Wainwright, where would you like your pieces shipped?"

She finished the transaction, chatted easily, even walked her customers to the door.

"Nice sale, boss. I love when they keep finding something else, adding it on."

"She was the one with the eye, he was the one with the wallet." It felt a little like floating, but Laine got back to the counter, lifted the dog. "Jenny, did you shelve this piece?"

"That? No." Lips pursed, Jenny walked over to study it. "Sort of cute, in a ridiculous way. A little flea market for us, isn't it? It's not Doulton or Minton or any of those types, is it?"

"No, it's not. I imagine it came in one of the auction shipments by mistake. I'll sort it out. Look, it's nearly five. Why don't you take off early? You covered for me for more than an hour this morning."

"Don't mind if I do. I've got a craving for a Quarter Pounder. I'll swing by the station and see if Vince is up to dining at Chez McDonald's. I'm as close as the phone, you know, if anything else pops to the surface and you want to vent."

"I know."

Laine shuffled papers until Jenny gathered her things and headed out the door. She waited another five full minutes, doing busywork in case her friend doubled back for any reason.

Then she walked to the front, put up the CLOSED sign, locked the door.

Retrieving the statue, she took it into the back room, checked those locks. Satisfied no one could walk in on her unexpectedly, she set the statue on her desk, studied it.

She could see the glue line now that she was looking for it, just a hint of it around the little cork shoved into the base. It was good work, but then Big Jack was never sloppy. Beside the cork was a faded stamp. MADE IN TAIWAN.

Yes, he'd have thought of little details like that. She shook it. Nothing rattled.

Clicking her tongue, she got out a sheet of newspaper, spread it on the desk. She centered the dog on it, then walked to the cabinet where she kept her tools. She selected a small ball-peen hammer, cocked her head, swung back her arm.

Then stopped.

And because she stopped, she realized, without a single doubt, she was in love with Max.

On a breath, she sat, staring at the dog as she set the hammer aside.

She couldn't do it on her own because she was in love

with Max. That meant they would do it together. And do whatever came next together.

And that, she thought, is what her mother had found with Robert Tavish. What she'd never really had with Jack, for all the excitement and adventure. Her mother had been part of the team, and possibly the love of Jack's life. But at the core, they hadn't been a couple.

Her mother and Rob were a couple. And that's what she wanted for herself. If she was going to be in love with someone, she damn well wanted to be half of a couple.

"Okay then."

She rose, got bubble wrap from her shipping supplies. She wrapped the cheap ceramic dog as carefully, as meticulously as she would've wrapped antique crystal. Over layers of bubble wrap, she secured brown shipping paper, then nestled the package into a tissue-lined shopping bag, along with a second item she'd taken from her stock and wrapped.

When the job was complete, she arranged for the shipping for her final sale of the day, then filed paperwork. At precisely six o'clock, she was at the front door waiting for Max.

He was fifteen minutes late, but that only gave her time to calm completely.

He'd barely pulled to the curb when she was walking out, locking the door.

"You're always on time, right?" he asked her when she got into the car. "Probably more like always five minutes early."

"That's right."

"I hardly ever am, exactly on time, that is. Is this going to be a deal with us down the road?"

"Oh yes. You get this initial honeymoon period where I just flutter my lashes when you show up and don't say a word about your being late. After that, we'll fight about it."

"Just wanted to check on that. What's in the bag?"

"A couple of things. Did you have any luck with the key?"

"That depends on your point of view. I didn't find the lock it fits, but I eliminated several it didn't."

He drove up her lane, parked behind her car. "How come Henry doesn't zip out his dog door when he hears a car drive up?"

"How does he know who it is? It could be someone he doesn't want to talk to."

She got out, waited for him to pop the trunk. And beamed at the bucket of fried chicken.

"You bought me chicken."

"Not only, but the makings for hot fudge sundaes." He lifted the two bags. "I thought about shrimp cocktail and pizza, but figured we'd both be sick. So just the Colonel and ice cream for you tonight."

She set the shopping bag down, threw her arms around his neck and crushed her mouth to his.

"I can hit up the Colonel every night," he said when he could manage it.

"It's those secret herbs and spices. They get me every time. I decided I love you."

She watched the emotion swirl into his eyes. "Yeah?"

"Yeah. Let's go tell Henry."

Henry seemed more interested in the chicken, but settled for a quick wrestle and a giant Milk-Bone biscuit while Laine set the table.

"You can eat that sort of thing on paper towels," Max told her.

"Not in this house."

She fancied it up in a way he found sweet and feminine. Her colorful plates turned the fast-food chicken and tubs of coleslaw into a tidy celebration.

They had wine and candles and extra-crispy.

"Would you like to know why I decided I love you?" She waited, enjoying the meal, watching him enjoy it.

"Because I'm so handsome and charming?"

"That's why I decided to sleep with you." She cleared the plates. "I decided I might love you because you made me laugh, and you were kind and clever and because when I played the next-month game, you were still there."

"The next-month game?"

"I'll explain that later. But I decided I must love you when I started to do something by myself, and stopped. Didn't want to do it by myself. I wanted to do it with you, because when two people make one couple, they do important things, and little things, together. But before I explain all that, I've got a present for you."

"No kidding?"

"No, I take presents very seriously." She took the first wrapped item out of her bag. "It's a favorite of mine, so I hope you like it."

Curious, he ripped the protective brown paper off, then broke into a huge grin. "You're not going to believe this."

"You have it already?"

"Nope. My mother does. Happens it's one of her favorites, too."

It pleased her to hear it. "I imagine she was fond of Maxfield Parrish's work or she wouldn't have named her son after the artist."

"She has a few of his prints. This one's in her sitting room. What's it called again?"

"*Lady Violetta About to Make Tarts*," Laine told him as

they both studied the framed print of a pretty woman standing in front of a chest and holding a small silver pitcher.

"She's pretty hot. Looks a little like you."

"She does not."

"She's got red hair."

"That's not red." Laine tapped a finger against the model's reddish-gold hair, then tugged a lock of her own. "*This* is red."

"Either way, I'm going to think of you every time I look at her. Thanks."

"You're welcome." She took the picture from him and laid it on the kitchen counter. "All right, now for the explanation as to why I decided I was in love with you and decided to give you a present to commemorate it. This couple in my shop today," she continued as she set the shopping bag on the table. "Upper class, second- or third-generation money. Not wealthy but rich. They worked as a team, and I admire that. The signals, the rhythm. I like that. I want that."

"I'll give you that."

"I think you will." She lifted the package out of the bag, retrieved scissors and went patiently to work on the wrap.

"While they were in the shop, buying some nice glassware, a gorgeous display table and a very unique chess table, the wife part of the team spotted this other piece. Completely *not* her style, let me tell you. But apparently her sister's. She got all excited, brought it to the counter while I was ringing up. She wanted it, but it wasn't priced. I hadn't priced it because I'd never seen it before."

She saw the jolt of understanding run over his face. "Christ, Laine, you found the pooch."

She set the unwrapped statue on the table. "Sure looks like it."

CHAPTER

12

He picked it up to examine it, just as she had. Shook it, just as she had.

"It looks like an ordinary, somewhat tacky, inexpensive ceramic dog." Laine gave it a quick tap with her fingers. "And just screams Big Jack O'Hara to me."

"You'd know." He hefted it, as if checking weight while he looked at her. "You didn't just bust it open and see for yourself."

"No."

"Big points for you."

"Major, but if we stand here discussing it much longer I'm going to crack, scream like a maniac and smash it into lots of doggie pieces."

"Then let's try this." Even as she opened her mouth to protest, he smacked the statue smartly on the table. Its winsome head rolled off so that the big painted eyes stared up in mute accusation.

"Well." All Laine could do was huff out a breath. "I thought we might do that with a little more ceremony."

"Quick is more humane." He dipped his fingers into the jagged opening and tugged. "Padding," he said and had her wincing as he smashed the body on the table.

"I have a hammer in the mudroom."

"Uh-huh." He unwrapped the layers of cotton, pulled out the small pouch. "I just bet this is a lot more upscale than anything I ever got out of a cereal box. Here." He handed her the jewelry pouch. "You do this part."

"And major points right back at you."

The buzz was there, that hum in the blood she knew came as much from holding something that belonged to someone else as it did from discovery. Once a thief, she thought. You could stop stealing, but you never forgot the thrill.

She untied the cord, pulled open the gathered top and poured a glittering rain of diamonds into her open palm.

She made a sound. Not unlike, Max noted, the one she made when he brought her to orgasm. And her eyes, when they lifted to his, were just a bit blurry. "Look how big and shiny," she murmured. "Don't they make you just want to run out and dance naked under the moon?" When he lifted an eyebrow, she shrugged. "Okay, just me then. You'd better take them."

"I would, but you've got them clutched in your fist, and I'd rather not have to break your fingers."

"Oh, sorry. Obviously, I still have to work on my recovery. Ha ha. Hand doesn't want to open." She pried her fingers into a loose curl and let the diamonds drip out into Max's open palm. When he continued to stare at her with that lifted brow, she laughed and let the last stone drop.

"Just seeing if you were paying attention."

"This is a new aspect of you, Laine. Something must be a little twisted in me because I like it. Maybe you could clean this mess up. I've got to go get a couple things."

"You're taking them with you?"

He glanced back at the doorway. "Safer for both of us that way."

"Just so you know," she called after him, "I counted them, too."

She heard him laugh and felt another click inside her. Somehow fate had tossed her the man who was perfect for her. Honest, but flexible enough not to be shocked or appalled by certain urges that still snuck up on her. Reliable, with a flicker of the dangerous about him to spice it up.

She could make this work, she mused as she swept the broken shards into the center of the newspaper. They could make this work.

He came back in, saw she'd put the dog's head on a lace-edged napkin, like a centerpiece. After a double take, he snickered.

"You're a strange and unpredictable woman, Laine. That sure suits me."

"Funny, I was thinking the same about you, except for the woman part. What've you got there?"

"Files, tools." He set the file folder down, opened it to a detailed description of the missing diamonds. Sitting, he took out a jeweler's loupe and a gem scale.

"You know what you're doing with those?"

"Take a case, do your homework. So, yeah, I know what I'm doing with them. Let's take a look."

He spread the diamonds on the pouch, selected one. "It's eye-clean." He held it up. "No inclusions or blemishes visible to my naked eye. How about yours?"

"Looks perfect."

"This one's a full-cut, weighing . . ." He laid it on the scale, calculating. "Whew, a whopping sixteen hundred milligrams."

"Eight gorgeous carats." She sighed. "I know a little about diamonds myself, and about math."

"Okay, closer look." Using a small pair of tongs, he lifted the stone and studied it with the loupe. "No blemishes, no clouds or inclusions. Terrific brilliance and fire. Top of the sparkle chart."

He set it to the side, on a small scrap of velvet he'd brought down with him. "I can cross the eight-carat, full-cut, Russian white off my list."

"It would certainly make a wonderful engagement ring. A little over the top, and yet, who cares?" His expression, one of mild horror mixed with hopeful amusement, made her laugh. "Just kidding. Sort of. I'm going to pour us some wine."

"Great."

He chose another diamond, repeated the routine. "So, does this talk about engagement rings mean you're going to marry me?"

She set a glass of wine by his elbow. "That's my intention."

"And you strike me as a woman who follows through on her intentions."

"You're a perceptive man, Max." Sipping her own wine, she ran a hand over his hair. "Just FYI, I prefer the square-cut." Leaning down, she brushed her lips over his. "A nice clean, uncluttered look, platinum setting."

"So noted. Should be able to afford one considering the finder's fee on these little babies."

"*Half* the finder's fee," she reminded him.

He gave her hair a tug to bring her mouth back to his. "I love you, Laine. I love every damn thing about you."

"There are a lot of damn things about me, too." She sat beside him while he worked. "I should be scared to death. I should be racked with nerves over what's happening between you and me. I should be terrified knowing what it means to have those pretty shiny rocks on my kitchen table, aware that someone's already been inside my house looking for them. And could come back. I should be worried sick about my father—what he'll do, what Crew will do to him if he finds him."

She took a contemplative sip of wine. "And I am. Under here," she said, with a hand on her heart. "All those things are going on under here, but over it, and through it, I'm so happy. I'm happier than I've ever been in my life, or expected to be. The worry, the nerves, even the fear can't quite outweigh that."

"Baby, I'm a hell of a catch. Nothing for you to be nervous about on that score."

"Really? Why hasn't anybody caught you before?"

"None of them were you. Next, whoever—and we'll assume it was Crew—broke in, tore the place up looking for these didn't find them here. Not much sense in coming back to go over the same ground. Last, your father's managed to land on his feet all his life. I bet he's still got his balance and agility."

"I appreciate the logic and common sense."

She didn't look like she was buying any. He considered showing her the snub-nosed .38 strapped to his ankle, but wasn't sure if it would reassure her or scare her.

"You know what we've got here, Ms. Tavish?"

"What have we got here?"

"Just over seven million—or one quarter of twenty-eight point four million in diamonds—almost to the carat."

"Seven point one million." She said it in a reverent whisper. "On my kitchen table. I'm sitting here, looking at them, and still I can't really believe he pulled it off. He always said he would. 'Lainie, one day, one fine day, I'm going to make the big score.' I swear, Max, most times he said it he was just conning himself. And now look at this."

She picked up a stone, let it sparkle in her hand. "All his life, he wanted that one, big, glittery take. He and Willy must've had the best time." She let out a breath, set the stone back with the others. "Okay, reality check. The sooner those are out of my house and back where they belong, the better."

"I'm going to contact my client, make arrangements."

"You'll have to go back to New York?"

"No." He reached for her hand. "I'm not leaving. We finish this out. Three-quarters of the pie is still out there. Where would your father go, Laine?"

"I don't know. I swear to you I don't have a clue. I don't know his habits and haunts anymore. I cut myself off from him because I wanted so much to be respectable. And still . . . God I'm such a hypocrite."

She rubbed her hands over her face, dragged them back into her hair. "I took money from him. Through college, a little here, a little there. There'd be an envelope stuffed with cash in my mailbox, or now and then a cashier's check made out to me. And after I graduated, too. A little windfall out of the blue, which I dutifully banked or invested. So I could buy this house, start my business. I took it. I knew it wasn't from the goddamn tooth fairy. I knew he'd stolen it or bilked someone out of it, but I took it."

"You want me to blame you for that?"

"I wanted to be respectable," she repeated. "But I took the money to build that respectability. Max, I wouldn't use his name, but I used the money."

"And you rationalized it and justified it. I could do the same. But let's just cut through all that and agree that it's a very shaky area. Let's agree you don't take it anymore, and make it clear to him the next time you see him."

"If I had a dollar for every time I tried to make it clear to him. Oh, that's right. I do. But I'll make it stick this time. I promise. Do me one favor?"

"Just ask."

"Put those away somewhere and don't tell me where. I don't want him coming back and talking me into giving them to him. It's not out of the realm."

Max slid the stones back into the pouch, tucked it in his pocket. "I'll take care of it."

"I want to help you get the rest of them. I want that for a few reasons. One, I guess it'll go a ways toward easing my conscience. Two, and more important, it's just the right thing to do. More important than that, I hope that recovering them, getting them back where they belong will protect my father. I couldn't stand for him to be hurt. And somewhere between the conscience and the right thing lies the two-and-a-half-percent finder's fee."

He took her hand and kissed it. "You know, you may have bought that respectability, but you must've been born with that style. I've got a few things to see to. Maybe you can see about warming up that fudge."

"If I wait a bit, both of us get our evening chores done, we could have those sundaes in bed with extra whipped cream."

"I believe I might just be the luckiest man alive at this point in time." His cell phone beeped, making Laine chuckle when she heard the digitized opening riff of "Satisfaction."

"Hold that thought," he said, and answered. "Gannon." His face broke into a wide grin. "Hey, Mama."

Since he leaned against the stove instead of heading out of the room for privacy, Laine started to ease out. But he grabbed her hand, pulled her back.

"So, you liked the glasses. That makes me the good son, right? Your favorite." He scowled, tucking the phone between his ear and shoulder so he could keep a hand on Laine and reach for his wine. "I don't think it's fair to put your grandchildren in the mix. It's not like Luke went out specially and picked them out to suit you. Stay," he said in a hushed aside to Laine, then transferred the phone to his other hand when he released her.

"Yeah, I'm still in Maryland. On a job, Mama." He paused, listening, while Laine puttered around the kitchen looking for something to do. "No, I don't get tired of hotels and eating in restaurants. No, I'm not sitting here chained to my nasty computer and working too hard. What am I doing? Actually, I'm two-timing you with a sexy redhead I picked up the other day. There's talk of whipped cream later."

Laine's shocked gasp only had him crossing his feet at the ankles.

"I am not making it up. Why should I? She's right here. Want to talk to her?" He tipped the phone slightly away from his ear. "She says I'm embarrassing you. Am I?"

"Yes."

"Guess you're right about that, Mama. Her name's Laine, and she's the prettiest thing I've seen in my life. How do you feel about redheaded grandchildren?"

He winced, held the phone out a good six inches. Across the room, Laine could hear the exclamations but couldn't tell the tone of them.

"No problem. I've got another eardrum. Yeah, I'm crazy in love with her. I will. Of course I will. She won't. As soon as . . . We *will*. Mama, take a breath, will you? Yes, she makes me very happy. Really? I want you to hang up and call Luke right now. Tell him he's been shuffled into second place, and I'm your favorite son. Uh-huh, uh-huh. Okay. I love you, too. Bye."

He clicked off, stuck the phone back in his pocket. "I'm her favorite son. That'll burn Luke's ass. Anyway, I'm supposed to tell you that she can't wait to meet you, and we have to come down to Savannah ASAP so she can meet you, and can have a little engagement party for us. Which in Marlene-speak means a couple hundred of her closest friends and family. You're not allowed to change your mind about me. And she'd like it very much if you'd call her tomorrow when she's calmed down so you can have a nice chat."

"Oh my God."

"She's prepared to love you because I do. Plus she's thrilled that I'm going to settle down and get married. Then there's you having the good sense to see what a prize I am. You've got a big leg up with Marlene."

"I feel a little sick."

"Here." He pulled his phone out again. "Call your mama, then you can tell her and put me on the spot. We'll be even."

She stared at the phone, stared at him. "This is real."

"Damn right."

"You really want to marry me."

"We're past the want to. I'm going to marry you. You don't follow through on this, Marlene will hunt you down and make your life a living hell."

She laughed, took two running strides, then jumped into his arms. Hooked her legs around his waist and covered his mouth with hers. "I've always wanted to visit Savannah." She took the phone out of his hand, laid it on the counter behind him.

"What about your mother?"

"I'll call her later. There's a two-hour time difference, you know. So if I call her in two hours, it's really the same thing as calling her now. That way we can do something else for two hours."

Since she was chewing on the lobe of his ear, he had a pretty good idea what the something else would be. Hitching her to a steadier position, he started out of the room. "What about those evening chores?"

"Let's be irresponsible."

"I like your thinking."

She ran her tongue down his throat, up again. "Can you make it all the way upstairs?"

"Honey, the way I'm feeling, I could make it all the way to New Jersey."

She bounced lightly as he started up the stairs. "We forgot the whipped cream."

"Save it for later."

She reached down to tug his shirt out of his waistband. "Big talk." Her hands snuck under the shirt, ran up the hard plane of his chest. "Mmm, I love your body. I noticed it right away."

"May I say, ditto."

"But it wasn't the kicker."

"What was?" he asked and turned into the bedroom.

"Your eyes. They looked into mine, and my tongue went thick, my brain went stupid. I thought . . . oh, yum, yum, yum." She kept legs and arms hooked tight around him when he tumbled them into bed. "Then when you asked me to dinner, I thought—in the far reaches of my mind I didn't quite acknowledge—that I'd have this rash, wild, impulsive affair with you."

"I think you did." He got busy undoing her blouse.

"Now I'm going to marry you." Delighted, she pulled his shirt over his head and threw it aside. "Max, I should tell you, I'd've slept with you if Henry didn't like you, but I wouldn't be marrying you if he objected."

He lowered his mouth to her breast, bit gently. "Fair's fair."

She arched, absorbed, then riding on the thrill rolled over to reverse positions. "I'd just sneak around behind his back and have sex with you. I'd feel bad about it, but I'd do it anyway."

"You're such a slut."

She threw back her head and hooted with laughter. "Oh God! I feel wonderful."

His hands ran up her sides, then in and over curves. "You're telling me."

"Max." The sweetness seeped into her, had her brushing her hands through his hair, then cupping his face. "I love you, Max. I'll be such a good wife."

She was everything he wanted and hadn't known he was looking for. The whole of her, all those strange and lovely layers that formed her fit the whole of him as no one ever had, or ever would.

He drew her down to him, stroking her hair, her back, as love swarmed inside him. And when she sighed, the long, contented sound of it was like music.

Soft, so soft, her skin, her lips, so that the moment took on a dreamy hue that made it easy to be tender. He could cherish her here, and wondered if anyone ever had.

Instead of seeing her as competent or clever, as practical and smart, had anyone ever shown her she was precious?

He murmured to her, foolish things, romantic things as he eased her over to undress her. His hands skimmed over her as if she were more fragile than glass, more splendid than diamonds.

Her breath caught, another quiet little sigh as she let him take her over, as she sailed over smooth, gentle waves of pleasure. Under his hands she was pliant, willing to lay herself open for whatever he gave, or took.

Long, lush kisses that shimmered through the blood and sent pulses skipping. Slow, indolent caresses that sent warm thrills over the skin. She floated on the lazy river of sensation.

As that river rose, she felt the sleepy passion wake to roll through her in an endless swell. She arched to him, once again wrapping herself around him so they sat, locked together in the middle of the bed.

Mouths met more urgently, with breath quickening as the air went misty, as heart kicked against heart. Need welled inside her, throbbing like a wound, spreading like a fever.

She murmured his name, over and over, as she pushed him back, as she straddled him and cupped his hands to her breasts.

She took him inside her, captured him in all that velvet heat. Watching him through the shadows, her hair gleaming through them, her eyes impossibly blue.

Angling back, she offered him the lovely white line of her. He could feel the canter of her heart, the shivers along her skin, the taunt brace of it as she set to ride him.

Then she leaned forward, her hair raining down to curtain her face, and his. She anchored her hands on his shoulders, dug her fingers in. And drove him mad.

Her hips charged like lightning, shooting sparks of shock through his blood. The pleasure stormed through him now, whipped by her energy. She threw her head back, crying out when she clamped around him, convulsed around him.

Clinging to the edge, he reared up, banded her in his arms and, with his lips hot on her throat, let her drag him over with her.

He had to work. It wasn't the easiest transition with his body sated with sex and his mind veering constantly back to Laine. But the work was vital. Not just for his client, or for himself, but for Laine.

The sooner this portion of the diamonds was back where it belonged, the better for all concerned.

But that was hardly the end of it, or of her problems.

He didn't expect Crew would come back searching for them in the house, but neither did he expect the man to just cut his losses and walk away. He'd killed for those stones, and he wanted all of them.

He'd planned to have all of them from the beginning, Max concluded while he shuffled his notes into another pattern to wait for some new piece to fall into place.

No reason that made sense to have lured Myers out for a private meeting unless he'd planned to eliminate him and increase his take. He'd have picked his other partners off and slithered away with the full twenty-eight million.

Had they sensed it? Wouldn't someone who'd lived a life on the grift catch the smell of a scam? That was his bet, in any case. Either Jack or Willy had sensed a double cross, or been spooked by Myers's disappearance.

So they'd gone into the wind.

And had both ended up here, assuming Laine would be the perfect place to hide the stones until they could liquidate them and vanish for good.

He'd kick Jack O'Hara's sorry ass for that later.

They'd led Crew right to Laine's doorstep. The stones were secure, but not in the way they'd planned. And Willy was dead, Laine a target.

And once more, he thought in disgust, Big Jack was under the radar and on the move.

He wouldn't go far, Max mused. Not with Willy's quarter share at stake.

He'd be holed up somewhere, working on the angles. That was good. It would give Max the time and the opportunity to run him to ground and collect another quarter share.

He'd keep his word to Laine. He wasn't interested in turning Big Jack over to the cops. But he was interested, in fact he was deeply invested, in tearing a strip off the man for putting Laine in jeopardy.

Which brought him back to Crew.

He wouldn't go far either. Now that he knew the investigation was centered right here in Angel's Gap—and Max could only lay that on his own head—he'd be more careful. But he wouldn't want too much distance between himself and the prize.

He'd killed for another quarter of the take. He sure as hell wouldn't hesitate to kill for another half.

In Crew's place, Max would set his sights on O'Hara. There was only one thing standing between O'Hara and twenty-eight million. That was Laine.

He'd hand the diamonds in his possession over to his

client, dust his hands and say that's the best I can do and scoop Laine up, tuck her away in Savannah. Of course, he'd have to sedate her, hog-tie her and keep her in a locked room, but he'd do it if he believed it would take her out of the mix and keep her safe.

But since he didn't think either of them would be very happy with her drugged, tied up and locked away for the next several years, it didn't seem like the way to go.

Crew would just wait, bide his time and come after her when he chose.

Best if Crew made the move while he was on their ground, with them both on full alert.

Because she had to know. Two things Laine wasn't, were slow and stupid. So she knew a man didn't steal millions, kill for it, then count his losses cheerfully and walk away from half that pie.

It wasn't just a case with the fun and challenge of the investigation, and a fat fee at the end of it, any longer. It was their lives now. To secure their future, he'd do whatever it took.

He scanned his notes again, stopped and nearly kicked back in the delicate chair before he remembered it wasn't suited to the move. He hunched forward instead, tapping his fingers along his own printout.

Alex Crew married Judith P. Fines on May 20, 1994. Marriage license registered New York City. One child, male, Westley Fines Crew, born Mount Sinai Hospital, September 13, 1996.

Subject filed for divorce; divorce granted by New York courts, January 28, 1999.

Judith Fines Crew relocated, with son, to Connecticut in November 1998. Subsequently left that location. Current whereabouts unknown.

"Well, we can fix that," Max muttered.

He hadn't pursued that avenue very far. His initial canvass of Judith's neighbors, associates, family had netted
him little, and nothing to indicate she'd continued contact
with Crew.

He flipped through more notes, found his write-up on
Judith Crew née Fines. She was twenty-seven when they
married. Employed as manager of a Soho art gallery. No
criminal record. Upper-middle-class upbringing, solid edu-
cation and very attractive, Max noted as he looked over the
newspaper photo he'd copied during his run of her.

She had a sister, two years younger, and neither she nor
the parents had been very forthcoming, nor very interested
in passing on information. Judith had cut herself off from
her family, her friends. And vanished sometime in the
summer of 2000 with her young son.

Wouldn't Crew keep tabs on them? Max wondered.
Wouldn't a man who took such pride, had such an ego,
want to see some reflection of self, some hint of his own
immortality in a son? Maybe he wasn't particularly interested in maintaining a relationship with the ex, or with a
small boy who'd make demands. But he'd keep tabs, you
bet your ass. Because one day that boy would grow up, and
a man wanted to pass on his legacy to his blood.

"All right, Judy and little Wes." Max wiggled his fingers
like a pianist about to arpeggiate. "Let's see where you got
to." He played those fingers over the keyboard and started
the search.

Walking voluntarily into a police station went against
the grain. Jack didn't have anything against cops. They
were only doing what they were paid to do, but since they

were paid to round up people just like him and put them in small, barred rooms, they were a species he preferred to avoid.

Still, there were times even the criminal needed a cop.

Besides, if he couldn't outwit the locals and wheedle what he needed to know out of some hayseed badge in a little backwater town, he might as well give it up and get a straight job.

He'd waited until the evening shift. Logically, anyone left in charge after seven was bound to be closer to the bottom of the police feeding chain.

He'd shoplifted his wardrobe from the mall outside of town with an eye to the personality he wanted to convey. Jack was a firm believer in the clothes making the man whatever the man might elect to be.

The pin-striped suit was off the rack, and he'd had to run up the hem of the pants himself, but it wasn't a bad fit. The clown-red bow tie added just the right touch, hinting at harmless.

He'd lifted the rimless glasses from a Walmart, and wasn't quite ready to admit they actually sharpened his vision. In his opinion, he was entirely too young and virile to need glasses.

But the look of them finished off the intellectual-heading-toward-nerd image he wanted to project.

He had a brown leather briefcase, which he'd taken the time to bang up so it wouldn't look new, and he'd filled it as meticulously as a man might when traveling to an out-of-town meeting.

A smart player became the part.

He'd browsed through Office Depot, helping himself to the pens, notepads, sticky notes and other paraphernalia the administrative assistant of an important man might carry. As usual, such office toys both fascinated and bemused him.

He'd actually spent an entertaining hour playing with a personal data assistant. He did love technology.

As he walked down the sidewalk toward the station house, his gait became clipped, and his big shoulders hunched into a slump that looked habitual. He tapped the glasses back up his nose in an absent gesture he'd practiced in the mirror.

His hair was brutally slicked back, and—courtesy of the dye he'd purloined from a CVS drugstore that afternoon—was a glossy and obviously false shoe-polish black.

He thought Peter P. Pinkerton, his temporary alter ego, would be vain enough to dye his hair, and oblivious enough to believe it looked natural.

Though there was no one around to notice, he was already in character. He pulled out his pocketwatch, just the sort of affectation Peter would enjoy, and checked the time with a worried little frown.

Peter would always be worried about something.

He climbed the short flight of stairs and walked into the small-town cop shop. As he expected, it boasted a small-ish, open waiting area, with a uniformed deputy manning the counter toward the rear.

There were black plastic chairs, a couple of cheap tables and a few magazines—*Field and Stream*, *Sports Illustrated*, *People*—all months out of date.

The air smelled like coffee and Lysol.

Jack, now Peter, tapped his fingers nervously at his tie and nudged up his glasses as he approached the counter.

"Can I help you?"

Jack blinked myopically at the deputy, cleared his throat.

"I'm not entirely sure, Officer . . . ah, Russ. You see, I was supposed to meet an associate this afternoon. One P.M., at the Wayfarer Hotel dining room. A lunch meeting, you see. But my appointment never arrived and I've been unable to reach him. When I inquired at the hotel desk, I was informed he never checked in. I'm quite concerned, really. He was very specific about the time and place, and I've come here all the way from Boston for this appointment."

"You looking to file a missing persons report on a guy who's only been gone, what, eight hours?"

"Yes, but you see, I've been unable to reach him, and this was an important appointment. I'm concerned something may have happened to him on his trip from New York."

"Name?"

"Pinkerton. Peter P." Jack reached inside his suit jacket as if to produce a card.

"The name of the man you're looking for."

"Oh yes, of course. Peterson, Jasper R. Peterson. He's a rare-book dealer, and was to acquire a particular volume my employer is most interested in."

"Jasper Peterson?" For the first time, the deputy's eyes sharpened.

"Yes, that's right. He was traveling from New York, into Baltimore, I believe, and through D.C. before taking some appointments in this area. I realize I may seem to be overreacting, but in all my dealings with Mr. Peterson, he's always been prompt and reliable."

"Going to ask you to wait a minute, Mr. Pinkerton."

Russ pushed back from the counter and disappeared into the warren of rooms in the back.

So far, so good, Jack thought. Now he'd express shock and upset at the news that the man he sought had recently met with an accident. Willy would forgive him for it. In fact, he thought his longtime friend would appreciate the layers of the ruse.

He'd probe and pick at the deputy and work his way around to learning exactly what effects the police had impounded.

Once he knew for certain they had the pooch, he'd take the next step and nip it from the property room.

He'd have the diamonds, and he'd take them—and himself—as far away from Laine as possible. Leaving a trail for Crew that a blind man on a galloping horse could follow.

After that . . . well, a man couldn't always plan so far ahead.

He turned back toward the counter, a distracted look on his face. And felt a quick lurch in the belly when instead of the bored deputy, a big, blond cop stepped out of the side door.

He didn't look nearly slow enough to suit Jack.

"Mr. Pinkerton?" Vince gave Jack one long, quiet study. "I'm Chief Burger. Why don't you step back into my office?"

CHAPTER

13

A thin worm of sweat dribbled down Jack's spine as he stepped into the office of Angel Gap's chief of police. In matters of law and order, he much preferred working with underlings.

Still, he sat, fussily hitching his trousers, then setting his briefcase tidily beside his chair, just as Peter would have done. The smell of coffee was stronger here, and the novelty mug boasting a cartoon cow with bright red Mick Jagger lips told Jack the chief was having some java with his after-hours paperwork.

"You're from Boston, Mr. Pinkerton?"

"That's right." The Boston accent was one of Jack's favorites for its subtle snoot factor. He'd perfected it watching reruns of *M*A*S*H* and emulating the character of Charles Winchester. "I'm only here overnight. I'm scheduled to leave in the morning, but as I've yet to complete my purpose I may need to reschedule. I apologize for bothering you with my problems, Chief Burger, but I'm really quite concerned about Mr. Peterson."

"You know him well?"

"Yes. That is, fairly well. I've done business with him for the last three years—for my employer. Mr. Peterson is a rare-book dealer, and my employer, Cyrus Mantz, the Third—perhaps you've heard of him?"

"Can't say."

"Ah, well, Mr. Mantz is a businessman of some note in the Boston and Cambridge areas. And an avid collector of rare books. He has one of the most extensive libraries on the East Coast." Jack fiddled with his tie. "In any case, I've come down specifically, at Mr. Peterson's request, to see, and hopefully purchase, a first-edition copy of William Faulkner's *The Sound and the Fury*—with dust jacket. I was to meet Mr. Peterson for lunch—"

"Have you ever met him before?"

Jack blinked behind his stolen lenses, as if puzzled by both the question and the interruption. "Of course. On numerous occasions."

"Could you describe him?"

"Yes, certainly. He's rather a small man. Perhaps five feet six inches tall, ah . . . I'd estimate about one hundred and forty pounds. He's in the neighborhood of sixty years of age, with gray hair. I believe his eyes are brown." He scrunched up his own. "I believe. Is that helpful?"

"Would this be your Mr. Peterson?" Vince offered him a copy of the photo he'd pulled from the police files.

Jack pursed his lips. "Yes. He's considerably younger here, of course, but yes, this is Jasper Peterson. I'm afraid I don't understand."

"The man you identified as Jasper Peterson was involved in an accident a few days ago."

"Oh dear. Oh dear, I was afraid it was something of the kind." In a nervous gesture, Jack removed the glasses, polished the lenses briskly on a stiff white handkerchief. "He was injured then? He's in the hospital?"

Vince waited until he'd perched the glasses back on his nose. "He's dead."

"Dead? *Dead?*" It was a fist slammed into the belly, hearing it again, just that way. And the genuine jolt had his voice squeaking. "Oh, this is dreadful. I can't . . . I never imagined. How did it happen?"

"He was hit by a car. He died almost instantly."

"This is such a shock."

Willy. God, Willy. He knew he'd gone pale. He could feel the chill under his skin where the blood had drained. His hands trembled. He wanted to weep, even to wail, but he held back. Peter Pinkerton would never commit such a public display of emotion.

"I don't know precisely what to do next. All the time I was waiting for him to meet me, growing impatient, even annoyed, he was . . . Terrible. I'll have to call my employer, tell him . . . Oh dear, this is just dreadful."

"Did you know any of Mr. Peterson's other associates? Family?"

"No." He fiddled with his tie, fussily, though he wanted to yank at it as his throat swelled. *I'm all he had,* Jack thought. *I'm the only family he had. And I got him killed.* But Peter Pinkerton continued in his snooty Harvard drawl. "We rarely talked of anything other than books. Could you possibly tell me what arrangements have been made? I'm sure Mr. Mantz would want to send flowers, or make a donation to a charity in lieu."

"Nothing's set, as yet."

"Oh. Well." Jack got to his feet, then sat again. "Could you tell me, possibly, if Mr. Peterson was in possession of the book when he . . . I apologize for sounding ghoulish, but Mr. Mantz will ask. The Faulkner?"

Vince tipped back in his chair, swiveled gently side to side with his cop's eyes trained on Jack's face. "He had a couple paperback novels."

"Are you certain? I'm sorry for the trouble, but is there any way to check, a list of some sort? Mr. Mantz has his sights set on that edition. You see, it's a rare find with the dust jacket. A first edition in, we were assured, mint condition—and he'll, Mr. Mantz, he'll be very . . . oh dear, insistent about my following through."

Obligingly Vince opened a drawer, took out a file. "Nothing like that here. Clothes, toiletries, keys, a watch, cell phone and recharger, wallet and contents. That's it. Guy was traveling light."

"I see. Perhaps he put it in a safe-deposit box for safe-keeping until we met. Of course, he wouldn't have been able to retrieve it before . . . I've taken enough of your time."

"Where are you staying, Mr. Pinkerton?"

"Staying?"

"Tonight. Where are you staying, in case I have something further on those arrangements."

"Ah. I'm at the Wayfarer tonight. I suppose I'll fly out as scheduled tomorrow. Oh dear, oh dear, I don't know *what* I'm going to say to Mr. Mantz."

"And if I need to reach you, in Boston?"

Jack produced a card. "Either of those numbers will do. Please do contact me, Chief Burger, if you have any word." He offered his hand.

"I'll be in touch."

Vince walked him out, stood watching as he walked away.

It wouldn't take long to check the details of the story, and to run the names Pinkerton and Mantz. But since he'd looked through those cheap lenses into Laine's blue eyes, he figured he'd find they were bogus.

"Russ, call over to the Wayfarer, see if they've got this Pinkerton registered."

He'd confirm that little detail, haul one of his men out of bed to keep tabs on the man for the night.

He'd have another look at the effects, see what O'Hara—if that was O'Hara—had been interested in finding. Since he was damn sure he didn't have a few million in diamonds sitting back in the property room, he'd just have to see if he had something that pointed to them.

Where the hell was it? Jack walked briskly for two blocks before he began to breathe easily again. Cop houses, cop smells, cop eyes tended to constrict his lungs. There was no ceramic dog on the list of effects. Surely even a suspicious cop—and that was a redundant phrase—would have listed something like that. So there went his tidy little plan to break into the property room and take it. Couldn't steal what wasn't there to be stolen.

The dog had been in Willy's possession when they'd split up, in the hopes that Crew would track Jack himself to give Willy time to slip away, get to Laine and give her the figurine for safekeeping.

But the vicious, double-crossing Crew had tracked Willy instead. Nervous old Willy, who'd wanted nothing more than to retire to some pretty beach somewhere and live out the rest of his days painting bad watercolors and watching birds.

Should never have left him, should never have sent him out on his own. And now his oldest friend in the world was dead. There was no one he could talk with about the old days now, no one who understood what he was thinking before the words were out of his mouth. No one who got the jokes.

He'd lost his wife and his daughter. That was the way the ball bounced and the cookie crumbled. He couldn't blame Marilyn for pulling stakes and taking little Lainie with her. She'd asked him, God knew, a thousand times to give the straight life a decent try. And he'd promised her that many times in return he would. Broken every one of those thousand promises.

You just can't fight nature, was Jack's opinion. It was his nature to play the game. As long as there were marks, well, what the hell could he do? If God hadn't intended for him to play those marks, He wouldn't have made so damn many of them.

He knew it was weak, but that was the way God had made *him*, so how could he argue the point? People who argued with God were prime suckers. And Kate O'Hara's boy, Jack, was no sucker.

He'd loved three people in his life: Marilyn, his Lainie and Willy Young. He'd let two of them go because you can't keep what didn't want to be yours. But Willy had stuck.

As long as he'd had Willy, he'd had family.

There was no bringing him back. But one day, when all was well again, he'd stand on some pretty beach and lift a glass to the best friend a man ever had.

But meanwhile, there was work to be done, thoughts to be thought and a backstabbing killer to outwit.

Willy had gotten to Laine, and surely he'd had the dog in his possession when he had or why make contact? He could've hidden it, of course. A sensible man would've locked it away until he was sure of his ground.

But that wasn't Willy's style. If Jack knew Willy—and who better?—he'd make book he had that statue with the diamonds in its belly when he'd walked into Laine's little store.

And he hadn't had it when he walked out again.

That left two possibilities: Willy had stashed it in the shop without Laine knowing. Or Daddy's little girl was telling fibs.

Either way, he had to find out.

His first stop would be a quiet little search of his darling daughter's commercial enterprise.

Max found Laine in her home office working some sort of design onto graph paper. She had several tiny cutouts lined up on her desk. After a minute's study he recognized them as paper furniture.

"Is this like an adult version of a doll house?"

"In a way. It's my house, room by room." She tapped a stack of graph paper. "I'm going to have to replace some of my pieces, so I've made scale models of some of the things I have in stock that might work. Now I'm seeing if they do, and how I might arrange them if I bring them home."

He stared another moment. "I'm wondering how anyone that careful about picking out a sofa ended up engaged to me."

"Who says I didn't make a scale model of you, then try it out in different scenarios?"

"Huh."

"Besides, I don't love a sofa. I like and admire it, and am always willing to part with it for the right price. I'm keeping you."

"Took you a minute to think that one out, but I like it." He leaned on the corner of the desk. "Looks like I've located Crew's ex-wife and kid. Got a line on them in Ohio, a suburb of Columbus."

"You think she knows something?"

"I have to speculate Crew would have some interest in his son. Wouldn't a man like that see an offspring, particularly a male offspring, as a kind of possession? The wife's different, she's just a woman, and easily replaced."

"Really?"

"From Crew's point of view. From mine, when you're lucky enough to find the right woman, she's irreplaceable."

"Took you a minute, but I like it."

"The other thing is, in my line when you pick loose any thread, you keep tugging until it leads to something or falls out of the whole. I need to check this out. So, change of plans. I'll be heading to New York first thing in the morning, with the diamonds we have. I'll deliver them personally, then bounce over to Ohio and see if I can finesse anything from the former Mrs. Crew or Junior."

"How old is Junior?"

"About seven."

"Oh, Max, he's just a child."

"You know the whole thing about little pitchers, big ears? Jesus, Laine," he added when he saw her face. "I'm not going to tune him up. I'm just going to talk to them."

"If they're divorced, it could be she doesn't want any part of Crew, and doesn't want her son to know what his father is."

"Doesn't mean the kid doesn't know or that Daddy doesn't drop in now and then. It needs to be checked, Laine. I'll be leaving first thing. If you want to come with me, I'll make the arrangements for both of us."

She turned back to her graph paper, used the eraser end of a pencil to poke the cutout sofa to a different angle. "You'd move quicker without me."

"Probably, but not as cheerfully."

She glanced up. "A quick trip to New York, a flip over to Ohio. Seems like old times, and it's appealing. But I can't. There's work, there's Henry, there's putting this house back together. And I have to practice calling your mother." She turned the pencil around to poke him when he laughed. "No comments on the last one, friend, it's how I do things."

He didn't want to leave her, not even for a day. Part of that, he knew, was the obsessive insanity of new love, but part was worry. "If you came with me, you could call her from wherever, you could leave Henry with the Burgers, close the shop for the day and deal with the house when we get back. You can take your graph paper."

"You're worried about leaving me while you go do your job. You shouldn't. In fact, you can't. I've been taking care of myself for a very long time, Max. I'm going to keep on taking care of myself after we're married."

"You won't have a homicidal jewel thief looking in your direction after we're married."

"You can guarantee that? Go," she said without waiting for his answer. "Do what you do. I'll do what I do. And when you get back . . ." She ran her hand along his thigh. "We'll do something together."

"You're trying to distract me. No, wait, you did distract me." He leaned down, kissed her. "How about this? I go do what I do, you stay and do what you do. I'll be back tomorrow night, earlier if I can manage it. Until I'm back, you'll go over and hang with the cop and his wife. You and Henry. You're not staying here alone until this is wrapped. Now, we can fight about that or we can take the compromise."

She continued to walk her fingers along his thigh. "I like to fight."

"Okay." He pushed to his feet as if preparing for the round.

"But not when I agree with the other person's point of view. It's an unnecessary risk for me to stay out here alone. So I'll impose on Jenny and Vince."

"Good. Well . . . good. Want to fight about something else?"

"Maybe later?"

"Sure. I'm going to go nail down my flights. Oh, any chance that sofa can be long enough for a guy to take a Sunday afternoon nap on?"

"That's a distinct possibility."

"I'm going to like being married to you."

"Yes, you are."

It was after one by the time Jack finished searching Laine's shop. Torn in two directions, he locked up after himself. He was bitterly disappointed not to have found the diamonds. Life would be so much simpler if he had the little dog tucked under his arm. He could be on his way out of town, leaving enough bread crumbs for Crew to follow that would lead him and any trouble away from Laine.

Then he'd vanish down the rabbit hole. Fourteen million in diamonds—even figuring on half of that due to a quick turnover—would provide a very plush rabbit hole.

At the same time he was struck with a kind of stupefied pride. Just look what his little girl had done, and in the *straight* world. How the hell had she learned to buy all those things? The furniture, the fancy pieces, the little fussy table sitters. It was a pretty place. His little girl had herself a very pretty business. And since he'd been curious enough to take the time to hack into her computer and check, it appeared she had herself a reasonably profitable one.

She'd made a good life. Not what he'd wanted for her, certainly, but if it was what she wanted, he'd accept that. He didn't understand it, and never would, but he'd accept.

She was never going to come back with him on the road. That fantasy had finally been put to rest after a good look at her house, her shop, her life.

A waste of considerable talent, to his way of thinking, but he understood a father couldn't push an offspring into a mold. Hadn't he rebelled against his own? It was natural enough for Laine to rebel and to seek her own path.

But it wasn't natural for her to try to scam her own blood. She had the diamonds. Had to have them. If she had some sort of twisted idea that she needed to hold out on him to protect him, he'd have to set her straight.

Time for a father-daughter chat, Jack decided.

It meant he'd have to boost a car. He really hated to steal cars, it was so common, but a man needed transportation when his daughter decided to live in the boondocks.

He'd drive out to see her, have that chat, get the diamonds and be gone by morning.

He settled on a Chevy Cavalier—a nice, steady ride— and took the precaution of switching its plates with a Ford

Taurus a few miles away. All things being equal, the Chevy should get him through Virginia and into North Carolina, where he had an associate who could turn it for him. With the cash, he could spring for a new ride.

He'd leave enough footprints for Crew to follow, just enough of a scent to draw the man away from Maryland and Laine.

Then Jack had an appointment in southern California, where he'd turn those sparkly stones into hard green cash.

After that, the world was his fricking oyster.

He was humming along to the classic rock station he'd found, his mood lifted by The Beatles' cheerful claim of getting by with a little help from friends.

Jack knew all about getting by.

As a precaution, he stopped the car halfway up the lane. The dog was the friendly sort when it wasn't wetting itself in fear, he recalled, but dogs barked. No point in setting it off until he scoped things out.

With his penlight, he started the hike. The dark was pitch, making him wonder again what had possessed Laine to choose such a place. The only sound he heard other than his own feet crunching on gravel was an owl, and the occasional rustle in the brush.

Why anyone would want brush anything could rustle in was beyond him.

Then he caught the scent of lilacs and smiled. That was a nice sort of thing, he thought. To walk along in the quiet dark and smell flowers. Nice, he added, for the occasional change of pace. Maybe he'd pick a few of the blooms, take them with him to the door. A kind of peace offering.

He started to follow his nose when his light hit chrome.

And scanning the beam over the car, Jack felt his mood plummet.

The insurance cop's car was at the end of the drive with Laine's.

Eyes narrowed, he studied the house. No lights glowed in the windows. It was near two in the morning. A man's car was parked in front of his daughter's house.

His little girl was . . . he searched for a word his father's mind could handle without imploding. Dallying. His little girl was dallying with a cop. To Jack's mind a private investigator was just a cop with a higher annual income than the ones who carried badges.

His own flesh and blood, with a cop. Where had he gone wrong?

With a huge sigh, he stared down at his feet. He couldn't risk breaking in a second time with the PI in there. He needed privacy, damnit, to talk some sense into his Lainie.

Cop had to leave sometime, Jack reminded himself. He'd find a place to stash the car, and wait.

It was a testament to her love, Laine concluded, that nudged her into altering her morning routine in order to see Max off at five forty-five A.M. She liked to think it also demonstrated she was flexible, but she knew better.

Her routine would snap right back into place once she and Max became more accustomed to each other. It might take on a slightly different form, but in the end, it would be routine.

She was looking forward to it and, thinking just that, gave him a very enthusiastic kiss at the door.

"If that's the goodbye I get when I'm only going to be gone a day, what do I have to look forward to if I have to be out of town overnight?"

"I was just realizing how nice it's going to be to get used

to you, to take you for granted, to have your little habits and quirks irritate me."

"God, you're a strange woman." He took her face in his hands. "Am I supposed to look forward to irritating you?"

"And the bickering. Married people tend to bicker. I'm going to call you Maxfield when we bicker."

"Oh, hell."

"I think that'll be fun. I really can't wait until we fight about household expenditures or the color of the bathroom towels." And as that was perfect truth, she flung her arms around his neck and kissed him enthusiastically again. "Travel safe."

"I'll be home by eight, earlier if I can manage it. I'll call." He pressed his face into the curve of her shoulder. "I'll think of something to bicker about."

"That's so sweet."

He eased away, leaned down to pet Henry, who was trying to nose between them. "Take care of my girl." He hefted his briefcase, gave Laine a quick wink, then walked to his car.

She waved him off, then, as promised, shut the door and locked it.

She didn't mind the early start. She'd go into town, take a closer look at her stock to see what she might want to transfer to her home. She'd take Henry for a romp in the park, then make some calls to see about repairing some of her damaged furniture, and make arrangements to have what she considered a lost cause removed.

She could indulge herself by surfing some of the bridal sites on-line, drooling over gowns and flowers and favors. Laine Tavish was getting married! Delight had her doing a quick dance that inspired Henry to race in mad circles. She wanted to buy some bridal magazines, but needed to go to the mall for that, where she could buy them without causing gossip in town. Until she was ready for town gossip.

She wanted a big, splashy wedding, and it surprised her to realize it. She wanted a gorgeous and ridiculously expensive dress. A once-in-a-lifetime dress. She wanted to spend hours agonizing over flowers and music and menus.

Laughing at herself, she started upstairs to dress for the day. Snapping back into place, she thought. Her normal life had taken a hard, unexpected stretch, but it was snapping right back into the normal. Was there anything more normal than a woman dreaming about her wedding day?

"Need to make lists, Henry. Lots and lots of lists. You know how I love that."

She buttoned up a tailored white shirt, slipped on trim navy pants. "Of course, we have to set a date. I'm thinking October. All those beautiful fall colors. Rusts and umbers and burnt golds. *Rich* colors. It'll be a bitch to get things organized in time, but I can do it."

Imagining, she twisted her hair into a single French braid, tossed on a jacket with tiny blue-and-white checks.

A romp in the park first, she decided, and slipped into comfortable canvas flats.

She was halfway downstairs when Henry gave a series of alarmed barks and raced back up again.

Laine froze where she was, then rolled to her toes as her heart slammed against her ribs. Before she could follow Henry's lead, Jack strolled out of the living room to the bottom of the steps.

"That dog go to get his gun?"

"Dad." She shut her eyes, caught her breath. "Why do you *do* this? Can't you just knock on the damn door?"

"This saves time. You always talk to the dog?"

"Yes, I do."

"He ever talk back?"

"In his way. Henry! It's all right, Henry. He won't hurt you." She continued down, letting her gaze pass over the dyed hair, the rumpled suit. "Working, I see."

"In my way."

"Looks like you slept in that suit."

"I damn well did."

The bite in his tone had her lifting her brows. "Well, don't snap at me, Jack. It's not my fault."

"It *is* your fault. We need to have a talk. Elaine."

"We certainly do." Voice crisp, she nodded, then turned on her heel and marched into the kitchen. "There's coffee, and some apple muffins if you're hungry. I'm not cooking."

"What are you *doing* with your life?"

His explosion had Henry, who'd bellied in to test the waters, scramble back to the doorway.

"What am *I* doing with my life? What am I doing?" She rounded on him, coffeepot in hand. Her heated response tore through Henry's fear to find his courage. He barreled in, glued himself to Laine's side and tried out a snarl in Jack's direction.

"It's all right, Henry." Pleased, and considerably surprised by his defense, Laine reached down to soothe the dog. "He's not dangerous."

"I could be," Jack muttered, but some of his temper faded into relief that the dog had some spirit.

"I'll tell you what I'm doing with my life, Dad. I'm *living* my life. I have a house, a dog, a business, a car—and payments. I have a plumber." She gestured with the pot, and nearly sloshed coffee over the rim. "I have friends who haven't actually done time, and I can borrow a book from the library and know I'll actually still be here when it's due back. What are you doing with your life, Dad? What have you ever done with your life?"

His lips actually trembled before he firmed them and managed to speak. "That's a hell of a way for you to talk to me."

"Well, it's a hell of a way for you to talk to me. I never criticized your choices, because they were yours and you were entitled to make them. So don't you criticize mine."

His shoulders hunched; his hands retreated to his pockets. And Henry, vastly relieved that his valor wouldn't be tested, stood down. "You're spending nights with a cop. A *cop*."

"He's a private investigator, and that's beside the point."

"Beside the—"

"What I'm doing is spending nights with the man I love and am going to marry."

"Ma—" He made several incoherent sounds as the blood drained out of his face. He gripped the back of a chair, slowly sank into it. "Legs went out. Lainie, you can't get married. You're just a baby."

"I'm not." She set the pot aside, went to him and put her hands gently on his cheeks. "I'm not."

"You were five minutes ago."

Sighing, she slid onto his lap, rested her head on his shoulder. Henry tiptoed over to push his head through the tangle of legs and lay it sympathetically on Jack's knee.

"I love him, Daddy. Be happy for me."

He rocked with her. "He's not good enough for you. I hope he knows that."

"I'm sure he does. He knows who I am. Who we are," she said, and drew back to watch Jack's face. "And it doesn't matter because he loves me. He wants to marry me, make a life with me. We'll give you grandchildren."

The color that had come into his cheeks faded away again. "Oh now, let's not rush that far ahead. Let me settle into the idea that you're not six anymore. What's his name?"

"Max. Maxfield Gannon."

"Fancy."

"He's from Savannah, and he's wonderful."

"He make a good living?"

"Appears to—but then, so do I." She brushed at his dyed hair. "Are you going to ask all the clichéd father-of-the-bride questions now?"

"I'm trying to think of them."

"Don't worry about it. Just know he makes me happy." She kissed his cheek, then rose to deal with the coffee.

Absently, Jack scratched Henry behind the ears, and made a friend for life. "He left pretty early this morning."

She glanced over her shoulder. "I don't like you watching the house, Dad. But yes, he left early."

"How much time do we have before he gets back?"

"He won't be back until tonight."

"Okay. Laine, I need the diamonds."

She took out a mug, poured his coffee. She brought it to the table, set it in front of him, then sat. Folded her hands. "I'm sorry, you can't have them."

"Now you listen to me." He leaned forward, gripped the hands she'd folded on the table. "This isn't a game."

"Isn't it? Isn't it always?"

"Alex Crew, may he rot in everlasting, fiery hell, is looking for those stones. He's killed one man, and he's responsible for Willy's death. Has to be. He'll hurt you, Laine. He'll worse than hurt you to get them. Because it's not a game to him. To him it's cold, brutal business."

"Why did you get mixed up with him?"

"I got blinded by the sparkle." Setting his teeth, he eased back, picked up his coffee. Then just stared into the black. "I figured I could handle him. He thought he had me conned. Son of a bitch. Thought I bought the high-toned game he was playing with his fancy fake name and patter. I knew who he was, what he'd been into. But there was all that shine, Lainie."

"I know." And because she did know, because she could remember how it felt to be blinded by the shine, she rubbed her hand over his.

"Had to figure he might try a double cross along the way, but I thought I could handle him. He killed Myers, the inside man. Just a greedy schmuck who wanted to grab the prize. That changed the tune, Lainie. You know I don't work that way. I never hurt anybody, not in all the years in the game. Put a hole in their wallets, sure, a sting in their pride, but I never hurt anybody."

"And you don't understand people who do, not deep down, Dad."

"You think you do?"

"Better than you, yeah. For you it's the rush. It's not even the score itself, but the rush of the score. The shine," she said with some affection. "For someone like Crew, it's the score, it's about taking it all, and if he gets to hurt somebody along the way, all the better because it only ups the stakes. He's never going to stop until he gets it all."

"So give me the diamonds. I can lead him away from

here, and he'll know you don't have them. He'll leave you alone. You're not important to him, but there's nothing in this world more important to me than you."

It was truth. From a man skilled as a three-armed juggler with lies, it was perfect truth. He loved her, always had, always would. And she was in the exact same boat.

"I don't have them. And because I love you, I wouldn't give them to you if I did."

"Willy had to have them when he walked into your shop. There's no point in him coming in, talking to you, if he didn't plan to give them to you. He walked out empty-handed."

"He had them when he came in. I found them yesterday. Found the little dog. Do you want that muffin?"

"Elaine."

She rose to get it, set it on a plate. "Max has them. He's taking them back to New York right now."

He literally lost his breath. "You—you *gave* them to the cop?"

"PI, and yes, I did."

"Did he hold you at gunpoint? Did you have a seizure? Or did you *just lose your mind*?"

"The stones are going back where they belong. There'll be a press release announcing the partial recovery, which will get Crew off my back."

He lunged up, pulling at his hair as he circled the room. Thinking it was a game now that they were friends, Henry scooped up his rope and pranced behind Jack. "For all you know he's heading to Martinique. To Belize. To Rio or Timbukfuckingtu. Sweet Baby Jesus, how could my own daughter fall for a scam so old it has mold on it?"

"He's going exactly where he said he was going, to do

exactly what he said he was doing. And when he gets back, you and I are going to give him your share, so he can do exactly the same thing with them."

"In a pig's beady eye."

To settle the dog, Laine got up and poured kibble into a bowl. "Henry, time to eat. You're going to give them to me, Jack, because I'm not going to have my father hunted down and killed over a sack of shiny rocks." She slapped her hands on the table between them. "I'm not going to lie to my own children one day when they ask what happened to their granddaddy."

"Don't you pull that shit on me."

"You're going to give them to me because it's the only thing in my life I've ever asked of you."

"Damn it, Laine. Damn it to hell and back again."

"And you're going to give them to me because when Max turns them over and collects the fee, I'm going to give you my share. Well, half my share. That's one and a quarter percent of the twenty-eight, Dad. It's not the score of a lifetime, but it's not sneezable. And we'll all live happy ever after."

"I can't just—"

"Consider it a wedding present." She angled her head. "I want you to dance at my wedding, Dad. You can't do that if you go to prison, or if Crew's breathing down your neck."

On an explosive sigh, he sat again. "Lainie."

"They're bad luck for you, Dad. Those diamonds are cursed for you. They took Willy away from you, and you're on the run, not from the cops but from someone who wants you dead. Give them to me, get the monkey off your back. Max will find a way to square it with New York. The insurance company just wants them back. They don't care about you."

She came to him, touched his cheek. "But I do."

He stared up at her, into the only face he loved more than his own. "What the hell was I going to do with all that money anyway?"

CHAPTER

14

Laine drummed her fingers on the steering wheel as she
sat parked on her own lane, studying the dark green Chevy.

"You know, precious, your mother used to get that look
on her face when . . ." Jack trailed off when she turned her
head, slowly, and stared at him. "That one, too."

"You stole a car."

"I consider it more of a lend/lease situation."

"You boosted a car and drove it to my house?"

"What was I supposed to do? Hitchhike? Be reasonable,
Lainie."

"I'm sorry. I can see how unreasonable it is for me to
object to my father committing grand theft auto in my own
backyard. Shame on me."

"Don't get pissy about it," he muttered.

"Unreasonable *and* pissy. Well, slap me silly. You're
going to take that car right back where you found it."

"But—"

"No, no." She lowered her head into her hands, squeezed her temples. "It's too late for that. You'll get caught, go to jail, and I'll have to explain why my father thinks it's perfectly okay to steal a car. We'll leave it on the side of the road somewhere. Not here. Somewhere. God."

Concerned by the tone of her voice, Henry stuck his head over the front seat to lap at her ear.

"All right. It'll be all right. We'll leave the car outside of town." She sucked in a breath, straightened. "No harm, no foul."

"If I don't have the car, how the hell am I supposed to get to New Jersey? Let's just consider, Lainie. I have to get to Atlantic City, to the locker, get the diamonds and bring them back to you. That's what you want, isn't it?"

"Yes, that's what I want."

"I'm doing this for you, sweetheart, against my better judgment, because it's what you want. What my baby girl wants comes first with me. But I can't walk to Atlantic City and back, now can I?"

She knew that tone. Using it, Jack O'Hara could sell bottled swamp water out of a tent pitched beside a sparkling mountain stream. "There are planes, trains, there are goddamn buses."

"Don't swear at your father," he said mildly. "And you don't really expect me to ride a bus."

"Of course not. Of course not. There I go being pissy and unreasonable again. You can take my car. Borrow," she amended swiftly. "You can borrow my car for the day. I won't need it anyway. I'll be busy at work, beating my head against the wall to try to find my brain."

"If that's the way you want it, honey."

She cast her eyes to heaven. "I still can't believe you left

millions of dollars' worth of diamonds in a rental locker,
then sent Willy here with several million more."

"We had to move fast. Jesus, Laine, we'd just found out
Crew killed Myers. We'd be next. Tucked my share away,
took off. Bastard Crew was supposed to come after me. I
all but drew him a damn map. Stash was safe. Willy gets
another chunk of it here, then he'd double back for the rest
while Crew's a thousand miles away tracking me. That was
going to be our traveling money, our cushion."

To live on like kings, Jack thought, on that pretty beach.

"Never figured Crew would track you down. I'd never
have brought that on you, baby. Crew was supposed to be
off chasing me."

"And if he'd caught up with you?"

Jack only smiled. "I wasn't going to let him catch up. I
still got the moves, Lainie."

"Yeah, you still got the moves."

"Just buying Willy time. He'd get to Mexico, liquidate
the first quarter of the take. We'd meet up, take off, and
with that much backing, we'd hide out in comfort until the
heat was off."

"Then slip back and pick up the rest from me."

"Two, three years down the road maybe. We were working it out as we went."

"You and Willy both had keys to the locker in AC?"

"Nobody on the planet I trusted like Willy. Except you,
Lainie," he added, patting her knee. "Cops got it now." He
pursed his lips in thought. "Take them a while to trace it,
if they ever do."

"Max has it now. I took it off Willy's key ring. I gave it
to him."

"How'd you get . . . ?" The irritation in his tone faded to
affection. "You stole it."

"In a manner of speaking. But if you're going to equate that with boosting a car, don't even start. It's entirely different."

"Did it right under their noses, didn't you?"

Her lips twitched. "Maybe."

He gave her a little elbow nudge. "You still got the moves, too."

"Apparently. But I don't want them."

"Don't you want to know how we pulled it off?"

"I've figured out most of it. Your inside man takes the blinds—the dog, the doll, et cetera—into his office. Innocuous things, who pays attention? They sit around in plain sight. The shipment or shipments come in, he replaces them—or some of them—with fakes. Tucks a quarter share of the score in each of the four blinds. And there they sit."

"Myers sweated that part. He was greedy, but he didn't have good nerves."

"Hmm. Couldn't wait long, or he'd crack. Besides, you wouldn't trust him longer. A couple of days at most. He puts out the alarm on the fakes himself, helps cover his ass. Cops swoop in, investigation starts. Blinds go out under their nose."

"We each took one. Fact is, I posed as one of the insurance suits, walked into Myers's office while everybody's swarming around, walked out with my share in my briefcase. It was beautiful."

He shot her a grin. "Me and Willy had lunch a couple blocks away at T.G.I. Friday's after the scoop, with fourteen million warming our pockets. I had the nachos. Not bad."

She shifted in her seat so they were face-to-face. "I'm not going to say it wasn't a great score. I'm not going to pretend I don't understand the rush either. But I'm trusting you, Dad. I'm trusting you to keep your promise. I need this life. I need it even more than you need that rush. Please don't mess it up for me."

"I'm going to fix everything." He leaned over, kissed her cheek. "Just you wait and see."

She watched him saunter to the stolen car. One for every minute, she thought. "Don't make me one of them, Dad," she murmured.

She had Jack drop her off at the park with Henry, and counted on it still being early enough that no one who knew her would be around to comment on the strange man driving off in her car.

She gave Henry a half hour to romp, roll and chase the town squirrels.

Then she took out her cell phone and called Max.

"Gannon."

"Tavish."

"Hi, baby. What's up?"

"I . . . you're at the airport?"

"Yeah. Just set down in New York."

"I thought I should tell you, my father came by to see me this morning."

"That so?"

She heard the chill in his tone, and winced. No point in mentioning her father's morning mode of transportation. "We settled some things, Max, straightened some things out. He's on his way to get his share of the diamonds. He's going to give them to me so I can give them to you, and you . . . well, et cetera."

"Where are they, Laine?"

"Before I get to that, I want you to know he understands he screwed up."

"Oh, which screwup does he understand?"

"Max." She bent to take the branch Henry dumped at her feet. She had to wing it like a javelin, but it had the dog racing off in delight. "They panicked. When they heard about Myers's death, they just panicked. It was a bad plan, no question, but it was impulse. My father didn't realize Crew knew about me, much less that he'd come here. He just thought Willy could get me the figurine, and I'd tuck it away for a few years while they . . ." She let it go as she realized how the rest would sound.

"While they fenced the remaining share of the stolen gems and lived off the fat."

"More or less. But the point is he's agreed to give them up. He's getting them."

"Where?"

"A locker in Atlantic City. Mail Boxes, Etc. He's driving up now. It'll take him most of the day for the round-trip, but—"

"Driving what?"

She cleared her throat. "I lent him my car. I had to. I know you don't trust him, Max, but he's my father. I've got to trust him."

"Okay."

"That's it?"

"Your father's your father, Laine. You did what you needed to do. But no, I don't have to trust him, and I'm not going to reel in shock if we find out he's living in a pretty casa in Barcelona."

"He doesn't trust you either. He thinks you're on your way to Martinique."

"Saint Bart's, maybe. I like Saint Bart's better." There was a moment's pause. "You're really stuck right smack in the middle, aren't you?"

"Just my luck to love both of you." She heard the change in background noise and realized he'd walked outside the terminal. "Guess you're going to catch a cab."

"Yeah."

"I'd better let you go. I'll see you when you get back."

"Counting on that. I love you, Laine."

"It's nice to hear that. I love you, too. Bye."

On his end, Max slipped the phone back into his pocket and checked his watch as he strode over to the cab stand. Depending on traffic, he could have the New York leg of the day knocked in a couple hours. By his calculation he could make the detour to Atlantic City without too much trouble.

If Laine was going to be stuck in the middle, he was going to make damn sure she didn't get squeezed.

Laine walked from the park to Market Street with Henry doing his best to swivel his head a hundred and eighty degrees to chew off the hated leash.

"Rules are rules, Henry. Believe it or not, I all but had that tattooed on my butt up to a couple of weeks ago." When his response to that was to collapse on his belly and whimper, she crouched until they were nose to snout. "Listen up, pal. There's a leash law in this town. If you can't handle that, and comport yourself with some dignity, there'll be no more playing in the park."

"Having a little trouble there?"

She jolted, cringed at the waves of guilt that washed hot over her as she looked up into Vince's wide, friendly face. "He objects to the leash."

"He'll have to take that up with the town council. Come on, Henry, I got part of a cruller here with your name on it. I'll walk with you," he said to Laine. "Need to talk to you anyway."

"Sure."

"Getting an early start today."

"Yes. I've had a lot of things piling up. Thanks," she added when he took the leash and dragged Henry along.

"Been an interesting space of time recently."

"I'm looking forward to it sliding back to dull."

"Guess you probably are."

He waited while she got out her keys, unlocked the front door of the shop. While she deactivated the alarm, he squatted down to unclip the leash and give the grateful Henry a rub.

"Heard you were in the station a couple days ago."

"Yes." To keep busy, she walked over to unlock the cash register. "I told you that I knew Willy, and I thought . . . I wanted to see about making arrangements."

"Yeah, you did. You can do that. Make the arrangements. That's been cleared."

"Good. That's good."

"Funny thing. Somebody else came in, last night, interested in the same guy. Only thing, he said he knew him by the other name. Name that was on the card he gave you."

"Really? I'm going to put Henry in the back."

"I'll do it. Come on, Henry." Bribed with half a cruller, Henry scrambled into the back room. "This guy who came in, he said Willy—or Jasper—was a rare-book dealer."

"It's possible he was. Or that he was posing as one. I told you, Vince, I haven't seen Willy since I was a kid. That's the truth."

"I believe that. Just a funny thing." He walked over to

lean on the counter. "Like it's a funny thing there were five keys in his effects, and when I looked through them last night, there were only four." He waited a beat. "Not going to suggest they were miscounted?"

"No. I'm not going to lie to you."

"Appreciate that. The man who came in last night, he had your eyes."

"It's more accurate to say I have his. If you recognized him, why didn't you arrest him?"

"That's complicated, too. Best to say you don't arrest a man because you see something in his eyes. I'm going to ask you for that key, Laine."

"I don't have it."

"Damn it, Laine." He straightened.

"I gave it to Max," she said quickly. "I'm trying to do what's right, what should be done—and not be responsible for putting my father in prison. Or getting him killed."

"One of those things that should be done is keeping me informed. The diamond theft might be New York's business, Laine, but one of the men suspected of stealing them died in my town. One or more of his buddies is in my town, or has been. That puts my citizenship at risk."

"You're right. I'm having a hard time keeping my balance on this very thin line. And I know you're trying to help me. I found Willy's share of the diamonds. I didn't know they were here, Vince, I swear it."

"If you didn't know, how'd you find them?"

"They were in some stupid statue. Dog—pooch. I've been trying to piece it together and can only conclude that he stuck it on a shelf when he was here, or put it somewhere—in a cabinet or drawer—and either Jenny or Angie shelved it. Angie, most likely. Jenny would've asked me about it, and when I asked her, she didn't remember seeing it before. I gave them to Max, and he's in New York right now, turning them over. You can check. You can call Reliance and check."

He said nothing for a moment. "We haven't run that far out of bounds, have we, Laine, that I have to check?"

"I don't want to lose your friendship, or Jenny's." She had to take a steadying breath. "I don't want to lose my place in this town. I wouldn't be insulted if you checked, Vince."

"That's why I don't have to."

She needed a tissue after all, and yanked one out of the box behind the counter. "Okay. Okay. I know where another share is. I found out this morning. Please don't ask me how I found out."

"All right."

"The key I took from Willy's things is to a locker. I called Max as soon as I could to tell him. In fact, I was talking to him about it when I was in the park with Henry. They're going to be turned in, too. That's half of them. I can't do anything about the other half. Max has leads, and he'll do what he does. But once the half of the diamonds is back where it belongs, I've done all I can.

"Am I going to have to move away?"

"Break Jenny's heart if you did. I don't want your father in the Gap, Laine."

"I understand. This should all be taken care of by tonight, tomorrow at the latest. He'll be gone."

"Until it's taken care of, I want you to stay close."

"That I can promise."

By the time Jack crossed over into New Jersey, he'd come up with a dozen reasons why taking the diamonds back was a mistake. Obviously, this Gannon character was stringing his little girl along so he could cop his fat fee. Wasn't it better for her to find that out sooner rather than later?

And going back to Maryland might lead Crew back to Maryland, and Laine.

Then there was the fact that turning over all those pretty stones fit him as well as a prison jumpsuit.

Besides, Willy would've wanted him to keep them. A man couldn't deny a dead friend's wish, could he?

He was feeling considerably better as he maneuvered through Atlantic City traffic. Enough to whistle cheerily between sips of his on-the-road Big Gulp. He parked in the lot of the strip mall and considered the best way out was to hop a flight at the airport and head straight to Mexico.

He'd send Laine a postcard. She'd understand. The kid knew how the game was played.

He strolled the walkway first, scanning faces, looking for marks, looking for cops. Places like this always gave him itchy fingers. Malls, shopping centers, little packs of stores where people breezed in and out with their cash and credit cards so handy.

Day after day. The straights buying their puppy chow and greeting cards, sold to them by other straights.

What was the point?

Places like this made him want to fall on his knees and give thanks for the life he led—right before he helped himself to some of that cash, some of those credit cards and made tracks to anywhere else.

He wandered into a Subway, bought a ham and cheese with hot pepper sauce to give himself more time to scope out the area. He washed it down with another big shot of cold caffeine, used the facilities.

Satisfied, he crossed to the Mail Boxes, Etc., strolled to the lockers, slid in his key.

Come to Papa, he thought, and opened the door.

He made a sound, something similar to a duck being punched in the belly, and snagged the only contents of the locker. A piece of notepaper with a one-line message.

Hi, Jack. Look behind you.

He spun around, one meaty fist already balled.

"Take a swing, I'll deck you," Max told him conversationally. "Think about running, consider that I'm younger and faster. You'll just embarrass yourself."

"You son of a bitch." He had to wheeze it, but even that had a couple of heads turning in their direction. "Double-crossing son of a bitch."

"Pots calling kettles only proves pots lack imagination. Keys." He held out a hand. "Laine's car keys."

In disgust, Jack slapped them into Max's hand. "You got what you came for."

"So far. Why don't we talk in the car? Don't make me haul you out," he said quietly. "We'd not only cause a scene that might bring the cops in on this, but Laine wouldn't like it."

"You don't give two damns about her."

"You're right, I don't. I give a hell of a lot more than that, which is why I'm not turning your sorry ass over to the cops. You've got one chance, O'Hara, and you've got it because of her. In the car."

Running occurred to him. But he knew his limitations. And if he ran, there was no chance to recoup the diamonds. He walked back out with Max, then settled himself in the passenger seat. Max took the driver's seat, set his briefcase on his lap.

"Here's the way it's going to be. You're sticking to me like gum on the bottom of my shoe. We're catching a flight to Columbus."

"What the—?"

"Shut up, Jack. I've got a lead to check, and until I'm done, you and me, we're Siamese twins."

"She told you. My own flesh and blood. She told you where I had the stash."

"Yeah, she did. She told me because she loves me, and she believes—convinced herself to believe—you'd keep your end and bring them in. Because she loves you. Me, I don't love you, Jack, and I figure you had other plans for this."

Opening his briefcase, Max took out a ceramic piggy bank. "I've got to give you points for the sense of the ridiculous. Me, you and the pig, we're going to Columbus, then heading back to Maryland. And I'm going to give you that chance. That one chance to deserve Laine. You're going to give her this." He tapped the pig, then put it away. "Just as if you'd planned to all along."

"Who says I didn't?"

"I do. You had fucking dollar signs in your eyes when you opened that locker. Let's show a little respect for each other here. My client wants the stones returned. I want my fee. Laine wants you safe. We're going to make all that happen." He started the car. "You finish this out, I'll see that your slate's wiped clean on this. You ditch me, you hurt Laine, and I'll hunt you down like I would a rabid dog. You'll be my goddamn life's work. That's a promise, Jack."

"You're not bullshitting. I know when a man's bullshitting. Son of a gun." Jack's grin spread wide and bright as he leaned over to embrace Max. "Welcome to the family."

"Briefcase is locked, Jack." Max pulled back, then set the briefcase out of reach in the back.

"Can't blame a guy for trying," Jack said cheerfully, and settled back for the ride.

In his cabin, Crew selected a shirt the color of eggplant. He'd ditched the mustache, replacing it with a soul patch he thought suited the sleek, chestnut-hued ponytail. He wanted an arty look for this trip. He selected a pair of round-lensed sunglasses from his supply and studied the effect.

It was probably unnecessary to go to such trouble, but he did enjoy a good costume.

Everything was ready for company. He smiled as he looked around the cabin. Rustic, certainly, but he doubted Ms. Tavish would complain about the accommodations. He didn't plan on her staying for long.

He hooked the little .22 on the back of his belt, covered it with a hip-length black jacket. Anything else he might need was in the bag he slung on his shoulder before he strode out of the cabin.

He thought he might have a bite to eat before he had his date with the attractive Ms. Tavish. He might be too busy to dine that evening.

"I did the legwork," Jack said as he and Max had a beer in the airport bar. "Courted Myers for months. Now, I'll admit, I never dreamed of a score that big. Was thinking small, taking a couple of briefkes, clearing a couple hundred thousand each. Then Crew came into it."

Jack shook his head, sipped through the foam. "For all his faults, that's a man who thinks big."

"Faults being he's a cold-blooded killer."

Frowning, Jack dug his big hand into a bowl of nuts. "Biggest mistake of my life, and I'm not ashamed to admit I've made a few, was hooking up with a man like Crew. He suckered me in, no question. I got dazzled by the idea of all those rocks. All those pretty, shiny rocks. He had the know-it-all for something like that, the vision. I had the connections. Poor Myers. I'm the one who brought him in, played him. He had a gambling problem, you know."

"Yeah."

"Far as I can see, any gambling's a problem. House is always going to win, so it's better to be the house. Gamblers are either rich people who don't give a shit if they lose, or suckers who actually think they can win. Myers was a sucker, word go. Had himself in deep, and with some nudging from me he was in deeper. He saw this as his way out."

Jack drank more beer. "Guess it was. Anyway, the deal went down smooth enough. Quick, clean. Had to figure they'd cop to Myers, but he was supposed to go straight under. Nobody was to know where anybody else was heading. Willy and me drove right out of the city, I dumped the pig in AC, and we dumped Willy's in a locker in Delaware. Got ourselves a nice hotel room in Virginia, had a fine meal, a couple bottles of champagne. Good time," he said, and toasted with his glass.

"Heard about Myers on CNN. Willy loved CNN. Tried to tell ourselves it was because of the gambling, but we knew. Switched cars, drove to North Carolina. Willy was spooked. Hell, we were both spooked, but he was nervous as a whore in church. Wanted to light out, just forget it all and head for the hills. I talked him down from that. God-damn it."

He studied his beer, then lifted it and drank deep. "I'd lead Crew off, and he'd double back, get his share, take it to Laine. She could put him up for a little while. I thought he'd be safe. Thought they both would."

"But he knew about her. Crew."

"I got pictures of her in my wallet."

He drew it out and flipped it open.

Max saw photos of a newborn with a bright thatch of red hair and skin as white as cream, and an expression on her little face that seemed to say, "What the *hell* am I doing here?"

There were several of Laine as a child, all bright hair and eyes, who from the grin had obviously figured out what she was doing here. Then of the nubile teenager, pretty and dignified in her graduation shot. Of Laine wearing cutoffs and a skinny top, laughing as she stood in the blue surf of what Max deduced was Barbados.

"Always been a looker, hasn't she?"

"Prettiest baby you ever saw, and she just got prettier every day. I get sentimental, especially after a beer or two." Jack shrugged. It was just another God-given weakness, after all. Closing the wallet, he tucked it away again.

"I must've shown her off to Crew sometime. Or he just dug down and looked for something he could use against me, should the need arise. There's no honor among thieves, Max, and anybody who thinks different is a sucker. But to kill over money? That's a sickness. I knew he had it in him, but I thought I could beat him at the game."

"I'll find him. And I'll put him down, one way or the other. That's our flight."

* * *

Laine fought not to pace, to just look busy. She checked the time again. Her father should be on his way back by now. She should've told him to call when he was on his way back. She should've insisted.

She could call Max again, but what was the point? He'd be on his way to Columbus. Maybe he was already there.

She just had to get through the day, that was all. Just this one day. Tomorrow, the news would hit that a large portion of the stolen diamonds had been recovered. She'd be in the clear, her father would be in the clear, and life would get back some semblance of normality.

Maybe Max would pick up Crew's trail from this Ohio connection. They'd track him down, put him away. She'd never have to worry about him again.

"You keep going away." Jenny gave her a little nudge as she carried a George Jones cheese dish to the counter for a customer.

"Sorry. I'm sorry. Wandering mind. I'll take the next one who comes in."

"You could take Henry for another walk."

"No, he's had enough walks today. He gets sprung from the back room in another hour anyway."

She heard the bells ring. "I'll take this one."

"All yours." Jenny lifted her brows as she glanced at the new customer. "Little old for that look," she said under her breath, and moved on.

Laine fixed on her welcome face and crossed over to greet Crew. "Good afternoon. Can I help you?"

"I'm sure you can." From his previous visits to her store, he knew the arrangements and exactly where he wanted her. "I'm interested in kitchen equipment. Butter crocks, specifically. My sister collects."

"Then she's in luck. We have some very nice ones just now. Why don't I show you?"

"Please."

He followed her through the main room, into the area she'd set up for kitchen equipment, furnishings and novelties. As they passed the door to the back room, Henry began to growl.

"You have a dog in here?"

"Yes." Puzzled, Laine looked toward the door. She'd never known Henry to growl at store sounds and voices. "He's harmless and he's secured in the back room. I needed to bring him in with me today." Because she sensed her customer's annoyance, she took his arm and led him to the crocks.

"The Caledonian's especially nice, I think, for a collector."

"Mmm." There were two customers and the pregnant clerk. As the customers were at the counter, he assumed they were paying for purchases. "I don't know anything about it, really. What in the world is this?"

"It's a Victorian coal box, brass. If she enjoys antique and unique kitchen items, this is a winner."

"Could be." He slipped the .22 out of his belt and jammed the barrel into her side. "Be very, very quiet. If you scream, if you make any move at all, I'll kill everyone in this shop, beginning with you. Understand?"

The heat of panic washed over her, then chilled to ice as she heard Jenny laugh. "Yes."

"Do you know who I am, Ms. Tavish?"

"Yes."

"Good, that spares us introductions. You're going to

make an excuse to walk out with me." He'd planned to take her out the back, but the damned dog made that impossible. "To give me directions, we'll say, to walk me to the corner. If you alert or alarm anyone, I'll kill you."

"If you kill me, you won't get the diamonds back."

"How fond are you of your very pregnant employee?"

Nausea rolled up her throat. "Very fond. I'll go with you. I won't give you any trouble."

"Sensible." He slipped the gun in his pocket, kept his hand on it. "I need to get to the post office," he said, lifting his voice to a normal tone. "Can you tell me where it is?"

"Of course. Actually, I need some stamps. Why don't I take you over?"

"I'd appreciate that."

She turned, ordered her legs to move. She couldn't feel them, but she saw Jenny, saw her glance up, smile.

"I'm just going to run to the post office. Just be a minute."

"Okay. Hey, why don't you take Henry?" Jenny motioned toward the back where the growls grew louder and were punctuated by desperate barks.

"No." She reached out blindly for the doorknob, snatched her hand back when it bumped Crew's. "He'll just fight the leash."

"Yeah, but . . ." She frowned as Laine walked out without another word. "Funny, she . . . oh, she forgot her purse. Excuse me just a minute."

Jenny grabbed it from under the counter and was halfway to the door when she stopped, glanced back at her customers. "Did she say she was going to buy stamps? The post office closed at four."

"So, she forgot. Miss?" The woman gestured toward her purchases.

"She never forgets." Gripping the purse, Jenny bolted for the door, pressing a hand to her belly as she dashed onto the sidewalk. She saw Laine's arm gripped in the man's hand as they turned the corner away from the post office.

"Oh God, oh my God." She rushed back in, all but knocking her customers aside as she snatched up the phone and speed-dialed Vince's direct line.

CHAPTER

15

It was a quiet suburban neighborhood, a middle-class bull's-eye with well-kept lawns and big leafy trees so old their roots had heaved up through portions of the sidewalks. Most driveways boasted SUVs, the suburbanites' transportation of choice. Many had car seats, and there were enough bikes and clunky secondhanders to tell Max the age of kids in the neighborhood ranged from babies to teens.

The house was an attractive two-story English Tudor with a pretty blanket of lawn decorated with sedate flower beds and neatly trimmed shrubs. And a SOLD sign.

Max didn't need the Realtor's sign to tell him the place was empty. There were no curtains at the windows, no cars in the drive, no debris a young boy might leave in his wake.

"Skipped," Jack said.

"Gee, Jack, thanks for the bulletin."

"Guess it's irksome to come all this way and hit a dead end."

"There are no dead ends, just detours."

"Nice philosophy, son."

Max stuck his hands in his pockets, rocked on his heels. "Irksome?" he repeated, and Jack just grinned. "Neighborhood like this has to have at least one nosy neighbor. Let's knock on doors, Jack."

"What's the line?"

"I don't need a line. I've got an investigator's license."

Jack nodded as they started toward the house on the left. "People in this kind of place like talking to PIs. Adds excitement to the day. But I don't think you're going to tell Nosy Alice you're looking for a lead on twenty-eight mill in stolen diamonds."

"I'm trying to locate Laura Gregory—that's the name she's using here—and verify if she is the Laura Gregory who's a beneficiary in a will. Details are confidential."

"Good one. Simple and clean. People like wills, too. Free money." Jack fussed with the knot of his tie. "How do I look?"

"You're a fine-looking man, Jack, but I still don't want to date you."

"Ha!" He gave Max a slap on the back. "I like you, Max, damned if I don't."

"Thanks. Now just keep quiet and let me handle this."

They were still several paces from the door of a modified split-level when it opened. The woman who stepped out was in her middle thirties and wearing a faded sweatshirt over faded jeans. The anthemlike theme music from *Star Wars* poured out the door behind her.

"Can I help you with something?"

"Yes, ma'am." Max reached for his ID. "I'm Max Gannon, a private investigator. I'm looking for Laura Gregory."

She looked hard at the identification, with a glimmer of excitement in her eyes. "Oh?"

"It's nothing untoward, Mrs. . . ."

"Gates. Hayley Gates."

"Mrs. Gates. I've been hired to locate Ms. Gregory and verify that she's the Laura Gregory named as a beneficiary in a will."

"Oh," she repeated as the glimmer spread to a sparkle.

"My associate and I . . . I'm Bill Sullivan, by the way." To Max's annoyance, Jack stepped forward, took Mrs. Gates's hand and pumped it heartily. "We were hoping to speak to Mrs. Gregory personally to verify that she is indeed the grandniece of the late Spiro Hanroe. There was a bit of a family schism in the previous generation, and several of the family members, including Mrs. Gregory's parents, broke contact." He lifted his hands in a shrug. "Families. What can you do?"

"I know just what you mean. Excuse me just a minute." She stuck her head back in the door. "Matthew? I'm right outside. My oldest is home sick," she explained as she eased the door closed but for a crack. "I'd ask you in, but it's a madhouse in there. You can see Laura sold the house." She gestured toward the house next door. "Put it on the market about a month ago—rock-bottom price, too. My sister's the realtor who listed it. Laura wanted to sell it fast, and the fact is, she moved even before it sold. She was planting her summer annuals one day and packing dishes the next."

"That's odd, isn't it?" Max commented. "She mention why?"

"Well, she *said* her mother in Florida was ill, seriously

ill, and she was moving down there to take care of her. She lived next door for three years, and I don't remember her ever mentioning her mother. Her son and my oldest played together. He's a sweet boy, her Nate. Quiet. They were both quiet. It was nice for my Matt to have a friend next door, and Laura was easy to get along with. I always thought she came from money though."

"Did you?"

"Just a feeling. And she worked part-time at an upscale gift shop at the mall. She couldn't have afforded the house, the car, the lifestyle, if you know what I mean, on her salary. She told me she came into an inheritance. It's funny she came into two, isn't it?"

"Did she tell you where in Florida?"

"No. Just Florida, and she was in a tearing hurry to get going. Sold or gave away a lot of her things, and Nate's, too. Packed up her car and zipped. She left . . . I guess it's three weeks ago. Little better than that. She said she'd call when she was settled, but she hasn't. It was almost like she was running away."

"From?"

"I always—" She cut herself off, eyed them both a bit more cautiously. "Are you sure she's not in trouble?"

"Not with us." Max sent out a brilliant smile before Jack could speak. "We're just paid by the Hanroe estate to find the beneficiaries and confirm identification. Do you think she's in trouble?"

"I can't imagine how, really. But I always figured a man—ex-husband—somewhere in the background, you know? She never dated. Not once since she's been here. And Laura never talked about Nate's father. Neither did Nate. *But*, the night before she listed the house, I saw a guy come by. Drove up in a Lexus, and he was carrying a box. All wrapped up with a bow, like a birthday present, but it wasn't Nate's birthday, or Laura's either, for that matter. He only stayed about twenty minutes. Next morning, she called my sister and put the house on the market, quit her job, and now that I think about it, she kept Nate home from school for the next week."

"Did she tell you who her visitor was?" Jack made the question conversational, as if they were all out here enjoying the spring weather and shooting the breeze. "You must've asked. Anybody'd be curious."

"Not really. I mean, yes, I mentioned I'd seen the car. She just said it was someone she used to know and clammed up. But *I* think it was the ex, and she totally freaked. You don't just sell your house and your furniture and drive off that way because your mother's sick. Hey, maybe he heard about this inheritance and was trying to wheedle his way back so he could cash in. People can be so low, you know?"

"They certainly can. Thanks, Mrs. Gates." Max offered a hand. "You've been very helpful."

"If you find her, tell her I'd really like her to call. Matt misses Nate something fierce."

"We'll do that."

"He got to her," Jack said as they started back to the rental car.

"Oh yeah, and I don't think there was a birthday present in the pretty box. She's running." He glanced back at the empty house. "Running from him, running with the diamonds, or both?"

"Woman runs like that's scared," was Jack's opinion. "Odds are even if he dumped the diamonds on her for safekeeping, she doesn't even know she's got them. Crew's not a man to trust anybody, especially an ex-wife. That's my take on it. So . . . are we going to Florida to work on our tans?"

"She's not in Florida, and we're going back to Maryland. I'll pick up her trail, but I've got a date with a beautiful redhead."

"You'll drive." Crew shifted the gun from Laine's kidney to the base of her spine. "I'm afraid you'll have to climb over. Do it quickly, Ms. Tavish."

She could scream, she could run. She could die. Would die, she corrected as she lowered herself into the passenger seat, maneuvered over the center console. Since she wasn't willing to die, she'd have to wait for a reasonable chance of escape.

"Seat belt," Crew reminded her.

As she drew it around to secure, she felt the lump of her cell phone in her left pocket. "I'll need the keys."

"Of course. Now, I'm going to warn you once, only once. You'll drive normally and carefully, you'll obey the traffic laws. If you make any attempt to draw attention, I'll shoot you." He handed her the keys. "Trust me on that."

"I do."

"Then let's get started. Head out of town and take Sixty-eight East." He shifted his body so she could see the gun. "I don't like to be driven, but we'll make an exception. You should be grateful to your dog. If he hadn't been in the back, we'd have gone out that way and you'd be taking this ride in the trunk."

God bless you, Henry. "I prefer this position." As she drove she considered, and rejected, the idea of flooring the gas or trying to whip the wheel. Maybe, just maybe, that kind of heroic action worked in the movies, but movie bullets were blanks.

What she needed to do was somehow leave a trail. And stay alive long enough for someone to follow it. "Were you what scared Willy into running into the street?"

"One of those twists of fate or timing or just bad luck. Where are the diamonds?"

"This conversation, and my existence, would both be over very quickly if I told you."

"At least you're bright enough not to pretend you don't know what I'm talking about."

"What would be the point?" She flicked a glance at the rearview mirror, let her eyes widen, then slid her eyes toward it again. It was enough to have him turning his head, looking behind. And when he did, she dipped her hand in her pocket, played her fingers over the buttons, praying she was counting correctly, and hit what she hoped was Redial.

"Eyes on the road," he snapped.

She gripped the wheel with both hands, squeezed once and thought, *Answer the phone, Max, answer the phone and listen.* "Where are we going, Mr. Crew?"

"Just drive."

"Sixty-eight East is a long road. Are you adding interstate abduction to your list?"

"It would hardly make the top of it."

"I guess you're right. I'd drive better if you weren't pointing that gun at me."

"The better you drive, the less chance there is it will go off and put an ugly hole in your very pretty skin. True redheads—as I assume you are, given your father—have such delicate skin."

She didn't want him thinking about her skin or putting holes in it. "Jenny's going to send out an alarm when I don't come back."

"It'll be too late to make any difference. Stay at the speed limit."

She sped up until she hit sixty-five. "Nice pickup. I've never driven a Mercedes. It's heavy." She ran a hand over her throat as if nervous and babbling. "Smooth though. Looks like a diplomat's car or something. You know, black Mercedes sedan."

"You won't distract me with small talk."

"I'm trying to distract myself, if you don't mind. It's the first time I've been kidnapped at gunpoint. You broke into my house."

"And if I'd found my property, we wouldn't be taking this little trip together."

"You made a hell of a mess."

"I didn't have the luxury of time."

"I don't suppose it would do any good to point out that you already have half the take when the deal was a quarter? And to say that once you get past, oh, say, ten million, the rest is superfluous."

"No, it wouldn't. You'll take the next exit."

"Three twenty-six?"

"South, to One forty-four East."

"All right. All right. Three twenty-six South to One forty-four East." She glanced over. "You don't look like the sort of man to spend much time in state forests. We're not going camping, are we?"

"You and your father have inconvenienced me considerably, and added to my expenses. He'll pay for that."

She followed his directions, carefully repeating them. She had to believe the call to Max had gone through. That her phone's batteries were still up, that she hadn't dropped out of range.

"Alleghany Recreation Park," she said as she turned off the macadam and onto gravel at Crew's instructions. "Really doesn't fit the Mercedes."

"Take the left fork."

"Cabins. Rustic, private."

"Bear right."

"A lot of trees. Deerwalk Lane. Cute. I'm being abducted to a cabin on Deerwalk Lane. It just doesn't sound menacing enough."

"The last, on the left."

"Good choice. Completely sheltered by the trees, barely within sight of the next cabin."

She had to turn off the phone. He'd find it, she thought. He was bound to find it, and if it was on when he did, she'd lose even that slim advantage.

"Turn off the car." He slapped it into Park himself. "Give me the keys."

She obeyed, turning her head, meeting his eyes, holding them. "I don't intend to do anything that gets me shot. I'm not going to be brave or stupid." As she spoke, she slipped her hand into her pocket, ran her thumb over the buttons and pushed End.

"You can start by climbing out this way." He opened the door at his back, slid out. The gun remained pointed at her heart as she hefted her hips over the console.

"Now, let's go inside." He nudged her forward. "And chat."

He'd made good time, Max thought as he strode across the terminal toward the exit. He'd be able to pick up Laine from Jenny's after he tucked Jack away. He didn't think it the best idea to take his future father-in-law to a cop's house.

The problem was trusting him.

He glanced back, noted Jack was still wearing a sickly tinge of green. They'd caught a prop plane out of Columbus to the local municipal, and Jack had been varying shades of green since takeoff.

"Hate those tin cans—tin cans with wings, that's all they are." His skin was still gleaming with sweat as he leaned against the hood of Max's car. "Need to get my legs under me."

"Get them under you in the car." Because he felt some sympathy, he opened the door, helped Jack settle his bulk inside. "You puke in my ride, I'm going to kick your ass. Just FYI."

He rounded the hood, got behind the wheel. He figured Big Jack could fake all manner of illnesses, but it took more talent than he could possess to change color. "Here's what else is going to happen. I'm taking you to Laine's, and you're staying there until I get back with her. You take off, I'll find you, haul you back and beat you senseless with a stick. Clear on that?"

"I want a bed. All I want's a bed."

Amused, Max backed out of his parking slot. Remembering his phone, he dug it out of his pocket. He'd had to turn it off during the flight. Switching it back on, he ignored the beep that told him he had voice mail and called Laine, cell to cell. He heard her recorded voice tell him to leave a message.

"Hey, baby, I'm back, heading out of the airport. Gotta make one stop, then I'll be by to pick you up. Fill you in when I see you. Oh, got a few things for you. Later."

Jack spoke with his head back, his eyes closed. "It's dangerous to drive talking on one of those things."

"Shut up, Jack." But because he agreed, Max started to put it aside, when it beeped for an incoming. Certain it was Laine, he answered. "You're quick. I was just . . . Vince?"

When fear bounced like an ice ball into his belly, he whipped the car to the side of the road. "When? For Christ's sake, that's more than an hour ago. I'm on my way."

He tossed the phone on the console, punched the gas. "He's got her."

"No, no, that's not true." Even the sickly green had died away, leaving Jack's face bone white. "He can't have her, not my baby girl."

"He got her out of the shop just after five o'clock. Vince thinks they're in a dark sedan. A couple of people saw her get into a car with a man, but he doesn't have a good description of the vehicle." He had the Porsche up to ninety. "Jenny's got a good description of the guy. Long brown hair, ponytail, soul patch, sunglasses. White male, forty-five to fifty, six-foot, average build."

"The hair's a blind, but it'd be him. He's got to get to me to get the diamonds. He'll hurt her."

"We're not going to think about that. We're going to think of how to find them and get her back." His hands were ice cold on the wheel. "He needs a place. If he thinks the stones are here, he won't go far. He needs a private place, not a hotel. He'll contact you, or me. He'll—*shit*!"

He fumbled for the phone.

"Give it to me. You kill us, we can't help her." Jack snatched it away, punched for the voice mail.

"You have two new messages. First new message received May eighteenth, at five-fifteen P.M.

They heard Laine's voice, dead calm. "Sixty-eight East is a long road. Are you adding interstate abduction to your list?"

"Smart," Max breathed. "She's very smart." He shot the Porsche like a bullet onto an off-ramp, spun it like a top and rocketed to backtrack toward the interstate.

He listened to every word, blocked the fear. When the call ended, he had to order himself not to tell Jack to replay it just so he could hear her voice. "Get Vince back, give him the vehicle description and the destination. Alleghany Recreational Park. Tell him we're en route and that Crew is armed."

"But we're not waiting for the cops?"

"No, we're not waiting for them."

He flew toward the forest.

*Laine stepped into the cabin, looked around the spa*cious living area with its stone fireplace and dark, heavy wood. It was time, she concluded, for a change of tack.

Stalling was fine, it was good. Anything that kept her from getting shot or beaten was fine and good. But it never paid to depend on a last-minute cavalry charge. Smart money depended on yourself.

So she turned, offered Crew an easy smile. "First, let me say I'm not going to give you any reason to hurt me. I'm not into pain. You could, of course, hurt me anyway, but I'm hoping you've more style than that. We're both civilized people. I have something, you want something." She strolled over to an overstuffed checked sofa, sat, crossed her legs. "Let's negotiate."

"This"—he gestured with the gun—"speaks for itself."

"Use it, get nothing. Why don't you offer me a glass of wine instead?"

He angled his head in consideration and, she thought, reevaluation. "You're a cool one."

"I've had time to settle down. I won't deny you scared me. You certainly did, and still could, but I'm hoping you're open to a reasonable dialogue here."

She flipped quickly through her mental file of what she knew of him and what she could observe.

Towering ego, vanity, greed, sociopathic and homicidal tendencies.

"We're alone, I've got no way out. You're in the driver's seat, but still . . . I have something you want."

She threw back her head and laughed, and could see she'd surprised him. Good. Keep him off balance, keep him thinking. "Oh God, who would have believed the old man had it in him? He's been second-rate all his life, and a serious pain in my ass. Now he comes along with the score of a lifetime. Hell, the score of ten lifetimes. And he drops it right into my lap. I'm sorry about Willy though, he had a sweet nature. But, spilled milk."

She caught a flicker of interest on Crew's face before he opened a drawer, took out a pair of handcuffs.

"Why, Alex, if there's going to be bondage fun, I'd really appreciate that wine first."

"You think I'm buying this?"

"I'm not selling anything." And maybe he wasn't buying, but he was listening to the pitch. She sighed as the cuffs landed in her lap. "All right, your way. Where do you want them?"

"Arm of the couch, to your right hand."

Though the idea of locking herself up had her throat

going dry, she did what he said, then sent him a sultry look. "How about that drink?"

With a nod, he walked over to the kitchen, took a bottle out of a cupboard. "Cabernet?"

"Perfect. Do you mind if I ask why a man with your skills and tastes hooked up with Jack?"

"He was useful. And why are you trying to play the hard-edged opportunist?"

She pretended to pout. "I don't like to think I'm hard, just realistic."

"What you are is a small-town shopkeeper who has the bad luck to have my property."

"I think it's remarkably good luck." She took the wine he offered, sipped. "The shop's a nice, steady game. Selling old, often useless items at a nice profit. Also gives me entry into a lot of places that have more old, often useless and very valuable items. I keep my hand in."

"Well." And she could see that while he hadn't considered that angle before, he was now.

"Look, you've got a beef with the old man, fine. He's nothing to me but an albatross. And if he ever taught me anything, it was to look out for number one."

Crew shook his head slowly. "You walked out of that shop with me without a sound, primarily to protect the clerk."

"I wasn't going to argue with the gun you were shoving into my side. And you're right, I didn't want you to hurt her. She's a friend, and for God's sake, she's nearly seven months pregnant. I've got some lines, Alex. I steer clear of violence."

"This is entertaining." He sat, gestured. "How do you explain the fact you're having an affair with Gannon, the insurance investigator?"

"He's terrific in bed, but even if he was a wash in that area, I'd have gotten him there. Keep your friends close, Alex, and your enemies closer. I know every move he makes before he makes it. And here's one for free, show of good faith: he's in New York today." She leaned forward. "They're cooking up a scam to smoke you out. There should be a press release by tomorrow, claiming Max recovered a portion of the diamonds. Max's bright idea is that will set you off, push you into doing something rash. He's smart, I'll give him that, but so far, he can't get a handle on you."

"I guess that makes me smarter."

"I guess it does," she agreed. "He's closing in on Jack, and God knows dear old Dad won't shake him for long. But he hasn't got a clue how to run you down." Ego, ego, ego. Pump his ego. "He's trying this Hail Mary pass."

"Interesting, but an insurance investigator hardly concerns me."

"Why should he? You took him out once already. I had to kiss his hurts." She chuckled. "And doing that, I've kept him busy enough to give you room."

"You want me to thank you. Consider the fact you're not currently in any pain my thanks. Where are the diamonds, Ms. Tavish?"

"Let's make it Laine. I think we're beyond formalities. I've got them. Jack's and Willy's." She shifted on the seat, put a purr in her voice. "What are you going to do with all that money, Alex? Travel? Buy a small country? Sip mimosas on a beach somewhere? Don't you think all of those things, all of the lovely, lovely things people can do with big, fat piles of money is more fun with a like-thinking companion?"

His gaze drifted to her mouth, back up to her eyes. "Is this how you seduced Gannon?"

"No, actually, in that case, I pretended to let him seduce me. He's the type that needs to chase and conquer. I bring a lot to the table. You can have the diamonds, and you can have me."

"I could have them both anyway."

She sat back, sipped. "You could. I find men who enjoy rape the lowest form. If you're one of them, I've misjudged you. You could rape me, beat me, shoot me. I'd certainly tell you where the diamonds are. But then . . ." She sipped again, and put a wicked gleam in her eye. "You wouldn't know if I was telling the truth. You could waste a great deal of time, and I could suffer considerable discomfort. Not very practical when I'm willing to make a deal that gives us both exactly what we want, with a little extra."

He rose. "You're an intriguing woman, Laine." Absently, he pulled off the wig.

"Mmm, better." She pursed her lips as she studied his pewter hair. "Much better. Could I have a refill?" She held out her glass, waggled it gently from side to side. "I'd like to ask you something," she continued when he went back for the bottle. "If you have the rest of the diamonds—"

"If?"

"I've only got your word you do. I don't consider my father a reliable source."

"Oh, I've got them."

"If you do, why not take the bird in the hand and fly rather than beating the bush for the rest?"

His face was stone, the smile carved onto it, and the eyes dead. "I don't settle for half of anything."

"I respect that. Still, I could make sharing very pleasant for you."

He filled her glass, set the bottle on the table. "Sex is overrated."

She gave a low, throaty laugh. "Wanna bet?"

"As attractive as you are, you're just not worth twenty-eight million."

"Now you've hurt my feelings." Get him closer, she thought, get him closer and distract him. It'll hurt, but it'll only hurt for a minute. Bracing herself for it, she leaned forward for the wine, then shifted so the phone in her pocket slapped against the arm of the couch.

He was on her like fury, yanking her hair to drag her down, tearing at her pocket. There were floating black dots of pain and fear whirling in front of her eyes, but she pushed herself up shakily and stared in what she hoped passed as disgust at the wine stains on her pants.

"Oh, for God's sake. I hope you've got some club soda."

He backhanded her so that the black dots exploded into red.

CHAPTER

16

Max angled his car across the gravel road, just out of sight of the last cabin on the left. If Crew tried to run, he'd have to go through the Porsche first.

It was quiet and near dusk. He'd seen little activity in the woods, or in the cabins he'd passed. Hikers would be back by this time of day, vacationers settling in for dinner or a drink.

He shut off the engine, then leaned across Jack to unlock the glove box.

"We can't just sit here."

"We're not going to just sit here." Max removed his gun, a second clip, then tossed a pair of binoculars in Jack's lap. "Keep an eye on the place."

"You go in there with that, somebody's going to get hurt. Guns are trouble," Jack added when Max merely looked at him.

"Right on both counts." He checked the clip, slapped it back into place, shoved the spare into his pocket. "Cops are on their way. It'll take them some time to secure the area, set up for a hostage situation. They know he's armed, they know he has Laine. They'll try to negotiate."

"How do you negotiate with a fucking lunatic? My girl's in there, Max. That's my baby girl in there."

"She's my girl, too. And I don't negotiate."

Jack swiped the back of his hand over his mouth. "We're not waiting for the cops here either."

"We're not waiting." Since Jack had yet to use the field glasses, Max took them, focused in on the cabin. "Closed up tight. Curtains are pulled over the windows. From this angle, I see one door, four windows. Probably a rear door, couple more windows on the other side, couple in the back. He can't get out this way, but if he gets past me, he could swing around the other side, take one of the side roads and loop to the main. I don't think we're going to let that happen."

Once again, he reached into the glove box. This time he pulled out a sheathed knife. When he drew the leather off, the blade was a sheen of bright silver with a vicious jagged edge.

"Jesus Christ."

"You take care of the tires on that Mercedes with this?"

"Tires." Jack breathed deep, in, out. "Yeah. I can do that."

"All right. Here's the way we play it."

Inside, Laine pushed herself up. Her ears rang from the blow, and under the pounding, she cursed herself for not moving quickly enough, not anticipating his reaction so she'd taken a swipe rather than a direct hit.

She knew her eyes were bright with tears, but she wouldn't shed them. Instead she burned them away with a hot stare as she laid a hand on her throbbing cheekbone. "You bastard. You son of a bitch."

He gripped her by the shirt, hauled her an inch off the couch. She stretched out her free arm as she stared back at him, but she was still short of her goal. "Who were you going to call, Laine? Dear old Dad?"

"You idiot." Her response, and the furious shove surprised him enough to have him dropping her back onto the couch. "Did you tell me to empty my pockets? Did you ask if I had a phone? It's off, isn't it? I always carry it around with me in the shop. You've been with me the whole time, Einstein. Did I make any calls?"

He seemed to consider, then turned the phone over and studied it. "It appears to be off." He powered it up. After it searched for and found service, the phone gave a little trill. "It seems you have a message. Why don't we see who's been trying to reach you?"

"Kiss my ass." She gave an annoyed shrug, scooted closer to the table, reached for the wine bottle and refilled her glass. Her hand remained perfectly steady when she heard Max's voice announce he was back.

"There, does that sound like I've contacted him by phone or the power of my mind? Jesus." He was a good four feet away now. Too far. Setting the bottle down, she cupped her injured cheek. "Get me some goddamn ice for this."

"I don't like orders."

"Yeah, well, I don't like getting clocked by some guy with an impulse-control problem. How the hell am I going to explain this bruise, and believe me, it'll be a beaut. You just complicated everything. And you know what else, hot-shot? My previous offer is now off the table. I don't sleep with men who hit me. Not ever, not for anything." She eased forward a bit, as if comforting herself, and continued to rub her cheek.

"Straight business deal now. No side bennies."

"You seem to forget, this isn't a negotiation."

"Everything's negotiable. You've got half, I've got half. You want all. I, on the other hand, am more realistic, and a lot less greedy. Take these damn things off," she demanded, rattling the cuffs. "Where the hell am I going?"

She saw his hand move, very slightly, toward his left pants pocket. Then drop away again. "I don't think so. Now . . ." He started toward her. "The diamonds."

"You hit me again, you lay a hand on me, and I swear, I'll see the cops get them before you get one more stone."

"You have a delicate build, Laine. Delicate bones break easily. I think you have a strong mind; it might take a great deal to break that. I could start with your hand. Do you know how many bones there are in the human hand? I can't quite remember, but I believe there are quite a few."

His eyes came alive as he said it, and nothing in the whole of her life had ever frightened her more than that amused gleam. "Some will snap, some will shatter. It would be very painful. You'll tell me where the diamonds are, and you'll tell me the truth, because even a strong mind can tolerate only so much pain."

Her pulse was pounding in her temples, in her throat, in her fingertips, drums of terror, all but deafening. "And only a sick one gets juiced at the thought of causing it. You know, without that little flaw, I would've enjoyed spending some time with you."

She had to keep her eyes on his, steady on his. Survival depended on it. "I like stealing," she continued. "I like taking what belongs to someone else and making it mine. It's such a rush. But the rush isn't worth pain. It's never worth my life. That's a little something I picked up from my father. I think we've reached a point where you want the diamonds more than I do. You want to know where they are? That's easier than you think. But getting to them, well . . ."

Her heart was thumping like a jackhammer as she curved her lips, curled her finger. "Come here, and I'll give you a little hint."

"You'll do better than that."

"Oh, come on. At least let me have some fun with it." She toyed with the pendant around her neck, held it up. "What does this look like to you?" She let out a soft laugh. "Come on, Alex, take a closer look."

She knew she had him when he stepped to her, when his gaze fastened on the pendant. She let it drop again, to free her hand, then leaned forward again as if to pick up her wineglass. "It's all about misdirection, really. Another little thing I picked up from my father."

She tilted her face up so his attention would lock on it. There would only be one chance. He reached down for the necklace, bending, angling his head so he could get a closer look.

And she came off the couch, swinging the wine bottle in a furious roundhouse. There was the hideous crack of glass on bone, the splatter of red wine like a gush of blood. The momentum had him spilling over backward as she stood in her half crouch, panting, the bottle still clutched in her hand.

She dropped to her knees, fighting off a wave of nausea as she stretched out to try to reach him. She had to get the key out of his pocket, get the gun, get the phone. Get away.

"No! Goddamn it." Tears of frustration burned in her eyes as she strained her muscles and found he'd fallen just out of her reach. She scrambled up again, climbed over the couch, ramming it with her shoulder to nudge it across the floor. Just a little closer. Just a little.

The blood roared in her ears, and her own voice, high and desperate, sounded miles away as she ordered herself to *Come on, come on, come* on!

She dove back on the floor, snatching at his pant leg, tugging his body toward her. "The key, the key, oh God, please, let him have the key."

She glanced over. The gun was on the kitchen counter eight feet away. Until she'd unlocked the cuffs, it might as well have been eight hundred. Bearing down, she stretched out until the metal cut into her wrist, but her free hand reached his pocket and her trembling fingers dipped in.

Those stinging tears spilled over when her fingers met the small piece of metal. Breath wheezing, she fumbled it into the lock, cursed herself again and gritted her teeth. The tiny click was like a gunshot. She offered incoherent prayers of thanks as she shoved the cuff off her wrist.

"Think. Just think. Breathe and think." She sat on the floor, taking a few precious seconds to cut through the panic.

Maybe she'd killed him. Maybe she'd stunned him. She was damned if she was going to check. But if he wasn't dead, he'd come after her. She could run, but he'd come after her.

She scrambled up again and, grunting, panting, began to drag him toward the couch. Toward the cuffs. She'd lock him down, that's what she'd do. She'd lock him down. Get the phone, get the gun, call for help.

Relief flooded in when she snapped the cuff on his wrist. Blood trickled down his face, dripped on her hand as she pushed his jacket aside, reached into the inside pocket for her phone.

The sudden blare of a car alarm ripped a short scream out of her throat. She jolted, looked toward the door. Someone was out there. Someone could help.

"Help." The word came out in a whisper, and she pushed herself to her feet. As she sprang forward, a hand grabbed her ankle and sent her slamming facedown onto the floor.

She didn't scream. The sounds she made were feral growls as she kicked back, crawled forward. He yanked, hooking an arm around her legs so she was forced to swivel, shoving herself up from the waist to use her fists, her nails.

The horn continued to sound, like a two-tone scream, over and over while she tore at him, while he pulled her closer. Blood matted his hair, streaked his face, gushed out of fresh wounds where her nails ripped.

She heard a crash, and one of her flailing arms landed on broken glass. The new jolt of pain had her rolling over, digging in with elbows to gain a few precious inches. Once again her hand closed over the wine bottle.

This time when her body jerked around she had it gripped in both hands like a batter at the plate. And she swung hard for the fences.

There was a pounding—in her head? In the room? Outside? Somewhere a pounding. But his grip on her released, his eyes rolled back and his body went still.

Whimpering, she scuttled back like a crab.

That's how Max saw her when he rushed into the room. Crouched on the floor, blood on her hands, her pants and shirt torn and splotched with red.

"Laine. Jesus God almighty." He lunged to her, the cold control he'd snapped on to get inside, to get to her, shattered like glass. He was on his knees beside her, running his hands over her face, her hair, her body. "How bad are you hurt? Where are you hurt? Are you shot?"

"What? Shot?" Her vision skipped, like a scratched film. "No. I'm . . . it's wine." A giddy bubble exploded in her throat and came out as a crazed laugh. "Red wine, and, oh, some of this is blood. His. Mostly his. Is he dead?" She said it almost conversationally. "Did I kill him?"

He brushed the hair back from her face, skimmed his thumb gently over her bruised cheekbone. "Can you hold on?"

"Sure. No problem. I just want to sit here."

Max walked over, crouched by Crew. "Alive," he said after he checked for a pulse. Then he studied the torn, battered and bloodied face. "Did a number on him, didn't you?"

"I hit him with the wine bottle." The room was moving, she realized, ever so slightly. And there seemed to be little waves in the air, like water. "Twice. You came. You got my message."

"Yeah. I got your message." He patted Crew down for weapons, then went back to Laine. "You sure you're not hurt?"

"I just feel numb right now."

"Okay then." He set his gun on the floor beside them and wrapped his arms around her. All the fear, the fury, the desperation he'd fought off for the last hour rolled into him, rolled out again. "I gotta hold on," he murmured against her throat. "I don't want to hurt you, but I've gotta hold on."

"Me too." She burrowed into him. "Me too. I knew you'd come. I knew you'd be here. Doesn't mean I can't take care of myself." She eased back a little. "I told you I can take care of myself."

"Hard to argue with that. Let's see if we can stand up."

When they gained their feet, she leaned into him, looked down at Crew. "I really laid him out. I feel . . . empowered and satisfied and . . ." She swallowed, pressed a hand to her stomach. "And a little bit sick."

"Let's get you outside, get you some air. I'll take care of things in here. Cops are on their way."

"Okay. Am I shaking or is that you?"

"Little of both. You've got a little shock going on, Laine. We'll get you out, and I want you to just sit down on the ground, lie down if it makes you feel better. We'll call for an ambulance."

"I don't need an ambulance."

"That's debatable, but he sure as hell does. Here we go."

He led her out. Jack sprang from the corner of the house, the knife in one hand, a rock in the other. Laine's first muddled thought was how silly he looked.

Then he lowered both arms, and the knife and rock fell from his limp fingers to the ground. He stumbled forward, swept her in.

"Lainie. Lainie." Pressing his face to her shoulder, he burst into tears.

"It's all right. I'm all right. Shh." She cupped his face, drawing back to kiss his cheeks. "We're all right, Dad."

"I couldn't've lived. I couldn't—"

"You came. You came when I needed you. Aren't I lucky to love two men who are there when I need them?"

"I didn't know if I was coming back," he began.

On a wave of tenderness, she brushed tears from his cheeks. "But you did, didn't you? Now you've got to go."

"Lainie."

"The police will be here any minute. I haven't gone through all this to see you arrested. Go. Before they come."

"There are things I need to say to you."

"Later. You can say them later. You know where I live. Please, Daddy, go."

Max stepped back out with the phone to his ear. "Crew's secured. Laine's banged up but she's okay. Crew's going to need some medical attention. Laine and I'll wait here. What's your ETA? Good. We'll wait." He clicked off. "Vince and the rest of them will be rolling in. You've got about five minutes," he said to Jack. "Better get moving."

"Thanks." Jack offered his hand. "Maybe you are—almost—good enough for her. I'll be seeing you. Soon," he added as he turned to Laine. "Soon, baby girl."

"They're coming." She heard the sirens. "Hurry."

"Take more than some hick cops to catch Big Jack O'Hara." He winked at her. "Keep a light burning for me." He jogged toward the woods, turned for a quick salute, then disappeared into them.

"Well." Laine let out a long breath. "There he goes. Thanks."

"For what?" Max asked as she kissed him.

"For letting my father go."

"I don't know what you're talking about. I've never met your father."

On a muffled laugh, she rubbed her eyes. "I think I'm going to do that sitting-on-the-ground thing now."

It wasn't difficult to win a debate about a visit to the ER with a man who was so relieved you were alive and whole he'd have given you anything you asked for. Laine took advantage of it, and of Vince's friendship, to go straight home.

She'd be required to give a more complete statement to the chief of police the next morning. But he'd accepted her abbreviated account of events.

She'd given it while she sat on the ground outside the cabin, with a blanket around her shoulders. Though she'd come through her ordeal with Crew with nothing more serious than cuts and bruises, she didn't object when Max cut off the police questioning, scooped her off the ground and carried her to his car.

It gave her a lot of satisfaction to watch Crew hauled out on a stretcher.

A lot of satisfaction.

Jack O'Hara's daughter still had the moves.

Grateful, was all Laine could think as she spent a full twenty minutes under the hot pulsing spray of the shower. She was so grateful to Max, to Vince, to fate. Hell, she was grateful for digital communication. So much so she was going to retire her cell phone, have it mounted and hung in a place of honor.

And she would never drink cabernet again as long as she lived.

She stepped out of the shower, dried herself gingerly. The numbness was long gone, and every bump, scrape and bruise ached like fury. She swallowed four aspirin, then gathered her courage and took a look at herself in the full-length mirror.

"Oh. Ouch." She hissed out a breath as she turned for the rear view. She was a colorful mess of bruises. Hips, shins, knees, arms. And the beaut she'd predicted on her right cheek.

But they'd fade, she thought. They'd fade and be forgotten as she went back to living her life. And Alex Crew would spend the rest of his behind bars. She hoped he cursed her name every day of that life. And she hoped he spent every night dreaming of diamonds.

As a concession to the bruises, she dressed in loose sweats, tied her damp hair back loosely. As a concession to vanity, she spent some time with makeup to downplay the mark of violence on her face.

Then she turned, spread her arms and addressed Henry, who'd shadowed her—even in the bathroom—since she'd retrieved him from Jenny's. "Not too bad, right?"

She found Max in the kitchen, heating the contents of a can of soup on the stove. "Thought you might be hungry."

"You thought right."

He stepped to her, played his fingers over the bruise. "I'm sorry I wasn't faster."

"If you're sorry, you're diminishing my own courage and cleverness and I've been congratulating myself on them."

"Wouldn't want to do that, but I've got to say, I feel cheated. You robbed me of a chance to beat that son of a bitch into pulp."

"Next time we deal with a homicidal sociopath, you can take him down."

"Next time." He turned back to stir the soup. Laine linked her hands.

"We've rushed into all this, Max."

"Sure have."

"People . . . I imagine people who come together in intense or dangerous situations often rush into things. All those emotions spiking. When things level off, they probably regret following those impulses."

"Logical."

"We could regret it if we move ahead the way we talked about before. We could regret rushing into a relationship, much less marriage."

"We could." He tapped the spoon on the edge of the pot, then set it down and turned to her. "Do you care?"

She pressed her lips together before they could tremble. There he was, at her stove, all tall and rangy, with those dangerous eyes and that easy stance. "No. No, I don't care. Not even a little." She flew into him, rising up on her toes when his arms clamped around her. "Oh God, I don't care. I love you so much."

"Whew. That's good." His mouth crushed to hers, then softened, then lingered. "I don't care either. Besides, I just picked this up for you in New York. It'd be wasted if you wanted to start getting sensible on me now."

He tugged the box out of his pocket. "Pretty sure I remember what you said you liked."

"You took time to buy me a ring in all of this?"

He blinked. "Oh. You wanted a ring?"

"Smart-ass." She opened the box, and her heart turned slowly, beautifully, over in her breast as she stared at the square-cut diamond in the simple platinum setting. "It's perfect. You know it's perfect."

"Not yet." He took it out, slipped it on her finger. "Now it is." He kissed her scraped knuckles just beneath it. "I'm going to spend my life with you, Laine. We'll start tonight with you sitting down there and me making you soup. Nothing intense about that."

"Sounds nice. Nice and normal."

"We can even bicker if you want."

"That doesn't sound so bad either. Maybe before we do, we should get the rest of it out of the way. Can I see them?"

He turned the soup down, opened the briefcase he'd set on the table. The sight of him taking out the piggy bank made her laugh and lower to a chair.

"It's horrible really, to think I might've been killed over what's in the belly of a piggy bank. But somehow it's not. It's just so Jack."

"A rep of the insurance company will be picking them up tomorrow." He spread a newspaper, picked up the little hammer he'd found in the mudroom. "Want the honors?"

"No. Be my guest."

It took a couple of good whacks before he could slide the padding out, then the pouch. He poured the sparkling waterfall in it into Laine's hand.

"They don't get less dazzling, do they?"

"I like the one on your finger better."

She smiled. "So do I."

While he dumped the shards and newspaper, she sprinkled the diamonds onto velvet. "They'll have half of them back now. And since Crew's been identified and captured, they might find the rest of them where he lived, or in a safe-deposit box under his name."

"Maybe. Might have a portion of them stashed that way. But he didn't go to Columbus, he didn't take something to that kid out of the goodness of his heart or a parental obligation. The ex and the son have something, or know something."

"Max, don't go after them." She reached out for his

hand. "Let it go. They're only trying to get away from him. Everything you told me says she's just trying to protect her child, give him a normal life. If you go after them, she'll feel hunted, she'll run again. I know what that's like. I know what it was like for my mother until she found some peace, until she found Rob. And my father, well, he's a thief and a con, and a liar, but he's not crazy, he's not a killer."

She nudged the diamonds toward him. "No amount of these is worth making that innocent boy live with the fact that his father's a killer. They're just stones. They're just things."

"Let me think about it."

"Okay." She got up, kissed the top of his head. "Okay. Tell you what. I'll put a couple of sandwiches together to go with this soup. You can cross-check the diamonds with your list. Then we'll put them away and eat like boring, normal people."

She got up to get the bread. "So when do you suppose I can get my car back from New Jersey?"

"I know a guy who'll transport it down. Couple of days." He set to work. "I'll run you around meanwhile, or you can use my car."

"See, boring and normal. Mustard or mayo on the ham?"

"Mustard," he said absently, then fell into silence with the dog snoring at his feet.

"Son of a bitch."

She glanced back. "Hmm?"

He shook his head. "Let me do this again."

Laine cut the sandwiches she'd built in two. "Doesn't add up, does it?" She set the plates on the table as Max tapped his fingers and studied her. "I was afraid of that. Or not afraid, really, just resigned. A little short of the quarter share?"

"About twenty-five carats short."

"Uh-huh. Well, your client would accept, I'm sure, that the shares might not have been evenly divided. That the portions that are left might be just a little heavy."

"But that wouldn't be the case, would it?"

"No. No, I doubt very much that was the case."

"He pocketed them. Your father."

"He'd have taken his share out, selected a few of the stones, just as a kind of insurance, then he'd have put them into another container—the pig—and kept the insurance on him. In a money belt or a bag around his neck, even in his pocket. 'Put all your eggs in one basket, Lainie, the handle's going to break. Then all you've got is scrambled eggs.' You want coffee with this?"

"I want a damn beer. I let him walk."

"You'd have let him walk anyway." She got the beer, popped the top for him, then slid into his lap. "You'd have taken the diamonds back if you'd known he had them, but you'd have let him walk. Really, nothing's changed. It's just a measly twenty-five carats." She kissed his cheek, then the other, then his mouth. "We're okay, right?"

When she settled her head on his shoulder, he stroked her hair. "Yeah, we're okay. I might put a boot in your father's ass if I ever see him again, but we're okay."

"Good."

He sat, stroking her hair. There were ham sandwiches on the table, soup on the stove. A dog snoozed on the floor. A few million—give or take—in diamonds sparkled in the kitchen light.

They were okay, Max thought. In fact, they were terrific.

But they were never going to be boring and normal.

Keep reading for an excerpt from

BIG JACK
by J. D. Robb

Available March 2010
from Berkley Books.

New York, 2059

She was dying to get home. Knowing her own house, her own bed, her own *things* were waiting for her made even the filthy afternoon traffic from the airport a pleasure.

There were small skirmishes, petty betrayals, outright treachery and bitter combat among the cabs, commuters and tanklike maxibuses. Overhead, the airtrams, blimps and minishuttles strafed the sky. But watching the traffic wars wage made her antsy enough to imagine herself leaping into the front seat to grab the wheel and plunge into the fray, with a great deal more viciousness and enthusiasm than her driver.

God, she *loved* New York.

While her driver crept along the FDR as one of the army of vehicles battling their way into the city, she entertained herself by watching the animated billboards. Some were little stories, and as a writer herself, and the lover of a good tale, Samantha Gannon appreciated that.

Observe, she thought, the pretty woman lounging pool-side at a resort, obviously alone and lonely while couples splash or stroll. She orders a drink, and with the first sip her eyes meet those of a gorgeous man just emerging from the water. Wet muscles, killer grin. An electric moment that dissolves into a moonlight scene where the now happy couple walk hand in hand along the beach.

Moral? Drink Silby's Rum and open your world to adventure, romance and really good sex.

It should be so easy.

But then, for some, it was. For her grandparents there'd been an electric moment. Rum hadn't played a part, at least not in any of the versions she'd heard. But their eyes had met, and something had snapped and sizzled through the bloodstream of fate.

Since they'd be married for fifty-six years this coming fall, whatever that something had been had done a solid job.

And because of it, because fate had brought them together, she was sitting in the back of a big, black sedan, heading uptown, heading toward home, home, home, after two weeks traveling on the bumpy, endless roads of a national book tour.

Without her grandparents, what they'd done, what they'd chosen, there would have been no book. No tour. No homecoming. She owed them all of it—well, not the tour, she amended. She could hardly blame them for that.

She only hoped they were half as proud of her as she was of them.

Samantha E. Gannon, national bestselling author of *Hot Rocks*.

Was that iced or what?

Hyping the book in fourteen cities—coast to coast—over fifteen days, the interviews, the appearances, the hotels and transport stations had been exhausting.

And, let's be honest, she told herself, *fabulous in its insane way.*

Every morning she'd dragged herself from a strange bed, propped open her bleary eyes and stared at the mirror just to be sure she'd see herself staring back. It was really happening, to her, Sam Gannon.

She'd been writing it all of her life, she thought, every time she'd heard the family story, every time she'd begged her grandparents to tell it, wheedled for more details. She'd been honing her craft in every hour she'd spent lying in bed as a child, imagining the adventure.

It had seemed so romantic to her, so exciting. And the best part was that it was her family, her blood.

Her current project was coming along well. She was calling it just *Big Jack,* and she thought her great-grandfather would have gotten a very large charge out of it.

She wanted to get back to it, to dive headlong into Jack O'Hara's world of cons and scams and life on the lam. Between the tour and the pretour rounds, she hadn't had a full hour to write. And she was due.

But she wasn't going straight to work. She wasn't going to think about work for at least forty-eight blissful hours. She was going to dump her bags, and she might just burn everything in them. She was going to lock herself in her own wonderful, quiet house. She was going to run a bubble bath, open a bottle of champagne.

She'd soak and she'd drink, then she'd soak and drink some more. If she was hungry, she'd buzz something up in the AutoChef. She didn't care what it was because it would be her food, in her kitchen.

Then she was going to sleep for ten hours.

She wasn't going to answer the telelink. She'd contacted her parents, her brother, her sister, her grandparents from the air, and told them all she was going under for a couple of days. Her friends and business associates could wait a day or two. Since she'd ended what had passed for a relationship over a month before, there wasn't any man waiting for her.

That was probably just as well.

She sat up when the car veered toward the curb. Home! She'd been drifting, she realized, lost in her own thoughts, as usual, and hadn't realized she was home.

She gathered her notebook, her travel bag. Riding on delight, she overtipped the driver when he hauled her suitcase and carry-on to the door for her. She was so happy to see him go, so thrilled that he'd be the last person she'd have to speak to until she decided to surface again, she nearly kissed him on the mouth.

Instead, she resisted, waved him off, then dragged her things into the tiny foyer of what her grandmother liked to call Sam's Urban Doll House.

"I'm back!" She leaned against the door, breathed deep, then did a hip-shaking, shoulder-rolling dance across the floor. "Mine, mine, mine. It's all mine. Baby, I'm back!"

She stopped short, arms still flung out in her dance of delight, and gaped at her living area. Tables and chairs were overturned, and her lovely little settee was lying on its back like a turtle on its shell. Her screen was off the wall and lay smashed in the middle of the floor, along with her collection of framed family photos and holograms. The walls had been stripped of paintings and prints.

Sam slapped both hands to her head, fisted her fingers in her short red hair and let out a bellow. "For God's *sake,*

Andrea! House-sitting doesn't mean you actually sit on the goddamn house."

Having a party was one thing, but this was . . . just beyond. She was going to kick some serious ass.

She yanked her pocket 'link out of her jacket and snapped out the name. "Andrea Jacobs. Former friend," she added on a mutter as the transmission went through. Gritting her teeth, she spun on her heel and headed out of the room, started up the stairs as she listened to Andrea's recorded message.

"What the hell did you do?" she barked into the 'link, "set off a bomb? How could you do this, Andrea? How could you destroy my things and leave this mess for me to come home to? Where the hell are you? You'd better be running for your life, because when I get my hands . . . Jesus Christ, what is that smell! I'm going to kill you for this, Andrea."

The stench was so strong, she was forced to cover her mouth with her hand as she booted open the bedroom door. "It *reeks* in here, and, oh God, oh God, my bedroom. I'm never going to forgive you. I swear to God, Andrea, you're dead. Lights!" she snapped out.

And when they flashed on, when she blinked her eyes clear, she saw Andrea sprawled on the floor on a heap of stained bedclothes.

She saw she was right. Andrea was dead.

She'd nearly been out the door. Five more minutes and she'd have been off-shift and heading home. Odds were someone else would have caught the case. Someone else would be spending a steaming summer night dealing with a bloater.

She'd barely closed the last case and that had been a horror.

But Andrea Jacobs was hers now. For better, for worse.

Lieutenant Eve Dallas breathed through a filtered mask. They didn't really work and looked, in her opinion, ridiculous, but it helped cut down on the worst of the smell when you were dealing with the very ripe dead.

Though the temperature controls of the room were set at a pleasant seventy-three degrees, the body had, essentially, cooked for five days. It was bloated with gases, had voided its wastes. Whoever had slit Andrea Jacobs's throat hadn't just killed her. He'd left her to rot.

"Victim's identification verified. Jacobs, Andrea. Twenty-nine-year-old mixed-race female. The throat's been slashed in what appears to be a left-to-right downward motion. Indications are the killer attacked from behind. The deterioration of the body makes it difficult to ascertain if there are other injuries, defensive wounds, through visual exam on scene. Victim is dressed in street clothes."

Party clothes, Eve thought, noting the soiled sparkle on the hem of the dress, the ice-pick heels kicked across the room.

"She came in, after a date, maybe trolling the clubs. Could've brought somebody back with her, but it doesn't look like that."

She gazed around the room while she put the pictures in her head. She wished, briefly, for Peabody. But she'd sent her former aide and very new partner home early. There wasn't any point in dragging her back and spoiling what Eve knew was a celebration dinner with Peabody's main squeeze.

"She came back alone. If she'd come back with someone, even if he was going to kill her, he'd have gone for the sex first. Why waste it? And this isn't a struggle. This isn't a fight. One clean swipe. No other stab wounds."

She looked back at the body and brought Andrea Jacobs to life in her mind. "She comes back from her date, her night out. Had a few drinks. Starts upstairs. Does she hear something? Probably not. Maybe she's stupid and she comes upstairs after she hears somebody up here. We'll find out if she was stupid, but I bet he hears her. Hears her come in."

Eve walked out into the hall, stood there a moment, picturing it, and ignoring the movements of the crime-scene team working in the house.

She walked back, imagined kicking off those sky-high heels. Your arches would just weep with relief. Maybe she lifted one foot, bent over a little, rubbed it.

And when she straightened, he was on her.

Came from behind the door, Eve thought, or out of the closet on the wall beside the door. Stepped right up behind her, yanked her head back by the hair, then sliced.

Lips pursed, she studied the pattern of blood spatter.

Spurted out of the jugular, she thought, onto the bed. She's facing the bed, he's behind. He doesn't get messy. Just slices down quick, gives her a little shove forward. She's still spurting as she falls.

She glanced toward the windows. Drapes were drawn. Moving over, she eased them back, noted the privacy screen was engaged as well. He'd have done that. Wouldn't want anyone to notice the light, or movement.

She stepped out again, tossed the mask into her field kit.

Crime scene and the sweepers were already crawling around the place in their safe suits. She nodded toward a uniform. "Tell the ME's team she's cleared to be bagged, tagged and transported. Where's the witness?"

"Got her down in the kitchen, Lieutenant."

She checked her wrist unit. "Take your partner, start a neighborhood canvass. You're first on scene, right?"

He straightened a little. "Yes, sir."

She waited a beat. "And?"

She had a rep. You didn't want to screw up with Dallas. She was tall, lean and dressed now in summer-weight pants, T-shirt and jacket. He'd seen her seal up before she went into the bedroom, and her right hand had a smear of blood on the thumb.

He wasn't sure if he should mention it.

Her hair was brown and chopped short. Her eyes were the same color and all cop.

He'd heard it said she chewed up lazy cops for breakfast and spit them out at lunch.

He wanted to make it through the day.

"Dispatch came through at sixteen-forty, report of a break-in and possible death at this address."

Eve looked back toward the bedroom. "Yeah, extremely possible."

"My partner and I responded, arrived on scene at sixteen-fifty-two. The witness, identified as Samantha Gannon, resident, met us at the door. She was in extreme distress."

"Cut through it. Lopkre," she added, reading his name tag.

"She was hysterical, Lieutenant. She'd already vomited, just outside the front door."

"Yeah, I noticed that."

He relaxed a little, since she didn't seem inclined to take a bite out of him. "Tossed it again, same spot, right after she opened the door for us. Sort of folded in on herself there in the foyer, crying. She kept saying, 'Andrea's dead, upstairs.' My partner stayed with her while I went up to check it out. Didn't have to get far."

He grimaced, nodded toward the bedroom. "The smell. Looked into the bedroom, saw the body. Ah, as I could verify death from the visual from the doorway, I did not enter the scene and risk contaminating same. I conducted a brief search of the second floor to confirm no one else, alive or dead, was on the premises, then called it in."

"And your partner?"

"My partner's stayed with the witness throughout. She—Officer Ricky—she's got a soothing way with victims and witnesses. She's calmed her down considerably."

"All right. I'll send Ricky out. Start the canvass."

She started downstairs. She noted the suitcase just inside the door, the notebook case, the big-ass purse some women couldn't seem to make a move without.

The living area looked as if it had been hit by a high wind, as did the small media room off the central hallway. In the kitchen, it looked more like a crew of mad cooks—a redundancy in Eve's mind—had been hard at work.

The uniform sat at a small eating nook in the corner, across a dark blue table from a redhead Eve pegged as middle twenties. She was so pale the freckles that sprinkled over her nose and cheekbones stood out like cinnamon dashed over milk. Her eyes were a strong and bright blue, glassy from shock and tears and rimmed in red.

Her hair was clipped short, even shorter than Eve wore her own, and followed the shape of her head with a little fringe over the brow. She wore enormous silver hoops in her ears, and New York black in pants, shirt, jacket.

Traveling clothes, Eve assumed, thinking of the cases in the foyer.

The uniform—Ricky, Eve remembered—had been speaking in a low, soothing voice. She broke off now, looked toward Eve. The look they exchanged was brief: cop to cop. "You call that number I gave you, Samantha."

"I will. Thank you. Thanks for staying with me."

"It's okay." Ricky slid out from the table, walked to

where Eve waited just inside the doorway. "Sir. She's pretty shaky, but she'll hold a bit longer. She's going to break again though, 'cause she's holding by her fingernails."

"What number did you give her?"

"Victim's Aid."

"Good. You record your conversation with her?"

"With her permission, yes, sir."

"See it lands on my desk." Eve hesitated a moment. Peabody also had a soothing way, and Peabody wasn't here. "I told your partner to take you and do the knock-on-doors. Find him, tell him I've requested you remain on scene for now, and to take another uniform for the canvass. If she breaks, it might be better if we have somebody she relates to nearby."

"Yes, sir."

"Give me some space with her now." Eve moved into the kitchen, stopped by the table. "Ms. Gannon? I'm Lieutenant Dallas. I need to ask you some questions."

"Yes, Beth, Officer Ricky, explained that someone would . . . I'm sorry, what was your name?"

"Dallas. Lieutenant Dallas." Eve sat. "I understand this is difficult for you. I'd like to record this, if that's all right? Why don't you just tell me what happened."

"I don't know what happened." Her eyes glimmered, her voice thickened dangerously. But she stared down at her hands, breathed in and out several times. It was a struggle for control Eve appreciated. "I came home. I came home from the airport. I've been out of town. I've been away for two weeks."

"Where were you?"

"Um. Boston, Cleveland, East Washington, Lexington, Dallas, Denver, New LA, Portland, Seattle. I think I forgot one. Or two." She smiled weakly. "I was on a book tour. I wrote a book. They published it—e, audio and paper forms. I'm really lucky."

Her lips trembled, and she sucked in a sob. "It's doing very well, and they sent—the publisher—they sent me on a tour to promote it. I've been bouncing around for a couple weeks. I just got home. I just got here."

Eve could see by the way Samantha's gaze flickered around the room that she was moving toward another breakdown. "Do you live here alone? Ms. Gannon?"

"What? Alone? Yes, I live by myself. Andrea doesn't—didn't—Oh God . . ."

Her breath began to hitch, and from the way her knuckles whitened as she gripped her hands together, Eve knew this time the struggle was a full-out war. "I want to help Andrea. I need you to help me understand so I can start helping her. So I need you to try to hold on until I do."

"I'm not a weak woman." She rubbed the heels of her hands over her face, violently. "I'm not. I'm good in a crisis. I don't fall apart like this. I just don't."

Bet you don't, Eve thought. "Everybody has a threshold. You came home. Tell me what happened. Was the door locked?"

"Yes. I uncoded the locks, the alarm. I stepped in, dumped my stuff. I was so happy to be in my own space again. I was tired, so happy. I wanted a glass of wine and a bubble bath. Then I saw the living room. I couldn't believe it. I was so angry. Just furious and outraged. I grabbed my 'link from my pocket and called Andrea."

"Because?"

"Oh. Oh. Andrea, she was house-sitting. I didn't want to leave the house empty for two weeks, and she wanted to have her apartment painted, so it worked out. She could stay here, water my plants, feed the fish . . . Oh Jesus, my fish!" She started to slide out, but Eve grabbed her arm.

"Hold on."

"My fish. I have two goldfish. Live fish, in my office. I didn't even look in there."

"Sit." Eve held up a finger to hold Samantha in place, then got up, stepped to the door and signaled to one of the sweepers. "Check out the home office, get me the status on a couple of goldfish."

"Huh?"

"Just do it." She went back to the table. A tear was tracking down Samantha's cheek, and the delicate redhead's skin was blotchy. But she hadn't broken yet. "Andrea was staying here while you were gone. Just Andrea?"

"Yes. She probably had someone over now and again. She's sociable. She likes to party. That's what I thought when I saw the living area. That she'd had some insane party and trashed my place. I was yelling at her machine through the 'link when I started upstairs. I said terrible things." She dropped her head into her hands.

"Terrible things," she murmured. "Then there was that horrible smell. I was even more furious. I slammed into the bedroom, and . . . she was there. She was there, lying on the floor by the bed. All the blood, that didn't even look like blood anymore, but, you know, somehow, you know. I think I screamed. Maybe I blacked out. I don't know."

She looked up again, and her eyes were shattered. "I don't remember. I just remember seeing her, then running down the stairs again. I called nine-one-one. And I was sick. I ran outside and got sick. And then I was stupid."

"How were you stupid?"

"I went back in the house. I know better. I should've stayed outside, waited for the police outside or gone to a neighbor's. But I wasn't thinking straight, and I came back in and just stood in the foyer, shaking."

"You weren't stupid, you were in shock. There's a difference. When's the last time you talked to Andrea?"

"I'm not sure. Early in the tour. From East Washington, I think. Just a quick check." She dashed a second tear away as if irritated to find it there. "I was awfully busy, and I didn't have a lot of free time. I called once or twice, left messages. Just to remind her when I was heading home."

"Did she ever say anything to you about being concerned? About anyone giving her trouble, making threats?"

"No. Nothing like that."

"What about you? Anyone making threats?"

"Me? No. No." She shook her head.

"Who knew you were out of town?"

"Ah . . . well, everyone. My family, my friends, my agent, publisher, publicist, editor, neighbors. It wasn't a secret, that's for sure. I was so juiced about the book, about the opportunity, I pretty much told anyone who'd listen. So . . . It was a burglary, don't you think? God, I'm sorry, I can't keep your name in my head."

"Dallas."

"Don't you think it was some sort of burglary, Lieutenant Dallas? Somebody who heard I was gone and figured the house was empty, and . . ."

"Possibly. We'll need you to check your belongings, see if anything's missing." But she'd noted the electronics, the artwork any self-respecting burglar would have taken. And Andrea Jacobs had been wearing a very nice wrist unit, and considerable jewelry. Real or knockoff, it hardly mattered. A B&E man wouldn't have left them behind.

"Have you had any calls, mail, any contact of an unusual nature recently?"

"Well, since the book was published, I've gotten some

communications. Mostly through my publisher. People who
want to meet me, or who want me to help them get their book
published, or want me to write their story. Some of them are
pretty strange, I guess. Not threatening, though. And there's
some who want to tell me their theory about the diamonds."

"What diamonds?"

"From the book. My book's about a major diamond heist
in the early part of the century. Here in New York. My grandparents were involved. They didn't steal anything," she said
quickly. "My grandfather was the insurance investigator
who took the case, and my grandmother—it's complicated.
But a quarter of the diamonds were never recovered."

"Is that so."

"Pretty frosty, really. Some of the people who've contacted me are just playing detective. It's one of the reasons
for the book's success. Millions of dollars in diamonds—
where are they? It's been more than half a century, and as
far as anyone knows, they've never surfaced."

"You publish under your own name?"

"Yes. See, the diamonds are how my grandparents met.
It's part of Gannon family history. That's the heart of the
book, really. The diamonds are the punch, but the love
story is the heart."

Heart or no heart, Eve thought cynically, a few million
in diamonds was a hell of a punch. And a hell of a motive.

"Okay. Have you or Andrea broken off any relationships
recently?"

"Andrea didn't have relationships—per se. She just
liked men." Her white skin turned flaming red. "That
didn't sound right. I mean she dated a lot. She liked to go
out, she enjoyed going out with men. She didn't have a serious monogamous relationship."

"Any of the men she liked to go out with want something more serious?"

"She never mentioned it. And she would have. She'd have told me if some guy got pushy. She generally went out with men who wanted what she wanted. A good time, no strings."

"How about you?"

"I'm not seeing anyone right now. Between the writing and the tour, juggling in the day-to-day, I haven't had the time or inclination. I broke a relationship off about a month ago, but there weren't any hard feelings."

"His name?"

"But he'd never—Chad would *never* hurt anyone. He's a little bit of an asshole—well, potentially a major asshole—but he's not . . ."

"It's just routine. It helps to eliminate. Chad?"

"Oh Jesus. Chad Dix. He lives on East Seventy-first."

"Does he have your codes and access to the house?"

"No. I mean, he did but I changed them after we broke up. I'm not stupid—and my grandfather was a cop before he went private. He'd have skinned me if I hadn't taken basic security precautions."

"He'd have been right to. Who else had the new codes?"

Samantha scrubbed her hands over her hair until it stood up in short, flaming spikes. "The only one who had them besides me is Andrea, and my cleaning service. They're bonded. That's Maid In New York. Oh, and my parents. They live in Maryland. I give them all my codes. Just in case."

Her eyes widened. "The security cam. I have a security cam on the front door."

"Yes. It's been shut down, and your disks are missing."

"Oh." Her color was coming back, a kind of healthy-girl roses and cream. "That sounds very professional. Why would they be so professional, then trash the house?"

"That's a good question. I'm going to need to talk to you again at some point, but for now, is there someone you'd like to call?"

"I just don't think I could talk to anyone. I'm talked out. My parents are on vacation. They're sailing the Med." She bit her lip as if chewing on a thought. "I don't want them to know about this. They've been planning this trip for nearly a year and only left a week ago. They'd head straight back."

"Up to you."

"My brother's off planet on business." She tapped her fingers against her teeth as she thought it through. "He'll be gone a few more days at least, and my sister's in Europe. She'll be hooking up with my parents in about ten days, so I can just keep them all out of this for now. Yeah, I can keep them out of it. I'll have to contact my grandparents, but that can wait until tomorrow."

Eve had been thinking more of Samantha contacting someone to stay with her, someone to lean on. But it seemed the woman's initial self-estimate was on the mark. She wasn't a weak woman.

"Do I have to stay here?" Samantha asked her. "As much as I hate the idea, I think I want to go to a hotel for the night—for a while, actually. I don't want to stay here alone. I don't want to be here tonight."

"I'll arrange for you to be taken anywhere you want to go. I'll need to know how to reach you."

"Okay." She closed her eyes a moment, drew in a breath as Eve got to her feet. "Lieutenant, she's dead, Andrea's dead because she was here. She's dead, isn't she, because she was here while I was away."

"She's dead because someone killed her. Whoever did is the only one responsible for what happened. You're not. She's not. It's my job to find whoever's responsible."

"You're good at your job, aren't you?"

"Yeah. I am. I'm going to have Officer Ricky take you to a hotel. If you think of anything else, you can contact me through Cop Central. Oh, these diamonds you wrote about. When were they stolen?"

"Two thousand and three. March 2003. Appraised at over twenty-eight million at that time. About three-quarters of them were recovered and returned."

"That leaves a lot of loose rocks. Thanks for your cooperation, Ms. Gannon. I'm sorry about your friend."

She stepped out, working various theories in her mind. One of the sweepers tapped her shoulder as she passed.

"Hey, Lieutenant? The fish? They didn't make it."

"Shit." Eve jammed her hands in her pockets and headed out.

Love blooms in the second novel
in the celebrated Bride Quartet series from
#1 *New York Times* bestselling author

N O R A   R O B E R T S

BED *of* ROSES

Florist Emma Grant is finding career success with her
friends at Vows wedding planning company, and her love
life appears to be thriving. And yet even though men
swarm around her, she still hasn't found Mr. Right. And the
last place she's looking is right under her nose.

But that's just where Jack Cooke is. He's so close to the
women of Vows that he's practically family, but the archi-
tect has begun to admit to himself that his feelings for
Emma have developed into much more than friendship.
When Emma returns his passion—kiss for blistering kiss—
they must trust in their history . . . and in their hearts.

M562T0809

Coming soon in paperback from
#1 *New York Times* bestselling author

Nora Roberts

BLACK HILLS

A summer at his grandparents' South Dakota ranch
is not eleven-year-old Cooper Sullivan's idea of a good
time. But things are a bit more bearable now that he's
discovered the neighbor girl, Lil Chance. Each year,
with Coop's annual summer visit, their friendship
deepens from innocent games to stolen kisses, but
there is one shared experience that will forever haunt
them: the terrifying discovery of a hiker's body.

Twelve years after they last walked together hand in
hand, fate has brought them back to the Black Hills
at a time when the people and things they hold most
dear need them most . . .

penguin.com